W9-AFS-108

WITHDRAWN

APR 2 5 2013

WITHDRAWN

the Slippage

Slippage
the

a novel

BEN GREENMAN

WHITCHURCH-STOUFFVILLE PUBLIC LIBRARY

HARPER  PERENNIAL

NEW YORK • LONDON • TORONTO • SYDNEY • NEW DELHI • AUCKLAND

HARPER ⬤ PERENNIAL

THE SLIPPAGE. Copyright © 2013 by Ben Greenman. All rights reserved. Printed in the United States of America. No part of this book may be used or reproduced in any manner whatsoever without written permission except in the case of brief quotations embodied in critical articles and reviews. For information address HarperCollins Publishers, 10 East 53rd Street, New York, NY 10022.

HarperCollins books may be purchased for educational, business, or sales promotional use. For information please write: Special Markets Department, HarperCollins Publishers, 10 East 53rd Street, New York, NY 10022.

FIRST EDITION

Library of Congress Cataloging-in-Publication Data is available upon request.

ISBN 978-0-06-199051-9

13 14 15 16 17 ov/rrd 10 9 8 7 6 5 4 3 2 1

To Gail—for being

Part I

———————

ALL HANDS ON DECK

William had told the Kenners not to worry if they were a few minutes late, and he was foresuffering the moment when he'd have to reassure the Fitches that it was okay to be the first ones to arrive. He had always had an ability to put people at ease, which was why he came on board quickly whenever Louisa proposed that they host a party. It was a chance to see himself in the best possible light, and there were fewer and fewer of those with each passing year.

They were on the deck, chopping vegetables on the narrow table next to the sliding glass door that led back into the kitchen. "Countdown to Tom," William said. There was a carrot that looked lost amid several stalks of celery, and he plucked it out, a rescue.

"Can't wait," Louisa said. She had mixed up three pitchers of punch: one red, one yellow-green, and a third that was an orange so chemically vivid that William wondered if anyone would want to drink it. "What should I call this one? It's like a sunrise."

"Or a sunset."

"Always the optimist." She hoisted a glass of the orange. "We could have had the party at midnight and put out bowls of this instead of lanterns. That is, if it was a festive occasion."

"It is, isn't it? Aren't you excited to have your brother back in town?"

"Don't I look it?" She did, but he didn't think Tom was the reason. Louisa, who could be quiet when it was just the two of them, came alive in groups. She loved to move from guest to guest, showing each of them an almost imperceptibly different version of herself. From where William stood, it looked like a gem being turned so that it sparkled.

"He's bringing a new girl. This one's more serious, he said."

"I don't believe him," Louisa said. "He's not the type." She slid her glass forward, let it come to rest for a second, slid it again and then again; it left a series of circles that reminded him of cartoon thought bubbles. "Although I didn't think I was, either."

"That was before I came along and swept you off your feet."

"Let the record show that there was no sweeping of any kind."

William reached for more vegetables, this time got mainly carrots, sliced lengthwise to multiply them into sticks.

"These all taste the same, even though they're different colors," Louisa said.

"Hey," William said. "Save some for the rest of us."

"Have you ever known me to drink too much at a party?"

"Comedienne," William said.

When William had first met Louisa, they were reporters at a small weekly newspaper. He was the veteran, with seven months of service; she had been there only three; they had taken to talking at a going-away party for an older editor. That first night she had talked mostly about her date, a designer at the paper who drank too much and wandered away from her side in the party's first minutes. "Do you know Jim?" she asked. William nodded dumbly, happy she'd asked a yes-or-no question, content to listen while this tall brunette with a constellation of freckles across her nose explained why two months with Jim was like an endless year with anyone else. Later, he convinced her that she was tipsy and should let him drive her home. Then he had kissed her on the strip of grass between the street and her apartment building, his hand inside the top of her waistband.

He did the same now.

"So presumptuous," Louisa said. "How could you be sure I wouldn't just haul off and flatten you?"

"Confidence of youth," William said. His youth had been filled with many things, but confidence was not one of them. When, a week later, Louisa had come to spend the night with William—she arrived carrying a turquoise backpack that she knelt to unzip—he could not believe his good fortune. In the morning, he tried to keep a straight face in front of the bathroom mirror but his expression shattered with sudden joy. Then one day six months later, in the midst of a fight that was not their first fight, she produced a soft black duffel he had never seen, stuffed her clothes into it, and was gone. A month after that, she was back with Jim. "He's different now," she told William, who was different also.

It didn't take, Louisa and Jim, even when she quit the paper after Jim gave her the idea that working together was straining their relationship. Within three months, they were on the rocks again. But she didn't come back to William. Instead, she became a story he told to other people. He used it with other women as proof that he was capable of listening, or fidelity, or sorrow. He used it with other men as proof of the unknowability of the human heart. Then, years later, they had met at a party. She was taking a spin around the room, sending up bright little flares of laughter, but when she saw him she froze. They embraced awkwardly, struck up a conversation; he found the courage to ask her to dinner the following week, and they were returned to one another with a velocity that surprised them both.

"Do you know her name?" William said. "Tom's new girlfriend?"

"No," Louisa said. "He likes to create mystery."

"Well, we'll meet her," William said. "And then, when no one's looking, I'll go into her wallet and see what her name is."

"Or we could just ask her."

"You always want to do things the easy way." He split the remaining stalks of celery and swept them into a bowl. "I'm ready for the party. Are you ready? It gives me a chance to get people out on the deck, which is always my secret ambition."

"If you talk about it constantly, it doesn't count as a secret ambition," Louisa said, digging a moat around the words. She had been pretty as a younger woman but was now beautiful: a certain indistinctness in her face had sharpened, and her eyes were streaked with traces of things both remembered and forgotten. "Though I'll admit that it's a nice deck." Her phone was ringing in the hollows of the house. She handed the orange punch to William. "Try," she said, and went inside.

William could not, at twenty-five, have anticipated the life he would live with Louisa. He had not been a genius of the present back then, let alone the future.

When they had gotten back together, he had lived in a little house just north of downtown. It fit him snugly, like a shell, and he could not imagine living anywhere else. But a month or so after he and Louisa started dating again, at the close of a restless weekend, she suggested a

drive through town, and they ended up on a quiet cul-de-sac punctuated at regular intervals by vaulting oaks. "Let's live here," she said. She
stepped out of the car and breathed in deeply to show him that she belonged in this new place. By year's end, they were there, along with a Lab
mix she'd rescued from a shelter. She asked William to suggest names
for the dog, but he came up mostly blank: he started with "Boy" and
then, when she reminded him it wasn't a boy, moved on to "Girl." He
was relieved when Louisa settled on Blondie. "Look at us," Louisa said.

William did, slowly at first. The house felt cavernous around him.
That first spring, he built a deck so he could sit outside, under trees
whose names he did not know, listening to birds whose names he did
not know. In the fall, he distinguished the place further by filling
the yard with a trio of vintage claw-foot tubs: an eagle, a lion, a tiger.
Before it got too cold, he put on shorts and got himself a beer and
stretched out in the center tub, the lion, the largest. Sometime between
that winter and the next summer, the television started to run an advertisement that showed older people in tubs as an illustration of ro-
mance, and Louisa asked William if he felt silly sitting in the tub after
seeing something like that. "Why?" William said. "Am I the kind of
person who gets scared off by what's on television?" She held up her
hands in surrender, but the damage was done. After that the tubs filled
up with leaves and he cleaned them out only for parties.

From the deck, the dog resting at his feet, William surveyed his
domain. The railing was lined with special lanterns he had bought in
Chicago, wrought-iron pieces silhouetted with icons of the American
West: cactus, cowboy, stagecoach. In the corner of the yard there was a
Wiffle ball that had been hit too hard by a kid in a neighboring yard,

or an adult acting like a kid. The house to the north had two little girls who sang sweet high-pitched nonsense songs to each other. The house to the south had a boy who spoke to his parents with chilling condescension. He was doing so now, his voice going sharply through the afternoon air. "Clearly, you don't understand," he said. "It's an assignment for school, which means it's required, which means I have to stay here and do it." There was a pause, and then an indistinct adult murmur. "And now tell me how that changes the facts," the boy said.

Louisa had a limit with the boy to the south, but also a fascination with him. "I don't know why they don't just clock him," she had said more than once. Now William called into the house. "Your friend out here is acting up," he said.

"On the phone," she said. At the sound of Louisa's voice, Blondie roused herself and trotted inside. William filled a big cooler with bottles of beer, removing the one that felt the least warm and settling down to drink it in a big wooden chair. The boy had stopped carping. The girls were not singing. There was a noise that pleased him, a spidery bass line from a car radio in the distance, and he followed it until it disappeared.

———

The doorbell rang. It was Eddie and Gloria Fitch, faces avid for approval. "Sorry we're so early," Gloria said. "I should have taken longer to get ready, as you can probably tell."

"Don't be ridiculous," William said. "It's not that you're here early. It's that everyone else is late."

Eddie, short and bald, piloted a bottle of wine into William's hands.

"I could use a drink," Gloria said. She was short, too, with round features and a sharp tongue.

"Your husband just gave away your wine."

"That?" Gloria said. "I wouldn't drink that." Blondie's collar jangled faintly on the deck. "Ooh," Gloria said. "Must pet dog."

William and Eddie worked for the same company, and they stayed by the door for a minute, faintly talking shop. "So they're changing the name of the division?" Fitch said with an anxious giggle. He had a nervous constitution. William imagined him fidgeting through his sleep.

"They seem to be," William said.

"I hope they're not focus-grouping it to death. That costs money, and don't they need that for our bonuses? Though we didn't get bonuses last year. Maybe I just answered my own question."

"I think you did," William said. "But it could always be worse. We could have no job at all. And then how could I afford to throw this party? And how could you afford to bring wine?" He held up the bottle, turned it until it was pointed toward the deck. "Let's go."

On the way out, he noticed that the door to the master bedroom was shut. "Hold on," he told Eddie. "I have to tell Louisa one thing." But Louisa wasn't in the bedroom. "Guess what," William said to the closed bathroom door. "Eddie and Gloria showed up first. Big surprise, I know. I'm taking them out back." When William made it outside, Eddie was unzipping wax from around a cheese, looking up at the overhang. "Painted the eaves and trim the other week," William said. "Doesn't look quite right now. Give it a few weeks of sun, though, and it'll fade to match."

"I know what you mean," Eddie said, waving the cheese. "New things just remind us that most things aren't new." It wasn't what William meant at all, but he nodded anyway.

The other guests were starting to arrive. Many of the men were bald and heavy. The women, with a few exceptions, fared better. Gloria Fitch was over in a corner, talking to sleek, epicene Paul Prescott, who held his thumb and finger just far enough apart to suggest he was indicating the thickness of a steak. He probably was. Graham Kenner, preceded by his aftershave, was lamenting the Congress. "Set phasers to socialism," he said.

William served drinks, refilled bowls of nuts and olives. "Hey," Graham said, reaching out to snag his elbow. "We missed you and Louisa the other week."

"Missed us how?"

"We had one of these at our place. A little get-together for Cassandra's fifty-first."

"Oh," William said.

"We sent real invitations and everything."

"Huh," William said. "I don't remember seeing it. Maybe we had a conflict. Louisa takes care of those things and doesn't always tell me."

"Speaking of Louisa," Gloria said, leaning in, "where is she?"

"She wasn't feeling great," William said. "Let me go check." He went back to the bedroom. The bathroom door was still closed. He tapped on it. No answer. He pushed it open slowly; the bathroom was empty. He checked the garage, the kitchen, even the laundry room, feeling increasingly foolish. On the way back out, he noticed that the junk room door was closed. That was what they called the spare bedroom off the main hall; they had marked it for a child when they moved in, and over the years it had filled with everything but. There was no answer when he knocked, though he thought he heard the jingling of Blondie's collar. "Hey," he said. "You in there, girl?" He tried the knob but it was locked. He jiggled it, knocked again, gave up.

Out on the deck he started to make hamburger patties for the grill, shaping rounds with his hands and then smashing them flat. Gloria Fitch had escaped Paul Prescott and was talking to a pair of young women William didn't know. Graham Kenner had buttonholed Helen Hull, by acclamation the prettiest woman in the neighborhood, to tell her about a study he'd read recently regarding parental favoritism. "You know how people say parents love their children equally?" he said. "That's not true. We're hardwired to prefer some of them to others, because we evolved from species that cull their young. You know: if you eliminate a third of the offspring, the rest have a better chance of surviving." He popped an olive in his mouth illustratively. The party had just started, and already the talk had turned to survival.

———

The doorbell rang, then rang again, its own echo. It was possible that it had been ringing for a while. "Someone get that?" William said, but no one did. He wiped his hands on a towel and went himself. It was Tom, wearing torn jeans and a T-shirt with a picture of a cartoon bird. William knew what kind of bird it was but he couldn't quite retrieve it: not a stork but something in that area. There was a woman behind him, a tall, voluptuous blonde in a white dress and a white hat. Her sunglasses were dark to the point of blindness.

"Billy Boy," Tom said. He stepped heavily into the foyer, long hair falling over his forehead, and clapped a hand on William's shoulder. The gesture wasn't overly emphatic, but it shifted William back all the same; Tom was as tall as his sister but twice as broad, with a deep chest and powerful arms. He resembled Louisa most closely in the eyes, which had the same distant brightness, like a ship coming in at nighttime. "My man," Tom said. The smell of alcohol rose off him like a cloud. "Good to see you. Point me toward the eats and drinks." Unguided, he wobbled past William.

William and the woman remained in the doorway. William smiled weakly.

"I am Annika," the woman said, extending her hand.

Tom was already deep into the house, but her voice turned him around. "Ah, yes," Tom said. "My lovely Swedish companion. Her grandfather was the minister of finance. They have finance in Sweden. It is one of their *in-dus-tries*." His finger made a spiral in the air through which the syllables of this last word passed.

Annika came into the house slowly, shaking her head as if she were getting water out of her ears. "I thought I would die in that car."

"The heat?"

"No. I thought Tom would kill us. He insisted on driving."

"His car?" William said.

"Have you seen his car?" she said. Tom owned a Charger of uncertain vintage, with a dented, crooked rear fender and tatty floor mats that covered but did not conceal a riot of discard: gum wrappers, receipts, hair, lint, pennies. It was in the shop more than it was out of it. "Mine, though I let him drive. He can be very forceful in his arguments. But there's no way he's driving us home."

"You don't have an accent."

"Neither do you." They squinted at each other until she remembered. "Oh, that. I'm not Swedish. I was born in Chicago. My mother's Swedish, though. She was a film actress there."

"Would I have heard of her?"

"It's possible." She pinched the bridge of her nose. "This is her dress I'm wearing. It was on-screen with Marcello Mastroianni."

William took the opportunity to stare. He was staring too much. The woman was too full. "My shirt was on local cable access," he said. "It was discussing the lagging housing market. It doesn't know what it's talking about."

"I never know what to say to celebrities," Annika said to William's shirt. Then, to William: "Should we go in? I should be a good date and fix Tom a drink. Maybe I'll water it down a little."

William sent Annika ahead and tried the junk room door again. "Louisa," he said. "Your brother's here. With a woman claiming to be his girlfriend, even." There was a shuffling and scraping from within, but still no answer. "You coming?" he said. "I'm going. There's hosting to do. We have guests to feed."

———————

Tom was already in demand, occupying the center of at least two conversations. He not only taught art at the local college but was an artist himself, which gave him the special status of a seer, or possibly a madman. "Sculpture is dead also," he was telling Helen Hull, which meant he'd already made the same pronouncement about painting. Tom billed himself as a chart artist. He made large-scale graphs that he transferred to canvas. Sometimes he called them meta-graphs, sometimes still lifes of information, sometimes "data tragedies." It depended on his mood, and to a lesser degree on his audience. Annika was evidently familiar with the performance as well; she stood off to the side, drinking white wine.

"Nice place you've got here," Tom said, catching sight of William. "It puts a man in mind of nature. Mother Nature, I mean, not human nature. Human nature, well, the less said about that the better." He laughed sharply and returned to the discussion, probably to drive a stake through drawing's heart.

The matte-black grill sat atop a white concrete island. From where William stood, he could see the window of the junk room, and he squinted to see if he could catch the curtain moving. He lost himself in the grilling. So many small pieces of meat about to disappear into larger pieces of meat. He put sausages on, took them off. Chicken followed. He added vegetables, peppers, and onions. The food hissed as it hit the grill.

Alcohol, a fuel, had increased the speed of the proceedings. Graham Kenner was explaining that city government had its own special brand of corruption, which he said was "homegrown and thus perfect for survival in the local ecosystem." Gloria Fitch was recalling how, in college, her boyfriend had rouged up her cheeks so she looked like a doll and made her sit cross-legged in bed, completely naked. People had moved closer to the edge of the deck, but no one had yet ventured

onto the lawn. A squirrel patrolled the zone between the eagle tub and
the lion tub.

Tom appeared at William's elbow. "Burgers?" he said.

"Getting there," William said.

Tom made to drain his beer, which was already empty. He puffed
and relaxed florid cheeks. "I haven't seen Louisa yet. She's around?"

"She is," William said. "I think she might have run out to the store
for more ice. Our ice maker is on the fritz."

"Fritz," Tom said. "Fritz." The way he said it made it sound ridiculous. He stepped up onto the concrete island that surrounded the grill,
where there was not quite enough space for both of them. "Damned
precarious up here," he said. "But the view is really something." Annika was coming across the deck now, and Tom hopped back off the
concrete onto the grass. "Well, well, well," he said loudly. "And they
told me there wouldn't be any women here today who would meet my
high standards."

"When I think of you," Annika said, "high standards aren't the
first thing that come to mind." She encircled his thick wrist with
her eloquently thin fingers and they wandered off, Tom weaving as if
avoiding obstacles. William plated the food.

———————

After another trip inside, and another session spent thumping on the
junk room door—lightly enough, so as not to draw the attention of
the guests—William went back outside and collected shards of conversation. He heard Graham Kenner on the fiction of a benevolent government and Paul Prescott on brandy's healing powers and Helen Hull

on how pleasure was a subdivision of something, though he didn't hear what.

He looked around for Annika and found her sitting on the stairs leading down into the yard, holding an unlit cigarette and smoothing her forehead with her fingertips. She wasn't talking to Tom, who was halfway across the deck with Eddie Fitch, swinging his drink like a pendulum. More precisely, she was not-talking to Tom: she stared in his direction, slightly baleful, every once in a while taking a sip of wine.

William walked up to Annika. "I'm going to have to ask you to leave," he said.

She blanched. Her wine was next to her, on the railing, and she picked it up as if that were the problem.

"You're not eating. That's against the rules."

"Oh," she said. "I was just admiring the lawn." She meant the tubs, but she didn't mention them. That happened often.

"Very admirable, I agree. But you have to eat."

"I'm a vegetarian."

"I know you are," he lied. "Tom told me. That's why we have grilled vegetables—for you and people like you."

"Okay," she said. "You sold me. I'll get myself something and be right back."

She returned a few minutes later, plate heaped high. She slid it onto the railing until it balanced and then she lit her cigarette. She was about the same height as Louisa, which meant that she was almost as tall as William. He looked toward the house, toward the junk room. Were the blinds moving?

"Well," Annika said after just one drag on her cigarette. "If I'm going to eat healthy, might as well get rid of this." She looked around for an ashtray, couldn't find one, then bent down and dropped the cigarette into a beer can.

"Don't do that on my account."

"I didn't," she said. "Although . . ."

"Although what?" William said. He was excited to hear.

"I think this was someone's beer. It belongs to that bald man over there." She pointed to Graham Kenner. "What if he wasn't finished?" She knelt to pick up the can.

"It's no matter now," William said. "That beer is, for all intents and purposes, no more. It has left our world for another world. We should wish it well."

Annika came up slowly, like she wasn't certain she wanted to. "I can't bear that tone," she said. "The tone like we're in a play. Don't you think I get plenty of that with Tom?"

"I can see how you might feel that way," William said.

"Or not," she said, frowning. "Who am I to complain? People are who they are. You either take them as they come or you don't take them at all." She had a look on her face like a lifeguard about to go into a churning sea. "Okay, then," she said, coming to her feet, "let's go find the boy."

———

The afternoon light was draining, and with it the specifics distinguishing one guest from another. William found Tom by height. He had no drink in his hand, but it was shaped like he was holding one. Fitch, beside him, was laughing so hard he was bent over.

"What's so funny?" Annika said.

"Milady," Tom said. "Allow me." He pulled out a chair with a flourish and then sat in it himself.

Annika got a chair for herself and pushed it alongside Tom's. William took a spot on a built-in bench across from Tom. "Did you have a nice talk?" Tom said. Annika slid out another cigarette, turned it over consequentially, returned it to the pack. Lines of strategy were visible between all of them, which made the whole thing beautiful, if unbearable. It was like a card game without cards.

One of the young women who'd been talking to Gloria Fitch wandered over. Sour-faced, eyes drenched in blue makeup, hitching a skirt that was already too short, she leaned on the deck rail. "Tamara," she said, blurrily enough that it was unclear whether she was calling out or identifying herself.

Tom stood and bowed at the waist. "Good evening," he said. "Do I know you? You look familiar."

"I'm Paul's niece," she said.

"I don't know Paul," Tom said.

Her eyes skittered from side to side. "I'm also a student at the college," she said. "I came to one of your summer lectures."

"Of course, of course," Tom said. "I don't know what's the matter with me." He gestured to his chair. "Sit, sit. A lady should not be kept on her feet."

Tamara waved him off. "Thanks, but I'm okay," she said. William slid over and made room for her.

"We were just talking about art," Tom said. "But if you came to my summer lecture, there's no reason to rehash it."

"Oh," she said.

"And yet," Tom said, "I'm interested in what an intelligent young woman has to say about the matter. Do you remember the distinction drawn between urban and rural art forms?"

"Well," she said. She ran a hand through her hair. "I was auditing."

Tom leaned toward her as if he was about to release a secret. Instead his head drooped forward until it was nearly in her lap. He brushed a fingertip across her knee and then, grasping that same knee, pulled himself in closer and looked up her skirt. "Ah, for the views of the countryside," he said.

"Come on, man," Tamara said. "Don't be a snake." She was smiling as if he had said something kind.

"I think I'll take a refill on that wine," Annika said, standing.

Tom had a hand on each of the girl's knees now, delicately, as if he were measuring tremors. He whistled faintly.

"You were drinking white?" William said.

"Anything." She wasn't looking at Tom or the girl.

"I'll get it," William said.

They walked briskly together, saying nothing. Annika stopped at the crackers and started to turn them like she was looking for the perfect one. William, affecting purpose, continued on into the kitchen, where he found a bottle of white wine in the refrigerator.

On the freezer door was a picture of him and Louisa, a Post-it note stuck just beneath it. "Family vacation?" it said. The question mark tripped William up. He marched to the junk room. Where knuckle had gone before, fist now went, a bass note against the door. "Louisa," William said. "This is ridiculous. I'm done entertaining your brother.

He's however many sheets to the wind a person can be. I'm going to have to drive him home."

"I thought there was a girlfriend," he heard her say. "Can't she do that?" She sounded far away, though the room was small.

"The mummy speaks," William said.

"I'm in here," she said.

"You should be out here." She didn't answer. "I'm losing my patience," William said, pretty sure it didn't matter. Just then he heard a noise, a pollen of alarm filtering in from outside.

———

Tamara, the young woman in the skirt, was pointing into the yard, and William followed her finger to find Annika sitting cross-legged on the grass, about five feet to the right of the rightmost tub, the tiger. She had grown tired of waiting for William to bring her wine and had switched to the orange punch. Tom was on the grass, too, though without his shirt, which lay crumpled at the foot of the stairs. He tottered toward the eagle tub, went slowly around it, and then shook his head, an unsatisfied customer. He did the same with the lion and arrived at the tiger, where he stood silent for a moment and then lowered himself into the tub. "Uh oh," Eddie Fitch called to William. "I think that's your cue."

William went down into the yard. The grass crackled under his shoes. He stood next to the tiger tub.

"Are you my father?" Tom said.

"No," William said.

"My father's dead," Tom said. He made a noise like a sob. His legs

were up and he had kicked off his shoes. He took an airline bottle
of single malt out of his pocket and emptied it into his mouth. "You
know," he said, "it seems at last that things are looking up." He lifted
the bottle as if to toast and then threw it as hard as he could toward
the eagle tub. "Shatter," he said, but it merely bounced once in the
grass and settled.

William extended his hand to Tom and pulled, aware as he did that
Tom was coming to his feet voluntarily; he was too thick for William
to move if unwilling. His belt was undone, buckle dangling, and his
belly hung out over his pants. "It's come to this," he said.

Everyone else at the party was lined up along the edge of the patio
now. Their mouths were parted slightly, as if they were tasting the air.
William looked toward the bedroom window. The curtain was pulled
aside now and he could clearly see Louisa. William wondered if she
could hear Tom. "I require the protection of a truly moral man. Are
you that man?"

William sensed that the question was in earnest. "I might be," he
said. "Though not by design. It just kind of happened that way."

"A good man designs," Tom said. "A great man submits to design."
He sat down hard, belt buckle clanging on the side of the tub. William felt something slide across the back of his legs and stepped free.
It was Blondie, sniffing the whiskey in the grass. William turned back
toward the house and saw Louisa there, at the edge of the deck, tasting
the air with the rest of them. Tom spotted her too. "Lou," he cried.
"It's good to see you! There's nothing more important than family, is
there?"

At this, Annika burst into tears. Her crying was arrhythmic and harsh and sounded, finally, foreign. Tom shouted at her from the tub. "Goddamn you," he said. "You're so beautiful." He stepped out of the tub, grabbed for her dress, got a bunch into his fist, and pulled. She reached for William to steady her, but he was no match for Tom's power. William pitched forward, a side of a tent collapsing. Annika's leg buckled. The punch, still orange in the dusk, splashed across the front of her dress.

––––––––––

Louisa sprang into action as if this were the moment she had been waiting for. She sped down into the yard, seized Tom by the arm, hustled him back up onto the deck; she located paper towels and club soda for Annika; she loaded Tom into Annika's car and waved as the car grumbled off down the gravel driveway; she returned to the deck, triumphantly smoking one of Annika's cigarettes and regaling the group with the story of what they had just seen. She grew animated in the retelling; a thin strip of perspiration appeared on her upper lip. "I don't know how, but I knew just what to do," she said, a note of surprise carbonating her tone.

William watched her with admiration. He wanted to keep the picture in his mind: his girl, on top of the world, and him right there with her. The cigarette burned down. Guests said their good-byes. Louisa stood to gather plates and cups. "Don't bother," William said. "I'll get it." When he looked for her again, she was gone, and he was alone in the thickening night.

Part II

———————

A HOUSE IS NOT A HOME

ONE

Most of the neighborhood was green, streets canopied by trees, lawns compassed by hedges, the houses themselves rarely exceeding complementary pastels, but about a mile north of William and Louisa was a stretch of highway that exploded simultaneously into tight-lipped gray and chattering color, a half mile of strip malls where buildings were densely packed in bric-a-brac and reader boards shrieked the latest specials. It was difficult to pass through this part of town without cringing, and for that reason its southern boundary was a site of welcome relief, as well as something of a local landmark. The last building on the strip had been a barbecue restaurant called the Pit, a faux log cabin topped by a stout iron pole, on top of which sat an enormous plastic pig wearing a chef's hat. The Pit had changed hands two or three times as a restaurant and then become a discount-retail outlet, though the new proprietor had wisely chosen to keep the sign. To get home, William turned right at the pig on the pole, which is what he was doing when the real estate agent waved to him from another car.

"Hi there," she said. He couldn't remember her name, but her face was the same as always, fully invested in a synthetic smile.

He returned her wave silently. It was Sunday morning and he was out for coffee only.

"Good news," she said. "We sold it."

"Great," he said. The light changed and he went around the corner.

It took him a few blocks to realize what she meant. The cul-de-sac where William lived was considered one of the most desirable in the area. His neighbors had not changed since shortly after he had moved in: Brooker and Pentz to his left and Eaton and Roth to his right, the other side running from Marker at the closed end of the street through Morgan, Johnson, and Kenner, with Zorrilla at the mouth. The houses were all one-story, Graham Kenner liked to joke, because that is what they told. More than once William had stepped out to collect his newspaper or water the lawn and seen at least one other man doing the exact same thing. There was a laugh of recognition and embarrassment they used in these situations. The structure of the street was as rigid as a crystal. Then one day at a party, Ron Johnson's wife, Paula, clinked on a glass and pulled her lips in with a secretive smile. "Someone has some news about sunny California," she said victoriously.

At first the neighbors had cheered the move, in part because it introduced some excitement into an otherwise uneventful April, and in part because most people disliked Ron Johnson and were glad to see him go. But after a month or so, with the FOR SALE sign still planted in the front lawn like a taunting flower, William began to resent the place on two counts. For starters, it bothered him that Ron Johnson could afford to move without selling. People whispered that the money came from Paula's parents, though Ron had assured William it wasn't true.

The second issue was that the vacant house began to look like a missing tooth in the smile of the street. It was directly opposite William, the first thing he saw when he left his front door in the morning, and he began to internalize its failure.

Now, finally, the place was sold. William went left on Conroy and right on Powell. He gunned the engine enthusiastically as he took the shallow turn off of Brashear, then coasted through the intersection of Jensen and Patrick. When he turned onto his street, he spotted the absence immediately: no sign at all, just the flat broad lawn, which was under the care of the Realtor and as a result far healthier and more manicured than it had ever been when Ron Johnson lived there.

———————

Louisa was on the phone in the other room. Her voice rose and fell in angry waves. He put her cup of coffee on the counter and drank the rest of his.

"Back already?" she said, coming into the kitchen. "Someone's here, cleaning. Your doing, I assume?"

"I thought it'd make things easier." Louisa, who could be lenient to the point of indifference about much of the house, was obsessed with keeping the kitchen in order, and so the day before, in a burst of foresight, William had arranged for a cleaning lady. The woman had arrived promptly at eight and stood with him on the deck. Beer bottles lined the edge of the railing; paper plates dotted the long table. Both had a faintly musical arrangement. William apologized for the mess, and she smiled. "Without mess, I don't work," she said. "This is three hours at least." Excitement clotted her voice.

"I'll go check on her," William said. But she was on a cigarette break, and he went down into the yard, where he found the whiskey bottle Tom had thrown. Ants rioted around it. In the house to the south, the boy who spoke to his parents as if they were children was already awake. He was crouched behind an overturned bench with a foam dart gun, carefully watching as another boy, a friend, pressed himself flat against the trunk of a tree. William copied the posture against the big tree in the corner of his own yard, but there was no one coming for him. One of the birds whose name he didn't know chirped loudly in the tree just overhead; its song was an exclamation point with feathers, a sharp whistle that went straight up.

In the kitchen, he paged through the newspaper, not quite reading. Louisa, spoon in hand, appraised a grapefruit that was titanic by any standard. "Hey," William said. "How about that party?"

"How about it?" Louisa said.

"You should have come out earlier."

"I had my reasons," she said.

"I don't doubt that," said William, even though he did. "So what were you doing that whole time?"

"What was I doing? I don't know. I read a little. I went onto my computer to listen to the radio, or whatever they call it now. If I'd known what was going to happen, I wouldn't have waited so long. I would have loved to see everyone before Tom went into the drink," she said.

"You mean the tub?" William said.

"I mean the drink," she said. "That's the last time we have a party for him."

"I hope he got home okay."

"He does his damage before he gets into the car. He's the world's oldest living child."

William lowered the newspaper. "Says the younger sister." Louisa pinched her mouth into a frown. "Seriously," he said. "Do you think it's okay that you hid out for the whole party?"

"Why?" she said. "Did you miss me?" She stood up and poured out her coffee, which was still mostly full. She wore tight aqua sweatpants that had not always been that tight and a cheerful pink T-shirt from the gift shop of the local history museum, where she worked as a curator.

"We're supposed to be in this together."

"You seem like you came through it with flying colors," she said without turning around.

"Says who?"

"You don't really want to fight about this, do you?"

"Fight, no. Talk, maybe."

"You don't really want to do that either." She fit herself into a safe place by the kitchen wall. "It was one party. I didn't make it out. No need to enter it into the permanent record." Her fingernails tattooed the countertop with a series of rapid taps.

"Fair enough."

"I'm going to shower and head to the grocery store."

"I'm fixing some things around the house," he said. "One of the lanterns on the deck is cracked, and the inside wall of the garage is damaged."

"The traditional couple," she said. "Traditionally maintaining their traditional home in their traditional neighborhood."

"Oh," he said. "That reminds me. The Johnson place sold."

"Bound to happen," she said. "Would have been more surprising if it didn't." What had happened? They had been taking it to Tom, and then William had started in after Louisa, and then the ground had reversed and she was bearing down on him. William rotated his coffee cup, suddenly eager for the day to start.

———

William hadn't been into the junk room in weeks, but things were just as he remembered. There was a scarred wooden desk and a ripped beanbag chair, an old computer that worked too slowly connected to a printer that William wasn't sure worked at all, a box of dog toys they had been sent as a promotion and never unpacked, discarded exercise equipment, a musical doll that had been Louisa's when she was a baby, a wall calendar from a previous year. A white plastic bag, fat bellied and rabbit eared, hung from the window crank. He emptied it onto the desk: there were magazines and advertising circulars and a letter from an old college roommate of William's who had made a killing online and now spent all his time plumping for environmental causes. He was soliciting donations and had included, as a personal appeal, a photograph from just after college, when he and William had driven to a music festival in New Orleans. William looked at the William in the picture: slimmer, lower hairline, more definition along the way. There was something in the eyes, too, a productive unknowingness. William had recently turned forty-two, a number he experienced as an atrocity. No man ever felt completely happy looking at a younger version of himself.

William left the mail in the bag, though he transferred the photo to the bottom drawer of the small table next to his bed—his museum of self, the place where he kept old letters and postcards, along with some dirty magazines and a coin collection he hadn't thought about in years. "Louisa," he said, coming into the kitchen. "Do you know why there's a bag of mail in the junk room?" But Louisa was gone to the grocery.

In the first years of their marriage, William and Louisa had fought often, and he had blamed inexperience, or high spirits brought on by the habits of the inexperienced: too much drinking, too little kindness. As time went on, a civility replaced the combat, and it wasn't until much later that it occurred to him that this placidity might be the result of what was absent rather than what was present. By that point, they mostly had only each other. Louisa had one close friend, Mary, who worked at the hospital across the municipal plaza from her office and whom she saw for lunch a few times a month. Her one ex-lover of note, Jim, was now living in Seattle with his wife and two children. William and Louisa had met Jim for dinner or drinks once every five years or so, when he was in town on business, and the meetings were cordial, heavily nostalgic, maybe a little longer than they needed to be, harmless.

For William's fortieth birthday, Louisa had taken him for dinner in a new restaurant attached to an old hotel downtown. She debuted a low-cut red dress for the occasion, and, after a few drinks, produced a room key from a matching purse. "Another round of drinks?" she said. "We're staying here tonight." He put a hand on the back of her thigh in the elevator and she showed him the hollow of her throat and said, "Yes, yes," the way she should have, but her voice came at him as if from the bottom of a well. He couldn't do anything much in the room, and she forgave him in that same distant voice. "Things can happen," she said. "Or not happen. That's just how it is."

Later that night, she shot awake and stared at the hotel walls with unfamiliarity in her eyes. "I'm not sure," she said, and just as quickly she burrowed back into her pillow, leaving him awake and alone in the inky blue air.

Her speech in the hotel was incomplete, but that didn't change the fact that it was essentially accurate. He had always counted on his ability to see Louisa clearly, but a part of the picture had smeared. In the months that followed, he started performing small gestures: flowers (she liked marigolds), candy (chocolate, the darker the better), the remote when they watched TV at night. He was surprised to find himself succeeding. She was ardent, generous, cooked him a meal as a surprise and placed the flowers in a prominent vase in the center of the table. "You know just what to do," she said, looking straight at him without giving the impression that she'd rather be looking away. He ate quickly, flushed with relief.

William was watching TV in the den when Louisa appeared beside him, hair piled atop her head except for one damp strand that snaked down her forehead, aqua sweats swapped for a yellow sundress. "Will you take a ride with me?" she said.

"You don't have to ask me twice," he said.

"Well, now I just don't know what to say," she said. She headed toward the front door. "Where are you going?" he said. His car, a nondescript sedan, was in the garage.

"I'm driving," she said. "My plan." Her car, a nondescript SUV, was in the driveway, and they climbed in.

The radio was playing a song Louisa liked, and she sang along. In the morning, she had been all nuance, impossible to untangle; now she was a bright, straight line and he had to blink against it a little.

She went along Ennis, turned on Arnold, and merged into Morton. "We're going to the mall?" William said.

"Quiet," Louisa said. "It's for your own good."

Inside the mall, the white floor was slick with light. Fake flakes of snow swirled on a giant video screen, even though it wasn't winter. Girls in high spirits laughed brightly on the perimeter of a carpeted pit where young mothers herded toddlers.

William and Louisa passed through the department store at the south end. Louisa stopped when they reached a clamor of oversize screens. "This is an appliance store," William said, trying to hide his disappointment.

Half a dozen salespeople were milling around in identical blue uniforms, and the closest of them, a young man with tight cornrows, stepped toward Louisa. "Can I help you?"

"We want to look at dishwashers," she said.

"How green?" She squinted and he stepped right, toward a row of low plastic boxes. "These do much better with water usage and energy expenditure. But if plates go in really dirty, they don't always come out really clean."

"I don't see the point of not getting things clean," Louisa said.

"It has to do with how much effort you're willing to put in at the sink."

"Does it come in stainless steel? I don't like the black or white."

The salesman pivoted to his left obligingly. "These are also good," he said. "It's turnover time so they're on sale."

"Green?"

"Not so much. To be honest, I hear there's not a huge difference between one kind and the other." His face suddenly fell, as if the beliefs upon which he was building his world had been disproven. "Here's my card," the salesman said. When Louisa moved to take it, he let it go quickly, as if it was hot.

"This way," Louisa said to William, gesturing broadly as if she were guiding him down a runway. They ended up two doors down, at an almost identical store where the salespeople wore red instead of blue. The man who approached them was older, with owlish glasses. "You came to the right place," he said, examining Louisa from head to toe in a manner that William did not find entirely reputable. He championed the stainless steel, and Louisa filed his card alongside the other one. "Well," she said. "I guess that's that." She turned to leave.

"I guess we didn't need the big car after all," William said.

One of the girls from before was on her hands and knees in the kiddie pit. It looked like a game at first, but she was wailing to her friends. "Those are my mom's earrings. She'll kill me if they're lost."

———————

In the car Louisa sat staring straight ahead, belt pulled partway so that the buckle bumped her shoulder. "Come to think of it, I want to check out one more place," she said.

"Just one more?"

"I can drop you at home if you want," she said. This was the impatient tone again, and William sensed now that it was concealing something.

Louisa backed out of the parking lot, went right on Kerrick, swung onto Francis, took a left at Harrow. She drove past one appliance store and then another. "Look," William said. "Dishwashers." But she said nothing, only drove, until there were no more buildings lining the roadside, just trees and scrub, and they went ten minutes beyond that, to a part of town he was not sure he had ever been to. She pulled over to the side of the road, switched the engine off, and got out to stand next to the car.

William joined her.

"So," she said.

"So," he said. "What are we looking at?"

"What do you think?" she said.

William tilted his chin up and tried to piece it together, but the land didn't look like anything: grass held down by sky.

"It's nice," he said.

"It's ours," she said.

"Ours?" William said. He didn't even flinch, which made him proud. "When did this happen?"

"A while ago," she said. "When my dad died, he left me some money in a trust. It matured. At some point, it was clear that it wasn't going to make any more money where it was, so I put it here instead. The rest is still in an account."

"The rest?" He tipped an invisible hat. "Nicely done," he said. "Really. Wow."

"It almost didn't happen. Yesterday they called me and said there was a problem with the sale."

"What kind of problem?"

"It turned out the bank had processed something incorrectly. That's why I didn't come out. I didn't want to face everyone while I was still reeling. It would have been just another thing I tried to do and failed."

The squint that came was from confusion. "But you didn't fail, right?" he said. "You said this is ours."

"We went through the paper trail and found it, and they remedied their error before I got off the phone with them." She'd been speaking slowly, but excitement was hurrying her along now. He stared down at the grass between his feet. His left shoe was coming undone at the toe, where Blondie had put her teeth into it.

He looked back up at the land. "It's big," he said.

"An acre," she said. "Is that big?" Louisa pointed to the end of the property line and back. It was mostly featureless, save for a tall elm at rear left and a browning knoll at front right. Fish-scale clouds roofed the afternoon and what was left of William's shadow lay down on the hill.

Suddenly she sprinted into the middle of the lot. "Land," she said, her voice bright and young. "Land, land, land." A crack in the clouds showed enameled blue sky. Then she was back at his side, up on her toes as if she were greeting him after a long time away. "I just wanted to show this to you." An artful pause followed. "Thanks for coming out."

"You're welcome," he said. "I like to know about every new investment."

"Is that what it is?" she said. She packed back into the car, fully proud now, face prim in profile. "I like thinking about the actual land. It's like a new country, but miniaturized. We don't know what will happen here."

William nodded, but not because he agreed. Mystery was for people whose desire to make life better outweighed their fear that it might become worse. William, for his part, had brokered a tentative peace with the flat line. It held its ground. And measured against the gravity of time, wasn't that a form of getting better, really?

———

She went on brightly through dinner, her conversation ventilating the kitchen, but then whatever motor was spinning inside her began to wind down. "I'm going to go watch TV," he said, and she just nodded.

A movie he didn't recognize was on one of the channels he paid extra for. It was about an older actor whose stardom in Westerns was built on the backs of his long-suffering family. He was trying to make peace with his grown daughter. The scene William came in on was played out over swelling strings. "I thought your cowboy hat was so big," the daughter was saying. "But the other day I tried it on and it almost fit me."

Louisa appeared at the door and knocked vertically along the frame. "Hi," she said.

"Hi," he said. He muted the TV.

"So," she said. "What do you think of it? The land, I mean."

"A lot," he said, but when she didn't answer right away he wondered if he'd been too glib.

The cowboy was alone now with a bottle of whiskey. He lifted it. He lowered it. He tipped it until the golden liquid was at an incline.

"I've been thinking about the things we have," she said, "and the things we don't have." Her sentence, split by the pause, fell open in two halves. "All of this," she said, casting her hands upward into the room.

"And all of the other, too," William said. "Land, land, land."

"I drove by there last week," she said. "It wasn't real yet, but I wanted to see how it felt. A few lots over, there's a construction site. Someone's putting up a house. The workmen were just driving away, and I walked up to the front where the doorway's going to be."

"Was it safe?"

"I even poked my head in. It had that distinctive smell, sawdust over earth, some faint electrical haze. The plans were tacked up near the front: they're going to have a sunken living room and a big island in the kitchen and a nursery with a little porch off the back."

"The best-tacked plans," William said.

Louisa eyes flashed out at him, but only for a second; then the anger was gone, like an arrow taken away by the wind. There were tears instead. "That girl's dress was so beautiful," she said. "And Tom ruined everything."

———

William watched a college basketball game, played along with an old game show whose answers he already knew, failed to laugh at a stand-up comedy special. The dog lounged beside a knife of lamplight on the rug. He kept flipping channels, high in the spectrum now: cooking class, home-design competition, travel documentary. He put his hand on his stomach in what he imagined was a Napoleonic manner. He crouched on the floor next to the dog and locked his ankles under the couch for sit-ups. They weren't hard until twenty, and then they were too hard. He went back through channels in descending order, the pictures washing over him in a rinse.

He had a brief idea that he might play some guitar, and he went into the garage and turned on the lights. When he was younger, he had learned the rudiments, mostly to impress a girl at college. He was mediocre at best, but when he moved to the house he had set up a guitar and an amp in a corner of the garage. Louisa called it his rehearsal space, which pleased him until he considered the possibility that she was mocking him.

In the corner by his guitar there was another plastic bag, tied up like a hobo's kerchief. He opened it to find even more mail, mostly advertising circulars and catalogs, along with a postcard from a distant cousin of Louisa's who had moved to Australia. This mail was dated earlier than the batch he had found in the junk room. He left the bag where it was, shut off the garage light, and wondered what it meant, if it meant anything at all.

Louisa was tough. It was something he used to tell his friends as a joke, admiringly but with a touch of exasperation, until he realized how true it was. She was tough when her father died and tough when her mother died. She was tough when she lost her job at the publicity firm and had to send résumés around for more than two months before the museum job came open. So what had rattled her now? He laid out the year in his mind. There was nothing out of the ordinary, no extreme misfortune. He could ask her but he doubted she'd even admit to the bags of mail.

The dog needed a reason not to rush after him down the hall. William pitched him a treat, which hit the floor with a little hop and disappeared into the narrow triangle between the garbage can and the counter. Blondie scrabbled for it and William made his getaway. In bed, Louisa was on her side, over the sheets, eyes closed. He went toward the bathroom with small, quiet steps, unsure if she was awake and unwilling to find out. When he came back to bed, Louisa was curled beneath the covers, pretending to hide. "You in there?" he said. But there was no noise and barely any life in the heart of that snow hill.

TWO

"Word around the office is, they're going with Domesta," said Eddie Fitch. He tipped his empty paper coffee cup, set it upright, tipped it again.

"Domesta is horrible," William said. "It sounds like a car, or a pill."

William worked for the Hollister Company, which occupied two floors of a mirrored office building downtown. The Hollister brothers, Leon and Julian, had started in residential development but maintained a sideline in mortgage brokering, and over time they had shifted into customized investment packages. Their flagship offering was TenPak, which had one foot in real estate and another in stocks, required an initial commitment of ten thousand dollars, and promoted, while not exactly promising, returns of 10 percent annually over a ten-year period. William was the editorial manager of the sales department, which meant that he was charged with preparing one-sheets and brochures for the salesmen when they went on sales calls. When people asked him what he did, he said financial writing, and over the years he had come to believe it.

"I used to drive a Domesta," Harris said. "Got terrible mileage."

Lunch was the spine of the day. Everything else moved away from it in both directions, at a constant speed. A group of them, what William thought of as his group, was eating in the lunchroom on the eighth floor, sandwiches brought from home or purchased from the ancient vending machine in the break room. "You'd just think they would have told us at the same time as everyone else." The week before, a memo had come down from nine announcing that the real estate and energy-investment divisions were being rebranded. Energy had quickly received a second memo informing them that they would hereby be known as Vyron. Real estate had been left to hang in a cold wind: sales had dropped for two consecutive quarters, and there were whispers that the staff would be thinned out before the end of the year.

Baker cleared his throat. Deep-voiced, caramel-skinned, always clean-shaven even on close inspection, he was the group manager. He had started at the same level as the rest, around the same time as William, but he had risen through the ranks like a flame on a curtain. "Pill is what they're going for," Baker said. "The economy has been sick, or perceived as such. So how do you cure it, or create the perception of cure? Take a pill. *Domesta has been proven effective in treating consumer debt and securing equity in your primary residence. Side effects may include nausea, hair loss, and ectopic pregnancy.*"

Harris and Fitch laughed. They were both easy laughs, though of much different species. Harris, tall and skinny, with hair that would have reached nearly to his waist if he were of average height, laughed like a cowboy, slow and appreciative, while Fitch erupted in childish giggles.

"The side effects include nausea?" William said. "You mean when people hear the word? I can understand why. I'm getting a little queasy myself."

Another pair of laughs. William didn't know if he deserved them. He was well liked, but the things he assumed people liked about him—his height, his voice, the fact that he had kept his hair and stayed relatively trim into his early forties—were things he had no control over. And so when people nodded at his comments or smiled at him in the hall he simply returned the gesture, neither pleased nor displeased, passing back something he had already decided had no value.

"Why change at all?" Harris said. "What was wrong with Hollister Homes? Don't people want a trusted name in an economy like this?"

Baker steepled his fingers. "These days," he said, "financial-services companies are among those most likely to rebrand, along with food services and technology."

"Maybe they're still making up their mind," William said.

"Minds," Fitch said.

"No, I think William is right," Harris said. "I think 'mind' is right."

"How can you say either, really?" Baker said. "Corporations are a highly specific form of organism that balances both collective and individual thoughts."

"That's exactly what I was thinking," William said.

"Me too," Harris said, and laughed.

"As long as my name's in the middle of the checks," Fitch said, "I don't care whose name is on the top." He looked to Harris for support. "That's my thing."

"Here's mine," Harris said. He wadded up his napkin and arced a shot toward the wastebasket in the corner.

"Perfect," Fitch said. "Two for Harris."

"That's a three-pointer," Harris said.

"No way," Fitch said. "Too easy. Shoot at a can that's farther away." He did, and missed.

"Pick that up, please," Baker said, flipping a hand toward the wad, lord to liege.

Fitch giggled. Lunch was over, with very little solved.

"William," Baker said. "Stay a minute. I need to discuss something with you that I have already discussed with Nicholas and Susannah." Baker called everyone in the office by the longest version of their first name. "We have an issue with O'Shea." He called customers by their last.

O'Shea was a local restaurateur who had bought into TenPak for a hundred thousand the previous January and doubled down in June. But then a cloud settled over him: his wife left him, his teenage son was in a car accident, and there was a kitchen fire that shut his restaurant for months. He had requested the return of his entire investment. "That can't happen," Baker had said. "When money goes out like that, it can start a stampede, especially in an economic climate like this one. Can you prepare a new one-sheet?"

"Sure," William said. "I have the spring brochure. I can revise and reprint that."

"Wonderful." Baker buttered the word. "Come by tomorrow and show me what you've done."

William tinkered with text and reviewed the accompanying artwork: a couple about his age, standing near what was probably a beach, holding hands. A boat in the distance distracted the eye. He marked it out with a circle and a line.

At four, he stretched his legs and went down the hall. He had read that each continuous hour of sitting shortened a man's life by ten seconds. Susannah Moore, who oversaw the office information network, was explaining the new e-mail protocol to another woman, her voice a colorless music. In the break room, Antonelli and Cohoe were holding cups of coffee; Harris was steeping tea. "How can you drink that stuff?" William said. "I'm going out."

"Done for the day?" Harris said.

"No," William lied. "I just need to get out of the office for a little while. I'll be back."

"Some people don't have real offices," said Cohoe, who did.

At the elevator, a man appeared at William's side. It was George Hollister, short and thick, his graying hair shaved tight, his features crowded into the center of his face. George was a nephew of the founders and the nominal boss of the division, though he didn't come in most days, and when he did, he mostly sat in his corner office watching a Japanese cable channel that none of the other TVs in the building seemed to get.

Hollister was standing next to the last elevator, which worked only by pass card. He and William had a checkered history, in the sense that there were a limited number of moves in the game. Years be-fore, Hollister had seen William out one evening at a performance of the *Symphonie Liturgique*, making use of subscription tickets Louisa had ordered. Hollister was alone, and possibly a little tipsy, and he had clasped Louisa's hand and expressed surprise to see William. "I didn't figure you for a music lover," he said. A few weeks later, in the office, Hollister asked if he could expect William at *Il Seraglio* that week-end, and the time after that he wondered if William had any opinion on Dohnányi and laughed aloud. The whole thing began to shade into malice, and William kept to the outer circuit of the hallway in a largely successful effort to avoid Hollister. This time, he had failed.

"Good afternoon," Hollister said.

"It's not bad," William said.

"How have you been?" Hollister said. And then, without waiting for an answer: "I thought of you the other day. I was at a Lyatoshynsky event, the *Mourning Prelude*." He held his fingers to his mouth and then opened them in a bloom of appreciation. "But I didn't see you there. Is everything all right?"

The elevator arrived in time to save George Hollister's life.

———

Tuesday came, rang its dampened bell. William rolled out of bed, shuffled to the bathroom, urinated, fished his toothbrush from the cup, brushed, showered, toweled dry, pulled comb through hair, pulled clothes onto body, breakfast table, cereal, car, road, parking space, el-evator. Somewhere along the way he became himself.

The morning passed without incident: he readied the presentation for O'Shea, reviewed the new brochure, visited the break room at regular intervals. At one, William walked over to the Red Barn, a dim, dingy restaurant on a small side street off Oakmont. Karla, a small forceful brunette who worked hard to seem relaxed, was waiting at a table. "Hi," she said. "I already ordered. Iced tea, right?"

"You're too good to me," he said.

William had been with Karla before Louisa—or, as he liked to say, between Louisas. Karla was a part-time Realtor with a sideline in floristry. She approached both jobs indifferently; her father, an engineer who had discovered a new material for industrial packing, had left her with enough money that she never needed to mention the amount. It was a mountain whose top she couldn't see. William had met her at work, when he was in advertising. They had been friends at first but had passed across the center of some odd chemical equation and become sporadic lovers. He had other girlfriends and she had other boyfriends. "We do this because we like it," she said, in a voice that made him unsure whom she was comforting. Then one night at dinner she pointed at his smiling face and said, "I'm about to change that." She was, she said, pregnant.

He was thirty-two years old, never married. He knew there was, at best, a one-in-four chance that he was the father, but he felt that fraction settle into him with a mix of thrill and misgiving. She kissed him and put her hand in his hair. "I need a sample to know for sure," she said, and pulled for science.

The DNA tests let him off the hook, pointing instead to a South American businessman who had been in town for the summer only, and then Karla stopped answering William's calls. When the baby was born, a boy named Christopher, she asked William out for coffee and apologized for cutting him off so abruptly. "For a little while I just couldn't," she said. Then Christopher's father had been piloting a small plane from Miami to the Bahamas when it crashed into the ocean. "It's not like he was around," she said. "He didn't want anything to do with us. But this is so permanent." Her lower lip trembled. He had never seen her so close to crying.

For a little while they were together again. William read the newspaper to the boy and fed him from a bottle and held him frequently enough that for the rest of his life he would be able to remember the hot little body with its rapid, rabbity heartbeat. When William and Louisa got back together, Karla wrote herself out of the scene, though they still met twice a year to mark the passage of time on each other's faces.

"Move your elbow," Karla said, pointing up at the waitress. "She's trying to give you your iced tea."

"Thanks, Mom," William said.

"You wish," Karla said.

"Speaking of which," William said, "I have a story." He had been at the park a few weeks before and had seen Christopher by the basketball courts, ringed by friends. When William had waved, the boy had returned a stiff reverse nod, chin lifted from chest as if by guide wire.

Karla laughed. "Ten years old and already treats you like a colleague."

"I could use a man like him down at the office."

"How's it going over there, anyway?"

"Been better," he said. "But things are tough all over."

"True," Karla said, blushing a bit because she had no idea. She was living in a large house in the best part of town and casually dating a young filmmaker, also independently wealthy, who took her on ski vacations twice a year and was teaching Christopher to ride a horse. "And how's the home front?"

"Ah, the home front," William said. "Smooth? Bumpy? Who can say? Louisa's brother moved to town. She threw a party for him and then refused to come out."

"For how long?"

"The whole party."

"Hmm," Karla said.

"The party's not the only thing," William said, and then had to think if it was. "I think she might be hoarding the mail."

"Hoarding?"

"Squirreling it away. I found two bags of it in the house, hidden in corners."

"Is she depressed?" Karla, precise in so many things, defaulted to the vaguest language when it came to the feelings of others.

"I don't think so," William said. "The other day, she drove me out to a plot of land in the middle of nowhere."

"Sounds like a mob hit."

"Turns out it's land she owns. We own."

"Congratulations," she said.

"I guess," he said. "I stood there in front of the land and felt empty."

"It's an investment," Karla said.

"But in what?"

"In your future," she said. "I hope you didn't make her feel bad about it."

"Sometimes people place the future between themselves and the present," he said. "I'm trying to figure out how to make things work now. If I do that, then the future's just the sound of that same note sustaining."

"That's beautiful," Karla said. The idea was something William had acquired from a magazine, which didn't make it less beautiful.

William paid, as always. It would have been nothing to Karla, and he wanted it to be something, at least. The cashier was the daughter of the owner. She smiled when she saw him looking at her. He had known the girl since she was six or seven and seen her at least yearly since then. She had been small and plump as a child but was now tall and angular, with a pleasant open face and skin as tight and fresh as an apple. Over the years she had absorbed hundreds of thousands of glances, touches, conversations, not to mention time itself, the minutes, the seconds, the smaller pieces that could not be casually measured but were still indisputable. She had grown thin in part because she had grown full with time. She was fifteen, maybe sixteen, and she had the body of a young woman, mostly there, never quite there. William wondered if Karla, looking at the girl, would think of the younger versions of herself, or of an older version of Christopher. William thought of the girl who had sat beside him in school when he was twelve; hair sprouted from beneath her arms and it shocked him. His arms felt leaden, not quite his own, both then and now. He thanked the girl, asked after her father, and went out to join Karla in the parking lot.

William's afternoon was oversold, a trio of conference calls laid end to end, and when he finished the third he went to the bathroom, wet his hands, and ran them through his hair. The office water was hard, or maybe it was soft: he didn't know which, but within an hour his hair would be stiff as a brush.

On his way down the hall, William saw Fitch standing outside Antonelli's office, pointing at the door. "I think I saw him in the break room," William said.

"Not today you didn't," Fitch said. "He's gone. Fired. There's a new guy coming to replace him next week from San Diego."

When William heard that changes were coming, he'd feared that this would be the first. Antonelli didn't always have his mind in the game—hadn't since that morning five years before when he had woken up early to play a round of golf on the course that bordered his backyard. He had eaten breakfast with his children, kissed his wife on the forehead, and made it to the first tee by seven. Antonelli was playing with an older Chinese man assigned him by the course, which was how he preferred it: "Less conversation means more concentration," he liked to say. He birdied the first hole and parred the second. The third hole was the one that backed his house; it had a water hazard in the form of a small lake. Turning to square himself with the tee, Antonelli noticed Linda, his three-year-old daughter, peering through a gap in his fence. He waved. She shouted something. Antonelli could not hear and so he pointed to his ear. She shouted again. *"Pete,"* the Chinese man said. "She say *Pete.*" Pete was Antonelli's son, six. Antonelli jogged closer to the wall. "What about Pete?" he said. "He fell in there," she said. She indicated the lake. Antonelli went in with all his clothes on. He didn't even drop his driver. Pete was in the shallows, not breathing, a lump on his head from where he had knocked against the rocks. Antonelli pulled him out onto the fairway and pumped his chest. The Chinese man called an ambulance. Antonelli's wife arrived just in time to watch her son expire on the lawn.

Like many personal tragedies, the incident was discussed frequently in Antonelli's absence but never in his presence. Two years after Pete's death, when Antonelli told the guys his wife was pregnant again, there was a moment of silence, a tensing, that preceded the round of congratulations. Once, William and Louisa had run into the Antonellis at a restaurant. William met the new baby, also a boy, and squeezed his foot. Louisa had praised him for this. "It's the normal thing to do, which is why I'm glad you did it," she said. But in the office, no one knew exactly how to handle the matter other than to ignore it, in part because they did not wish to do further injury to Antonelli, and in part because they feared, like all superstitious men—that is, like all men—that any mention of the drowning might begin an invisible process by which they, too, would be robbed of that which was most precious to them. Most of the other guys had kids, too, mostly sons, and on slow weeks they would bring the boys around and charge them with delivering paperwork or making copies or carrying out other duties that were not significantly more trivial than what went on at Hollister on an average day. William looked forward to opening his office door to a miniature Fitch or Cohoe. The last time, Elizondo had instructed his five-year-old son to walk into Antonelli's office and say,

"Lou, I really appreciate all that you've done for the company, but I think it's time we go our separate ways." Antonelli had laughed at that. Everyone had agreed it was a good sign. But it was a bad one.

———

William was heading for the elevator when he saw Harris standing in Baker's office, pointing out through the glass. William moved and Harris's finger moved with him. William stepped in. "O'Shea dropped out of TenPak," Baker said.

"What?" William said. "I was just about to send over the presentation."

"No point," Baker said. "He's gone for good." He rose up slightly behind his desk: broad, mahogany, it was like a ship at the head of a fleet.

"So what should we do?"

Baker pinched his chin and stared past William. Behind him there was a painting of an island, a conical mountain, ringed by clouds, rising from its center. William had heard the story of the mountain: Baker had climbed it as a young man, though the painting was made decades earlier. One of the other climbers who'd scaled the mountain with Baker had said that, after reaching the summit, most of the men on the expedition acted as if they had survived a tragedy. Their behavior became indefensibly risky, and for a number of days base camp became a blur of sex and drugs and gambling. Baker, by contrast, was exactly the same coming down the mountain as he had been going up. His only concession to the ascent was to acquire the painting, a testament to his calm mastery of the world.

"I think we should go down the line to make sure it doesn't happen again," Harris said.

Baker frowned and nodded. "That's prudent," he said. "There's another gentleman, a Mr. Loomis, who put in about eighty. I was just telling Arthur, I think you should clean up what you did for O'Shea and then Arthur and Edward will take it over to him. Can that be tomorrow?"

"If for William, then for me," Harris said.

"It works," William said. "I heard about Antonelli."

Baker lowered his head slightly. For a second, William thought the gesture was a guilty one—clearly, he'd known Antonelli was about to get the ax—but his head rose back up on a tide of purpose. "Louis was a valued part of this company," Baker said. "This economy can sometimes make harsh demands. Which is why it's all the more important that we keep this company running as smoothly as possible. If the Loomis meeting happened tomorrow, that would be best."

William made for the elevator. At the head of the hallway, he saw George Hollister again. Twice in three days: it had the feel of premeditation. William stopped at the stairwell. "No elevator for me," he called down the hall. "I have to go up to nine to pick up a file." George Hollister started to give him a thumbs-up but then extended his right index finger and, for a few excruciating seconds, conducted an imaginary orchestra. "Friday," he said. "Scriabin. They're staging the full *Mysterium*. I can only imagine that a man of your refinement will be there." William pushed into the stairwell, where a man of his refinement took a step upstairs, as if he were actually going for a file, then turned and hurried downstairs. In the lobby, he bought a bottle of water and an energy bar and handed the woman a five-dollar bill. "Keep the change," he said.

"Big spender," she said brightly. It occurred to him that he was. He unwrapped the energy bar and nibbled the edge. His phone buzzed. "Hello?" William said.

"Hey," Tom said. "Want to come over? I'm hanging."

THREE

Most of the university campus was done in Collegiate Gothic, but the art gallery occupied a sleek new glass-and-steel structure that had been endowed by a hedge-fund billionaire with roots in the community. The permanent collection filled the flat disk of the main building; new exhibits went into the wing, which extended to the north like a tonearm. William entered through the front door and gave Tom's name to a fiercely tattooed brunette whose face was almost entirely obscured behind a Japanese graphic novel. "That way," she said, extending a finger elegantly.

Tom was alone in the middle of a mostly empty large room, head lowered, looking like someone else's artwork until William got close enough to see the phone in his hand. "Send him over," Tom said. "I need him to make sure the projector works." There was a word for what Tom was, with his thick limbs and his large head and his jaw always set.

"Billy Boy," he said, turning. "Just firming up a few last things." He waved toward the far wall and his shoulder muscles shifted beneath his shirt. "Video loop over there." Burly: that was the word.

Tom was a graphist. Not a graphologist—"that's handwriting analysis, and everyone types these days," he said—but a visual artist whose work consisted entirely of charts and graphs, most drawn on paper, a few painted on canvas. His subjects were self-referential and possibly philosophical: he made charts, he said, about the way people looked at charts. Before Tom came back to town, Louisa, in a burst of sisterly pride, had shown William an online interview with Tom. "Graphs are supposed to help us see clearly," Tom said. "But what if they teach us that seeing clearly is impossible?"

The interviewer, a young man with early gray at his temples, leaned forward into his next question: "The untrained eye might say these are just comic versions of ordinary graphs, the kind you might see in a newspaper."

"As Kepler said," Tom said, "the untrained eye is an idiot."

That video was not in the exhibit. Instead there was another short feature, narrated by a young woman, that called him a "prop comedian whose props are some of our most commonly held ideas" before giving way to a montage of his graphs: bars, pies, points. The final was a line graph that rose sharply and then fell off as it went. It was titled *How Well You Understand This Graph Over Time.*

Next to the video were three huge gray bars stretching from the floor toward the ceiling, and over them an equally huge caption that read *Percent Chance That, in the Original Full-Color Graph, Each of These Bars Was the Color It Claims to Be.* The first one, labeled "red," rose to 60 percent, "green" went to 70, and "blue" left off around 25.

Tom was off the call now, coming toward William with a purposeful stride. "Funny," William said.

"Funny slash sad," Tom said. "If a color isn't what it says it is, what is it?"

"I'm no philosopher," William said. "But I would say that color is a liar."

"Isn't a lie just a deeper truth?" Tom said. "Each of these works is a way of conducting an experiment into what we believe: into conventional ways of organizing ideas, conventional narratives, conventional morality. And all convention leaves something to be desired. Here, let me show you the new pieces." A hand went on William's shoulder again, and William felt the weight of Tom's attention.

Beyond the smoked-glass door at the corner of the room was the lobby for the entire exhibit, which was called *Faculty Voices*. Participants included, according to a brochure, a Native American woman who rendered biblical scenes on parfleche and a Frenchman who created grotesque miniature sculptures and set them before distorted mirrors that reflected them back as normal. The tattooed brunette from the front desk was there, sitting behind the same book. "Jenny," Tom said. "This is Billy, my brother-in-law. I'm going to show him all the important work in the show, by which I mean all of my work." The girl lowered the book, beaming. Was she his next-in-line? Or maybe she'd already passed through.

Beyond the lobby was a small rectangular room. "Here you are," Tom said. His eyes flashed impatiently. "Take a look." The room had three pie graphs printed in bright colors; he could read only the first, which said *Is This Pretty Much the Roundest Thing You've Ever Seen?* One hundred percent of respondents had answered in the affirmative. There were also half a dozen black circles on the floor. "Percent chance that someone will walk on me?" William said.

"Not bad," Tom said. "But wouldn't be accurate. We strive for accuracy." He patted the near wall, which was fully white save for a stenciled title: *Heights of Visitors*.

"Nice," William said. He wasn't sure what he was looking at.

"Hang on," Tom said. "Nate should be here any second." And he was, a young man whose T-shirt was emblazoned with a logo of a skull and crossbones, the former made from a paint can, the latter from paintbrushes. "Right on time," Tom said. "This is Billy. He's here to see the piece. Fire up the standing circles?"

"Certainly," Nate said. He went back to the small door and slid his finger along the space to the right of it. "Stand on one of the circles," Nate said to William. "Any one." William picked the one closest to him; suddenly a gray bar materialized on the wall.

Tom stood on another circle, and a slightly taller bar appeared next to the one William had generated. "You too," Tom said to Nate. He stepped onto another, which produced a third bar.

"How does it work?" William said. "There's a hidden projector?"

But Tom wasn't listening. He was staring coldly at Nate. "Go back to that other circle," he said.

"Which other?"

"The one right by the door. It didn't even flicker, but you went right on past it." Tom was not raising his voice but rather lowering it, which shrank Nate.

"I don't think so," Nate said.

"Don't need to think so," Tom said. "I saw."

Surrender came into the boy's eyes. "I just wanted a good demonstration. There's something wonky about the sensor."

"Fix it." Now his voice went up in volume. "That's your job. When you're hired to do something, you do it. You don't skip it and think that people are so blinkered or so timid or so used to settling that they're not going to look you in the face and ask you exactly what I'm asking you, which is why you can't figure that out without a reminder." His anger was like another person in the room.

Nate slunk away through the door. Tom looked up at the ceiling and rolled his head around like it was loose on his neck. "Dim bulb," he said.

"He's just a kid," William said.

"No," Tom said. "The problem is a dim projector bulb. The circle works fine. If he'd been paying attention, he would know that."

"You're not going to tell him?"

"Can't," Tom said. "His senior thesis is about the psychological aspects of gallery shows. He has to figure it out for himself." Tom restaged the demonstration, stepping on the circles in quick succession, including the culprit by the door, which produced a faint outline. "The thing about this piece," Tom said, "is that the projector is also a recorder. When it's all done, you can review the entire history of visitors." He had William step on every circle and then played the set back. The bars appeared on the wall one by one, shadows of things that were no longer there. "I hope it works on opening night," Tom said. "Because that's what the world needs more of: hope."

———

Tom snaked back past the lobby and then through another small door, which opened into a large bright room with a rectangular snack counter and ten or fifteen circular tables. He sat for a second, then sprang up violently. "What are we doing here?" he said. "The coffee is terrible. Let's go to that place on Gerson. Can you drive?" And then, when they were in the car: "I might need a favor."

"Isn't this a favor?"

"Something bigger," Tom said. "Not too big, but a slightly larger investment. I can't say much, only that it requires an automobile. And let's keep it between us for now."

"What about Annika?"

"What about her?" Tom said. "Oh, her car? She wouldn't be right for this. And anyway, she's gone with the wind." He gave a dismissive wave. "She couldn't accept my demeanor, which I understand. Many things are said when a man is in the demon's grip. *In vino vulgaritas.* She's not the first to object. In fact, there are certain countries I can't go back to as a result of my high spirits."

"Which ones?"

"Mexico. Egypt. Assorted island nations." Tom had lived as an itinerant academic for more than a decade, and he kept his past whereabouts frustratingly vague. "All good options for Annika. She'll be safe from me there."

"Too bad," William said. "She seemed nice."

"And people are always how they seem." Tom laughed. "If you're not careful, you'll end up a philosopher yet." He smiled thinly, as if he could see what was coming for William and had nothing particularly good to say about it. "It's probably better that she got gone. This way, I get free. I'm no expert at relationships. Never saw the point of them. They always say 'a marriage of two equals,' and it always ends up as an Anschluss. As it turns out, Thomas does not play well with others, and so Thomas does not play with others at all, not for the long run at least. He gets what he can, and then he gets back to work." The weather had turned when they were inside, and the sky looked like a window with the curtains drawn. "It's like Horace said: *'Aut insanit homo, aut versus facit.'* 'The man is either insane or he is composing verses.' "

"Why not both?" William said. His voice was filled, suddenly, with a vehemence that surprised him.

———

As they neared the intersection of Rosten and Sawyer, William noticed a man coming across the park. He was walking funny, wobbling side to side with every step. Then William noticed a second man, then a woman, and then he saw the fingers of thin, dark smoke at the corner of the office building at the far end of the park. Before long, nearly two dozen people were in the park. They were dressed for the workday—the men wore suits, the women dresses—but several were without shoes or had their shirts unbuttoned. One man, tall and reedy, with a receding hairline, came near enough that William and Tom could hear him talking on his telephone. "Fire," he said, after which he doubled over and began to cough.

William took a bottle of water from the door pocket of the car, hopped out, and rushed to the man. "Here," he said. The man braced himself and downed the entire bottle of water. "What happened?" William said.

The man jerked a thumb backward. "Started in the electrical closet, I think." The man worked for an insurance company, Birch Mutual, which shared a broad two-story building with attorneys, a consulting service, home health care, and tax preparers. They'd had dozens of false alarms over the years, the man explained, so many that the employees learned to ignore them. "They usually tell us to wait for an update on the condition, and then they vanish for a few minutes," the man said. "But this time they came right back on. This time you could hear the fear a little bit." The man had been in the east wing. "They told us not to move. The west had to evacuate out the front door, but we were told to stay where we were." So they remained, working, or trying. "We all were looking up to the second floor. Then there was a noise over by the central stairwell, and they all came running downstairs."

Others leaving the building had gathered around them. Some had sooty faces. All smelled like smoke. A few of them came near William's car. "Hi there, Fred," said one man, holding out his hand. Fred didn't reach out to take it. William was relieved; a handshake would have seemed inappropriate. Someone came from the park house with more water bottles, and they were passed from hand to waiting hand. Tom rolled down the car window to listen.

About five minutes after the first alert, Fred said, the alarm sounded again. A part of the roof had collapsed. "They told us in the drills that that was only a faint possibility," said the man who had offered his hand.

"They don't know," Fred said. "At that point, everyone started grabbing what they wanted to take with them: family photos, cell phones, food."

Tom came out of the car. "People grab to flee a fire like they grab to flee a flood," he said. Fred nodded, though William didn't know if he was agreeing or just acknowledging the idea.

Just then a woman gasped and pointed; the crowd turned, almost in unison. A man was going across the far edge of the meadow—at least William thought it was a man. It was a plume of fire with a dark core, and it was making a noise that was not quite a shriek but not quite a word: a high note, eerily pure. "Andy," a woman said. The figure lurched forward a few more steps and then collapsed onto the grass. Another man appeared from the building and started hitting at the fire with his coat. "Is it Andy?" another woman said. Paramedics rushed toward the middle of the field like water to a drain.

Louisa's friend Mary liked to say that there were two kinds of people: those who couldn't stand to see people fresh from an accident, all busted up, and those who couldn't stand to see people who were terminal, slowly withering on the inside. Louisa had announced she was the second type and waited expectantly; William said nothing, but they both knew he was the first. A few years earlier, Louisa, who never complained of pain, had felt a stabbing in her belly. Bleeding had followed. The doctor ran tests, and in the days of waiting, as William worried over every terrible possibility, he wanted nothing more than to escape, to get in the car and drive north as fast and far as he could. The tests came back, and the doctor explained what had happened, pointing to pink areas on a chart of the female anatomy. Louisa wept. A pamphlet outlining fertility treatments was pressed into William's hands by an overeager nurse. On the drive home from the doctor's office, Louisa stopped crying, and William made his peace with the almost lunar silence that followed.

Now, with the paramedics still on the burning man, William took out his keys and opened the car door. "What?" Tom said. "We're not leaving, are we?" They could see the burned man's legs, clothes in shreds, in the gaps between the paramedics. The man moved for a little while on the ground and then stopped moving. Orders were shouted, skin was wrapped, a stretcher procured, the body hoisted. There must have been sirens, but William did not hear them.

———

The coffee shop, the Bean Counter, was the small dream of a pair of married accountants. They had been fixtures in the place, greeting guests and always finishing each other's sentences, until something snagged after a year or so and they split up. People now called it Grounds for Divorce, with not a little sadness. William and Tom ordered from a stringy young man with a faint caterpillar of a mustache and carried the cups to a table by the front. A pair of women fake-hugged another pair of women they didn't seem happy to see. Three five-year-old boys were banging hell by the counter.

"You know what I was thinking about when we were by the fire?" Tom said. William shook his head. "I was thinking about the man who was running across the field."

"That's understandable," William said.

"But not about his pain, or his misfortune, or anything like that. I was thinking about the physics of it." Tom bent his head, dug a thumb into the hinge of his jaw. It was a gesture William had seen on Louisa. "You know Aristotelian physics? He said that certain elements seek certain locations. It's in their essential nature. Earth moves toward the center, or down. Fire moves toward the sky, or up. By his reckoning, a man who's mostly fire would fly away, but that man went down to the earth. I wondered what Aristotle, or someone who believed his philosophy, would have thought as he watched the man go down. He might have wondered, suddenly, if he knew anything at all. But people can't really entertain that idea, because that's when the slippage starts."

William nodded and said yes, the slippery slope, and Tom interrupted him right back. "No," he said. "The slippery slope is for politicians and propagandists. The slippage is a specific thing. It's the moment when you start to lose your footing." He held up a hand, rigid and horizontal, to represent the X-axis of some invisible graph. "See," he said, "any graph is a set of expectations. It tells you what's normal and what's exceptional, where there are gains and losses. But what if you suddenly find that you're plotting all your data on a graph that's coming loose? What if the graph itself is unmoored, if you no longer know where you're standing in relation to it?" The hand flipped so that the thumb and fingers switched positions. "Is the hand reversed now? Is it even the same hand? You don't know if you can trust the graph, not because of its inaccuracy, but because of your disorientation. The slippage isn't the moment when a graph turns upward or downward. It's the moment when it turns on you."

"I'm not sure I know what you mean."

Tom rapped on the tabletop. "Well, then," he said. "You're halfway there." He blinked fiercely. The right hand, the one that had been the baseline, fell into his lap. The performance had not gone unnoticed by those around them. The quartet of women snickered among themselves.

FOUR

William woke. He rolled to his right and nearly turned an ankle standing up. The darkness was smooth, the visual equivalent of silence. He could see the outline of the dog sleeping near the entrance to the bathroom. When he was a child, he would sometimes stand in the hallway in the middle of the night and wonder if perhaps he had died. "You awake?" he said to Louisa, but Louisa wasn't there.

He found her in their rarely used living room, sitting with her legs folded under her. The television was on, but not the volume. "Hey," she said.

"What time is it?"

"Ten thirty? Maybe not quite. When I got home you were zonked out in bed with all your clothes on."

"I had quite an afternoon. Long day at work, and then guess what happened." He set the scene dramatically, starting with the color-coded graph in Tom's studio and the gray bars on the wall. "They're like teleporters," he said. Louisa didn't seem to be listening. She was holding a tube of lipstick in her hands, swiveling it up and down, and William started to feel transfixed by the way it always went back where it came from. When he got to the part where the first man had made his shaky way across the field, Louisa didn't even look up at him. Now he was sure she wasn't listening.

Suddenly, Louisa stood. "I need to talk to you." She wielded the lipstick.

"Okay," he said. "What about?"

"I need you to tell me that there's a next step in all of this."

"In the story? I just got to the fire."

"I mean the land," she said. "Our land."

And then it came to William, all at once; he was like an explorer in a jungle at the moment the vegetation cleared. "Oh," he said. "You want a new house."

———

"I do," she said, like she was making vows.

"But there's no house on that land," he said.

"Right. So we build one."

"Build?" It was an idiot's echo.

"I'll make it worth your while." She shifted so that her sweatshirt slid off one shoulder, exposing the swell of a breast.

"Come on," he said, and she covered up, frowning. "Are you serious? You think we should build a new house?"

"People do it all the time. I told you: I peeked into one that's just going up."

"Right," he said. "Because we have all the time and money in the world."

"Is that what we need?" she said. "All the time and money in the world?"

"Can't we redo a room here? Is it change you want?"

Her frown hadn't lifted. "I just want to know for sure that life is moving forward."

"What's the alternative?"

Louisa stood, smoothed her shirt in front, and turned away, murmuring something he couldn't quite hear.

"What?" he said.

"There's nothing here for me." She headed down the hall.

"So that's it? That's our evening?"

"It's a bed you made," she said in a gratified way. "Lie in it. I can't stay out here with you when you're being a child." She forced capital letters onto the last few words.

Blondie lolled beneath one of the front windows and William went to pet her. Kneeling there, he took a measure of the night sky. There was a nearly full moon, a coin no one could spend, and he moved side to side to hang it in the center of the pane. He had read recently that Earth might have a second moon, invisible to the naked eye. The scope of it all disconcerted him. He couldn't even really get a grasp on the minuscule portion of existence in his window. William was increasingly convinced that he was a man of limits.

———

William usually treasured his weekend mornings, grateful for the extra hours in bed, but the image of the man coming across the field was still high in his mind, and he got to the shower by eight, grateful for the water. The late news had furnished some details, and more were on the radio in the morning. The man was not Andy. His name was

Karim and he had been one of the security guards at the building. He had been rushed to the hospital, only to be pronounced dead a few minutes later.

The deck was the most reliable place of comfort William knew, and he sat there, the dog at his feet. The sky was filled with dark clouds in strange shapes, and the sun coming through them gave the tubs the look of old bone. "Garcia," the radio said, calling the security guard by his last name, "is survived by one son, age fifteen. His wife was killed last year in a car accident."

William's parents had died at either end of his twenties, both uneventfully, if such a thing was possible. His father's death had come as a sorrow but not a surprise; he was a cancer survivor by the time William was born, a young man who moved like someone much older. William remembered him as pale, precise, and almost pathologically quiet, as if he were hiding from something and worried that the smallest noise would reveal his location. Maybe he was: between William's junior and senior years in college, the cancer had returned with new ferocity. William, home for the summer, visited him frequently in the hospital, unsure what to say to the silent figure stretched out on the bed. He did not know how he had come from the man, who hardly seemed to have enough energy to produce a sentence, let alone a child. On the day before William went back to school, his father clasped one of William's nervous hands between both of his papery ones. "Thank you," he said, his voice filled with emotionlessness. It was a humiliation William would never forget and almost all he could remember at the funeral a month later.

His mother had been quiet in life as well, but when she was widowed, a dam within her opened, and judgments poured forth: the art on the wall of the lawyer's office was depressing (William agreed), the waitress at lunch dressed like a streetwalker (William disagreed), the oceans had been polluted beyond repair by the shortsighted greed of the human species (William felt the matter needed more study).

Then she fell ill, with a different cancer from the one that had killed his father. The treatment took her hair and gave her the look of a fortune-teller, scarf wrapped around a head that seemed larger than ever, and that lent her pronouncements a dramatic weight. When she visited his apartment, she stood in the front doorway and said that it was no place for him if he wanted to be consequential in the world. "Get yourself a house," she said. "Don't be a coward."

He flew out for her funeral within the year, made remarks at her graveside to no real effect, and put a bid in on a house—a modest one-bedroom with a small screened porch on the north side of town. When the Realtor called him to tell him the place was his, he was at his desk at the advertising agency where he worked as a copywriter, and he went to the bathroom and stared at himself in the mirror.

His first night there, he brought a girl over to help him christen the place. The girl was Karla, and she lay down on an air mattress, which was all he had, in her underwear, which was all she had. "Certificate of occupancy," he said, pointing at the deed, and she laughed and bucked up her hips rakishly. "You may own the house," she said, "but you're a renter here."

Then Louisa, returning to him, had taken him away from all that, into what she insisted was his first true home. He found himself agreeing without feeling any inner snag or catch. Was that love? Now, in the dim afternoon light beneath the clouds that would not rain, she came outside, having forgiven him for the fight of the night before, carrying mugs in both hands as proof.

"Thanks," he said.

"No problem," she said. "It's not very good coffee." She leaned on the rail. "Looks like the people who bought the Johnson place are finally moving in," she said. "I saw a man the other day. About our age, short, hairy."

"A caveman?" he said. "In that case, I would definitely consider getting out of here. Drives down property values."

"Funny, but not so funny," she said. "Let me read you something. I was going to read this out at the lot the other day, but I lost my nerve." She took a piece of paper out of her pocket. "'We make a pact with another person to follow as far as they go, but we do not really mean it. We mean that we will follow so long as we do not start to feel lost. Love, or what passes for it, is about believing that we are never truly lost.'"

"That's nice. Who wrote that?"

"I did, in college. I found it the other day during the party."

"I'm glad you were keeping busy."

Louisa turned, the paper still in her hand, and he thought she was going to start in on the idea of a new house again. But speculation was running ahead of evidence. She sat down without a word. Adjacent yards supplied the sounds of children.

———

The next day, he woke early, kissed Louisa good-bye, and made like he was going to work. Instead he drove to the triangular park on the corner of Keeler and Martin, where he sat and watched knives of light pierce the surface of a small lake.

Louisa and William had come to this lake during their first try at love, twenty years before. They passed the time naming ducks, or rather William did, mostly for historical figures. The one in front of the line, looking around imperiously: Churchill. The one in the water, flapping its wings: Archimedes. The one off to the side, tilting its head and considering a family at a picnic table: Albert Einstein. Louisa named them all Duck, and every once in a while pointed excitedly into the middle of the pack and shouted, "Goose!"

He had crisscrossed the town hundreds of times over the years, never with any particular emotion, but now it contained the possibility of loss—or, rather, he saw the possibility of loss that had always been there—and it made him sad. That was the apartment building where, twenty years before, he and Louisa had considered renting a place. That was the tree where he had pretended to carve their initials. That was the Italian restaurant where he had thought to take her during their first relationship, but she had broken up with him and he had never been able to work up the courage. Most of these, he conceded, were somewhat abstract.

He crossed back through town in search of more concrete examples. There was a park bench where Louisa had kissed him roughly. There was a canal where William had, half in jest, thrown a pebble he pretended was his wedding ring. There was the pig on a pole, presiding over discount retail. The theater on Loomis and Bell contained a longer story. A few months after their second first date, he had taken Louisa to see an old film about a young woman from a small town in the Upper Midwest. She took training as a singer, made a striking entrance in a big-city nightclub, fell in love with both a waiter and a captain of industry. Two of the sides of the triangle were shot to death.

Afterward, out on the sidewalk, William seized Louisa's hand. She wore gloves, which he mocked as an affectation but secretly admired. "What?" she said.

"I have a question," he said. "You don't have to answer right away."

"What is it?"

"Well, you know how you start life alongside everyone else and then, when you're young, detach from the mainland? You drift out on your little floe. At first it's exciting. Then it's scary. Then you look and see that all around you there are other people on floes of their own. They look close to each other, because they're far from you. If you could get close enough, you would see that they're all feeling the same terror. But you can't get close enough."

"I wish your mouth would shut sometimes," Louisa said, but when she covered it with hers she made sure it stayed wide open. He woke in the morning to find her sitting on a chair beside his bed, already fully dressed, even down to the gloves, and the morning breeze slowly ballooning the curtains in the bedroom.

"I can't believe you remembered all that," Louisa said. She had coaxed him out onto the deck with a bottle of red left over from the party. The sun had just disappeared behind the rear fence, but she had lined up the wrought-iron lanterns on the railing. A big-band song, clarinet in prominence, sailed in from a radio in a neighboring yard. "Who would pick a girl who wears gloves?"

"I would," he said. "I did."

"Come here," she said, but she pulled her chair closer to him. She hid her head in the space beneath his chin and he smelled her hair, now a sugary vanilla, and when she sighed and blew hot breath against his neck he understood that he had miscalculated by telling her about the drive through town. He had wanted it to ignite the same fire in her, but it lit the wrong wick. It had put her in mind of his love for her, not for the neighborhood.

She kissed him on the side of the face, and then on the lips. "I'm heading off."

William went from deck to garage, tried to exercise a little, stood with barbells in his hands and his full weight pressing down on the soles of his feet. He picked up his guitar, ran his fingers over the body and the neck. There was a scar near the bridge that he wished he had the story for, but it had been there when he bought the thing. So much in the world had happened before he arrived.

Coming through the kitchen, he was stopped by a flicker in the corner of his eye. It was another white plastic bag, handles tied, belly full, in the center of the counter. He dumped the contents out. The first bag, the one in the junk room, had contained June's mail; the bag in the garage had been May. This had everything they had and then some: notices from professional associations, postcards announcing special offers at local stores, catch-up chronicles from friends they hadn't seen in years. The invitation to the Kenners' cocktail party was in there. There were no bills or checks or even subscription renewals—

anything of consequence had been removed—but along with the mail there was a strange assortment of objects: a spare key for his car; a baseball cap he had thought was lost forever; a bottle cap that, upon closer inspection, appeared to have been saved from the party they'd thrown for Tom. The collection was at once curated and entirely haphazard.

He went down the hall. The hall was endless. The junk room door was closed. He put a knuckle to it but got no answer, though he thought he heard the faint strains of the music box. He had better luck with the bedroom door. "Yes?" Louisa asked.

"I found this bag you left here."

"What bag?"

"The giant bag of mail and things. What do you want me to do with it?"

"I don't know what you mean," she said. And then, "Deal with it, I guess."

He removed the spring top of the trash can, slid it to the corner of the counter, and started transferring the contents of the bag: catalog, catalog, magazine, catalog, magazine, bottle cap. He put the baseball cap on his head.

On the back of one catalog, stuck diagonally, there was a cream-colored envelope, note card size. He peeled it free. His name was handwritten across the face, and the return address was one he didn't recognize, from Chicago. He scrutinized the cancellation, which was dated more than three months ago. He looked again. He had seen his name written that way before, with a loop atop the central peak of the W. He could not think of the hand that made the loop but thought he might if he concentrated. Concentrating meant overlooking the pooling noise of the refrigerator, the thrum of a car going by, Blondie's barking and the distant commiserating howl of some other dog. But it came to him. And when it finally did, it came with force, and his knees rubbered out from under him.

Part III

———————

THE SEARCH PARTY

A little more than a year before, William had been in the same position, though it was nighttime, and the air was cool from recent rains. Louisa drank coffee and read the paper. Blondie toyed with a bug she had trapped between her paws. William set up an old boom box that was busted unless you put a foot on it to hold the cassette door closed. That's what he was doing, and singing along: "Would you miss your color box, and your soft shoe shining?"

"Don't sing," she said. "It offends my ears." He whistled instead, and his favorite bird joined in above, the one that sounded like a firework. "Hey," Louisa said, shaking the paper, "here's one thing that might interest you: it's an article about a deck and porch trade show in Chicago next month."

"What exactly do you think of me?"

She laughed. "It looks pretty impressive. You should go." She started reading, suddenly serious on his behalf. "'For two days in July, the convention center will be host to the world's largest deck and porch event . . .' See? It's an *event*. You would have a good time. I'll buy you the tickets, even."

"With my money? You're too good to me. Are you trying to get rid of me?"

"I'm trying to be nice to you. You like these kinds of things, even when you don't admit it."

"I admit it," he said. He pulled her chair to his and brushed his fingertips along the side of her head.

"Put your mouth where your fingers were," she said. The surface of her face did not change except to admit that there was more beneath it. She led him, her fist around a single finger of his. That was all it took sometimes.

He got in under the wire for conference registration, overstuffed an overnight bag—toothbrush, toothpaste, deodorant, two days' worth of clothes, phone, cord, a few books in the corners—and drove himself to the airport, filling with the lightness he always felt before a trip.

———

Coming down in the plane over Chicago William read the city as a text, each block a paragraph, each building a word. What did that make the people? Characters, maybe.

He checked into the hotel and then wandered back downstairs, past the tables with fliers, the posted schedules, a banner connected to another convention advertising something called "Legislative Karaoke." In the hotel lobby, he struck up a conversation with a fellow conventioneer named Pete, who had inherited a series of camping lodges in Wisconsin. Pete convinced him to come out for drinks. "I have a cousin here," he said. "She's young, and her friends are even younger. They know a bar near here." The bar was lined by curved wooden beams, and after hours spent watching young women pretending to resist the advances of men, William began to feel the whole place sinking. "I'm feeling tired," he told Pete, who was making inroads with a pale girl whose face was tilted up to show long thin nostrils. He went back to the hotel and slept partly dressed, atop the comforter.

The second day was William's first in the crass cathedral of the convention hall. All around him, farther than he could see, people stood hawking additions to decks, techniques for perfecting them, plans for care and upkeep. One woman sprayed a piece of wood with what looked like silver paint. Another demonstrated fireproofing by holding a match to a square of fabric from lawn furniture. A tall redhead, in a blindingly pink bikini, struck a bored pose in a hot tub that had no water in it.

William looked at post caps in the shape of lions and welcome mats that showed pictures of famous baseball players and lawn sculptures of fantastical animals like unicorns and dragons. Eventually he came to a booth that displayed craftsman lanterns decorated with regional filigree: one set had a Western theme, cacti and cowboys, another mountains and pines, a third a lobster and a sailboat. A young blond woman was also in the booth. When she turned around, she showed bright eyes beneath dark eyebrows and a full, rounded mouth that contained teeth that were neither too small nor too white.

"I'm just browsing," he said.

"Oh," she said. "Oh, no. I don't work here. I thought you did." She sounded Southern, but lightly so.

"No," he said. He put on a loud stage whisper. "We can steal these lanterns and run."

She reached out and touched the nearest lantern. "I wish they had the whole New England set out. I might steal that. But this is an odd assortment, one of each. It's all over the place. I wonder if there are other booths that have the same thing but different."

Together they went to explore. At the next booth, surf music was playing from speakers hidden in plastic rocks and a small man with a flowered bow tie was bending and straightening, bending and straightening. Looking closer, William saw that he was applying a sheet of PVC to a flat surface. "Imagine this is a balcony," he said. "We treat them like they're roofs. We lock the PVC in place mechanically, using trained applicators, because we have learned over thirty-five years not to trust adhesives."

"I've learned the same thing," the woman said. "But with men."

The small man blinked. "We've put down more than a hundred million square feet of this material."

Deep in the hall someone dinged a digital bell.

"Well," the woman said. "I think I hear a Sunbrella calling my name."

"Which is what?" William said. But she was too far to hear.

———

The end of the day's program was signaled like an intermission, a tug on the lights to dim them. William went to the hotel bar, where a small combo measured out mediocre jazz and the pretty bartenders brightened coldly in anticipation of the coming tide. What was William drinking in those days? What wasn't he drinking? Probably he started with scotch. He liked the way it glowed in his glass and even the way he hated the smell. Pete popped up on the other side of the bar, came to thump William on the back, said he was sitting in the back with some friends and William should join them. From a distance, William gave Pete's group the once-over: two older men, one older woman, one younger man. They laughed and tipped forward into the light, which was not what he had in mind. He spoke to the bartender for a little while. She was trying to break in as an actress. "I can do either comedy or drama," she said, doing neither.

Midway through his second glass, William saw a woman step into the bar, look around as if lost, and then proceed to Pete's table: she had blond hair cut short, tan shoulders, a slight curve to her back, like an archer's bow. She was walking away from William, mostly, but he saw that it was the woman from the convention, his friend from the lantern booth. He steeled himself with what was left of his scotch and then headed over to return Pete's thump. "Hey," he said.

"Mr. Bill," Pete said. "Meet my people." He rounded the table counterclockwise. Alan was a mortgage broker in Ontario. Roy was a musician turned forest ranger. Ana was a Cuban artist and, apparently, Pete's date while in town. William nodded at each description, absorbing little. The young blonde was in the middle of a conversation with a young man who was scouting locations for a new television drama about deep-sea divers. "The shadows of the palm trees are like dazzle paint," the man said. William leaned over to shake hands. "Simon," he said. "And this is Emma. She's a caterer, working at the show."

"I'm not working it," she said. "I'm looking for supplies for deck catering."

"Whatever," Pete said. "It still doesn't explain why she knows so much about the ocean." William nodded, introduced himself, said that it was nice to meet everyone, looked at Emma as he said it.

About an hour later, the waitress appeared at William's arm to see if he wanted a refill on his whiskey, except that it wasn't the waitress; it was Emma. "Pete was looking for you," she said. "He wanted to know if you want to go out with a bunch of us tomorrow night."

"What are you?" William said. "The search party?"

She moved up, as if by levitation, onto the stool beside him. The small band was stuck wetly in the middle of "How Long Has This Been Going On?" "I'm here," she said, "to tell you how I know so much about the ocean."

She was thirty-one years old. She had been born in the eastern suburbs of New Orleans, to a chemist father who worked in an oil lab and a dancer mother, Russian-born, who had forgone her own career and opened a small studio instead. Emma had danced, too, hated it, been delivered out of bondage by injury in her late teens, had switched over to marine biology in college, and had seriously considered a career in it. "Which is how," she said. College was Chicago and summers spent working in restaurants, and an older boyfriend who taught her to cook and encouraged her to start catering. "The money was good enough that I postponed grad school for a year," she said. "Then it got better." She had been a caterer for almost ten years, and had been good at it for five. "It's the kind of thing where commitment really matters. When you run an event, it's like conducting an orchestra. So many moving pieces." She paused and flipped her hand outward like it was hinged. "I'm sorry," she said. "I should shut up."

"No," William said. "I mean, maybe about work. I could live with that. But how about the rest of life?"

"Ah," she said. "The rest of life." There was a disorderly silence and no strong indication that she wished to go on talking, though eventually she did. "Married for about two years. His name is Stevie. He works for Arrow, the car company, in marketing." She drew a line on her forehead with a finger wet from ice. "One of his commercials was on the TV a little earlier."

"How did the two of you meet?"

"At a party his company threw. I was sort of seeing another guy, but Stevie came up and started talking to me and he was attentive and funny and handsome. I was in high cotton."

William downed his second scotch and then a third. Emma nursed a gin fizz. It must have rained while they were in the convention center, because the sun was coming off of wet concrete, and then it was low in the sky, and then it was gone.

"Hey," William said. "Is that his commercial?" He pointed at the television, but it was too late. They were on to advertising computers.

Emma set her legs apart, on either side of his. "You don't have any idea," she said, "do you?" William shook his head. She was right. He didn't. But then he realized that he didn't even know what part of his ignorance was being identified. "Let's go," she said.

They took the elevator up in silence. William was tall enough that he didn't mind crowded elevators; sometimes he enjoyed them. He was standing behind Emma, watching the seam where her roots darkened and disappeared into her scalp. When the doors opened, she turned left and then right and then stuck her card key into the chrome box hanging below the door handle. The panel blinked green and she put her shoulder into the door. William followed her in and went straight to the bathroom. "Hope you don't mind," he said.

"Not at all."

When he came out, he noticed a man's suit hanging on the closet door. "What's this?" he said. "Is Steve here with you?"

"Stevie," she said. "And no." He looked around the room. It was his room. "Remember when I asked to see your wallet?" He nodded, more to try to locate the memory than to agree. "Well, I just took your key."

Or maybe he was remembering it wrong. Maybe he had given it to her, laughing as if he was returning it, and they had ridden up in the elevator under the spell of this fiction. Or maybe he had interrogated her further about her job and her marriage, asking questions in rapid-fire delivery until she sighed and said *Pochemuchka*," which was, she explained, an affectionate insult for an overly inquisitive friend. They had held hands in the hall and looked at their joined shadow. They had duplicated the pose in front of the mirror and looked at their joined reflection. Or had they?

What he did remember for certain is that she had taken off her shoes, and that their removal had the opposite of the effect it should have, making her seem taller, and that by now he accepted the paradox of her physical stature and realized that the only way to resolve it was to render her horizontal, which he did, lightly pushing her backward onto the bed. Out loud, though not to her, he said, "We really should turn on the television." He didn't think she had heard him, but she reached back and found the remote control and switched it on. He lay down on the bed beside her. They were both fully clothed. The only bit of come-on, except for the fact that she was in his room, was the shoes, and that was hardly anything at all. Maybe it was just going to be the TV.

For a little while they lay on the bed that way, rigid as skis, and watched the closed-circuit convention channel, which was showing footage from that morning. She switched channels until she found an ocean documentary, and she started to tell him about the animals of the deep, how their eyes had a reflective curtain just behind the retina that kept light in, a *tapetum lucidum*, and her chest was gently rising and falling, and the hollow at the base of her neck was fluttering. William propped himself up on one elbow so that his face was above hers. He traced the line of her jaw with his finger. There was something comical about her at that moment, despite her beauty, and she seemed to sense it, and she crossed her eyes and jutted out her tongue. "Oh my," she said. "What's a nice girl like me doing with two gentlemen like you?"

This set her to giggling, and she kept it up all through the kiss, and the unbuttoning of her shirt, and the unhooking of her brassiere. Only when William squeezed the side of her skirt to pop open the bar fastener did she stop, and it was to draw a deep breath and continue. William tried a steady voice. "I don't know," he said. "This isn't . . ."

He never got to say what it wasn't. Emma clapped a hand over his mouth and, with her other hand, tugged at his belt. He excused himself and leaned on the bathroom counter weakly, telling himself that he was in the grip of excitement rather than fear. When he came out of the bathroom, the nice girl was naked on top of the sheets. He breathed in sharply, as a reflex, and went to his knees by the edge of the bed, where he put his mouth on her breast. She gasped and he moved down, away from the source of the gasp.

He woke before her. There was a noise somewhere in the hotel, a shallow scraping. He tried to block it out without success. Emma shifted and frowned, opening her eyes, and William saw her seeing him. What did she see? A man who was in bed with another woman, feeling so many things that it wasn't easy to locate regret among them. He was sure that her face would have been cool to the touch if he had been brave enough to reach out.

The night had made not the slightest difference to their manner or appearance. They got dressed and went downstairs for breakfast. The hostess, an overripe young woman stuffed hopefully into black pants and a white dress shirt, waved a merry hand across the buffet: waffles, pancakes, omelets, donuts, cereals.

Emma clapped. "I was dreaming of this," she said.

"Was it was a good dream?" the hostess said.

"Not this good."

"We keep her dreams on a tight budget," William said.

William joked that way with Louisa, sometimes with desperate regularity, but she reacted like transition lenses: the brighter his tone, the darker the look she returned. Emma laughed easily. She was tired of some other man.

Later, in the lobby, she looked small inside a green armchair. A cherrywood staircase behind her led up into the hotel, toward the room they were done with forever. "I wish we didn't have just a single morning," William said.

She frowned at him and fretted the button of her coat. "Don't say that," she said. "You're not part of my life. My life is fine as it is. It's life, right? Not worth escaping but hard to completely embrace. So I do what I have to do." Courage pooled in her eyes.

He went home after breakfast. She saw him out to the edge of the curb and shook his hand crisply, as if she had done business with him. From the plane, the city receded beneath him until it was, to his relief, unreadable.

———

Back at home Emma was a constant presence in William's mind, a layer beneath everything, and so he moved rapidly to conceal it. He made good on the deck show, ordering the Western-themed lanterns, though when they arrived in the mail they were flimsier than he had remembered. Other attempts to take his mind off Chicago fell similarly short. He bought himself a new alarm clock, but the face was too bright and he could not sleep with it beside his bed. He upgraded his car stereo, but there were not enough gradations in the volume dial and music was either too soft at the fourth click or too loud at the fifth. He told himself that he was more alive to the world around him, and then, when that idea came to seem too romantic, that he was simply agitated. He waited for ordinary life to seal him in again, and a month later the alarm clock's glare was no longer keeping him awake. He commended time for passing.

But now, the unthinkable had happened: a year had gone by and her letter was open on the kitchen counter, heating up the place. "Dear William," it said. "I have some very surprising news I need to share with you. I am moving. Stevie got transferred to a new division of Arrow that's based in your town. We will be neighbors. And when I say neighbors, William, I mean near neighbors. I looked up the address, and it's right across the street. Life's funny sometimes, and sometimes it's anything but. See you soon."

He read the note a second time and let his finger rest on words he thought he was supposed to understand. He threw the rest of the mail away but put the letter in his pocket, and when he reached the bedroom, he transferred it quickly to the drawer in the table beside his bed. He could not see it but he could sense it there still, and so he lay in bed and forced his mind to rise, like mist off a river, and hover at the top of the bedroom, before it passed through the ceiling. He could take the sky, bit by bit, until he saw it all stretched out before him: the houses, the cars, the lights twinkling in the dark carpet of the town at night. And so he rose and the letter did not. It stayed there in the bottom of the table, a small white rectangle that shrank until it was a scrap, a shred, nothing or even less than that, so long as he stayed aloft.

Part IV

THE NEIGHBOR POLICY

ONE

William waited for signs of life in the house across the way. At first he was casual about it, angling his kitchen chair during meals so he could see out the front window. It looked just like a house: nondescript cream-colored façade punctuated by a few shuttered windows. A bright green vine climbed calligraphically alongside the front door. The first Saturday he set an alarm for seven and walked Blondie up and down the street, a surveillance pass. The Monday after that, he invented an excuse to go out to the garage, where he pushed the weightlifting bench up against the small vertical window and remained at his post until Louisa called him in to watch TV with her. Then, at ten or so on the morning of the second Saturday, the front door disgorged a young woman. She knelt by a green puff of shrubbery, rearranged something William couldn't see, and then made her way along the narrow path toward her garage. It was Emma, unmistakably, if only from the wide swing of her right hip when she walked. She touched the handle of her door, tested it for tightness, appeared to adjust it slightly, and passed back inside the house. He had seen it all from his post, through the dusty pane of duty glass. The whole thing had taken ten seconds, tops.

Sunday, errands; Monday, work; Tuesday-to-Friday's assault on meaningful memory. Then Saturday again, and a rare rain that pattered on the glass door that led from the kitchen to the deck. The weather cleared at lunchtime, and Louisa went to run errands, and that was his cue to walk across the street and knock on the door. Emma answered. Her hair was shorter than before, and slightly darker. Her face was holding back nearly everything. He sensed someone behind her. "Hello," she said. "Can I help you?"

"Hi," he said. "Bill Day."

"Bill?" she said, smiling uncertainly. A book was wedged under her arm. He didn't recognize the cover and couldn't see the full title—something about a mirror.

"William, I guess. Most people call me William, though whenever I meet new people, I try to go by Bill. Sounds friendlier. But it never seems to stick. Anyway, I live right across the way there." He lifted an index finger and pointed it, so deliberately that no reasonable observer could have perceived it as casual.

"Nice to meet you," she said.

"You're moving in?" He heard his own foot dragging across the bricks of the walk.

"Trying to. We're box people at the moment."

"Completely," he said, not sure what he was agreeing with.

A man's voice came from inside the house. "Who is it?"

"A neighbor."

The man appeared beside her, wearing tight blue metallic shorts. "Hey," he said. "I'd shake your hand but I've been oiling up my bicycle so I can take a ride." He laughed at a joke that maybe he thought he had made. Emma had described him as tall, or at least compared him to someone tall. He was not. He put his arm around his wife. "Stevie," he said.

"William," William said.

"Emma," Emma said.

There was a silence. "Where are you guys coming from?" William said.

"Chicago," Stevie said.

"Great city," William said. "I haven't been there for years." He grimaced. What if that remark wound its way back to Louisa? He would write it off as a misunderstanding. Everything is not always perfectly understood. His foot was scuffing faster now. A brown parcel-post truck rumbled around the corner. It was probably headed for the Zorillas'; the wife had lost her job and was working from home, buying and selling collectibles. But it pulled up at the head of William's driveway and a young black man with dreadlocks hopped out. "Oh, look, a package," William said. "I should go get that." He bid a quick good-bye and went back to his house. The package was addressed to Louisa, a box of unrevealing size and weight from a catalog house he didn't recognize. He carried it inside, flipping a waist-height wave back across the street, but the door was already closed.

That night, he and Louisa were watching TV, a crime drama they had joined halfway through and were trying to piece together. "Your phone," Louisa said. William shook his head and let it ring. Later in the bathroom, he checked for a message; there was none, but he had her number now. He slept encircled by the memory of Emma as she stood there in the doorway, saying his name like a question.

———————

Louisa was up before him, already in the kitchen, menacing the coffeemaker. "This machine," she said murderously. "It won't listen."

The old machine had expired with an electrical puff. "I'll get a new one," William said, but he preferred store-bought coffee, and so he forgot, and Louisa reminded him, and he forgot again, and finally she sighed with exasperation and said she was going online to call in the cavalry.

The cavalry, which had been designed by an award-winning Swiss architect, was a chrome sphere with a recessed instrument panel that promised, according to the box, "total control over the coffee-making experience." For the moment, it seemed to be exercising total control over Louisa. "Damn it," she said. "I can't get this to do what it's supposed to do." She put both hands on the sphere and lifted it off the table as if it were a head.

"Which is?"

"Turn on?"

A piece that looked important gleamed on the counter. "Maybe that's something," William said.

"That's from the old one. I think. Or the rice cooker. I don't know." Louisa returned the head to the counter and scooped food into the dog's dish. She had set out a small bowl of cereal for William and a glass decorated with the Statue of Liberty. "So what's your day like?"

William filled his glass up to the crown. "I don't know. The usual. Tote that barge, lift that bale." He began to hum.

"Don't sing," she said. "I don't want to have to stay in a hotel." Marriage, having grown tired of labor, resupplied old plots and conflicts, snippets of familiar dialogue. "It could be worse. At least you don't have to deal with curators all day long. Nothing's worse than a female martinet."

"You're going to have to help me out with that one," he said. "I failed zoology."

Louisa laughed, but only briefly, and William moved into the space the silence created. "Hey," he said. "I ran into Eddie Fitch and he invited us to a party. It's a theme party, kind of."

"They always are," Louisa said. "What's this one?"

"Southern Christmas." It was based on something that Helen Hull had told Gloria: "She was talking about how when she was growing up in Manitoba, she had so many signs that autumn was changing into winter. Now there's no good way to tell."

"So Gloria decided to do it for her?"

"I guess." William opened the gate the rest of the way. "It's kind of a welcome-wagon party for the new people, too, I think. Have you met them yet?"

"Not really," Louisa said. "So this will be a good way." She put the butter back.

"Yeah," William said. But he pinched the bridge of his nose when he said it. An old affair across the street: it was a secret he had to keep, a spot of frostbite on his memory. Tom had said that conventional morality left something to be desired, but William thought the problem was that it left nothing to be desired. It was a dull steady heartbeat that trailed off over time. In Chicago, he had put the paddles to this slowly dying heart. He had clobbered his expectations of himself and then convinced himself not to think about the consequences. But now the past had surfaced, and there was movement in water he needed to be placid.

Louisa cleared his bowl and glass from in front of him and then started in on the counter: she folded up a newspaper, rolled up catalogs she didn't want, dumped them all into the garbage. "I hope there was nothing in there for me," he said. He hadn't brought up the issue of the mail since she had left the bag on the counter, and things seemed back in swing, with a steady stream of publications they didn't need.

She leaned across him to get the pitcher of water. She had missed a button on her nightshirt and he widened the opening. "Hey." Louisa gripped him at his wrist. "Got to go," she said. "I've got bales of my own to lift." The museum was opening an exhibit on the history of local signage. Louisa had written the wall text and had to proof the plaques before they were placed. One night, Tom had come by to help her out with what he called "the intentionally dead language of museum writing." He pretended to be cynical, took on a tone, but William heard something else instead: Tom's pride in his sister.

"Ready to go," William said. "I need to be at the office fifteen minutes ago." He had Loomis work to do. It was piled up on his desk, heating up the place. "So we're not going to get any coffee from this UFO?"

"I'll return it," Louisa said. "But I'm very disappointed. I thought Swiss engineering was the best in the world."

"I don't see how," William said. "Even their cheese has holes."

Louisa untangled her purse strap from the back of the kitchen chair. "You want to walk out with me?"

"I'm not quite ready." He figured he could take a few minutes to watch the house across the street, maybe catch sight of Emma. He'd seen her the night before, coming in from a supermarket trip. She was wearing a tank top and he got the curve of her shoulder into his mind and couldn't get it out.

William went to the den, took a magazine from the table. He noticed, maybe for the first time, that the design on the wallpaper was a four-blade pinwheel cornered by a quartet of birds. He surveyed the rest of the room. There was the shallow blue ceramic vase on the windowsill, the strange broken-neck lamp over the recliner. How could he fairly move to a new house when he knew so little about this one?

He lay down on the couch and balanced his phone on his chest. Suddenly it buzzed, a tiny heart attack. William flipped the phone open. It was a text from Louisa. "Make sure water bowl before you go," it said. "Dog thirsty."

———

William gazed out his office window into the park across the street and wondered what it had all looked like a thousand years before, and whether the change had been for the better. To his left was a legal pad on which he had block-printed the name o'shea, then crossed it out and written loomis. He turned to his computer, opened up the brochure file, and got to it. He needed to create the impression that any TenPak investor, but especially a principal, was in for the ride of his life. He moved words from one sentence to another, shifted punctuation. He polished the paragraph until he could almost see himself in it.

Through lunch, beyond lunch, into afternoon, conversation came to him as if through water. The reason was simple. The reason was

Emma. He still hadn't called her back, hadn't even dialed a single digit of the number. She had called him again, this time leaving a message. It wasn't much—a slow *hello*, then a quick *call me back*—but he snapped the phone shut without deleting her voice mail and tried to make sense of the hectic jazz in his chest.

An alert blinked on William's screen for a meeting down the hall. In Baker's office, an intern was tending to a reference shelf in the corner. He was tall and slim and possibly Baker's nephew. Fresh energy came off him in waves. "I have some information about our new employee," Baker said. He paused to invite speculation.

"The one from San Diego?" Fitch said.

"He's starting any day, right?" Harris said. It seemed like it. A cubicle had been cleaned, except for a note taped at shoulder height that said "Hold All Walls for Harry." A replacement chair had come down from Vyron—Antonelli, always rocking, had damaged the last one's spine. Someone had even tacked up a California postcard on the wall over the desk, though it was of the Bay Area. Approximate hospitality was better than none at all.

"Well," Baker said. His voice was even deeper and more resonant when it carried news. "George came to me the other week to ask if I thought it was a good idea to bring the man in immediately or let him finish out the quarter in San Diego. Because when he comes here, he's going to be part of the team. And that means that he'll need to understand everything about the way we're selling TenPak." He pointed at William. "When you write, you make customers believe. But you also make these men believe." He pointed at Fitch, Harris, and Cohoe.

"And when they believe they sell, and their sales create more belief. It's a virtuous circle." His voice dropped another half step. "The new hire is a true son of this company."

"Meaning what?" Cohoe said.

"Meaning that he's shattering sales records. Not just in San Diego, but for any city, any division." Baker patted the desk emphatically. "That's one of the reasons I decided to delay him. For these weeks, especially, I don't want him to make the rest of you think too much about what you are or aren't doing, especially given the circumstance with O'Shea and Loomis. Because you know whose team it is?"

"All of ours?" Fitch said.

"No," Baker said. He looked confused. "It's Arthur's team." Now Harris looked confused. "He's senior by a month and he consistently tops sales figures. Six months from now, it might be the new guy's, but that remains to be seen. We're having some issues with TenPak, as I'm sure you all know, and we need to remedy them. So for now Arthur is the main character in this movie. The rest of you are in supporting roles."

"I'm the main character?" Harris said. He didn't sound convinced.

"Wait," William said to Baker. "If he's the main character, what are you?"

Baker tilted his large head and considered the question. Its difficulty seemed to please him. "Well," he said finally, "I'm the director."

Fitch went for the door. Cohoe followed.

"William," Baker said. "Wait a moment." He squared himself at his desk. "Loomis," he said softly. The word was hard inside the whisper.

"Yes," William said. "I just finished those up this morning. You want Harris and Fitch to take them over?"

"He dropped out."

"Impossible," William said.

"Not only is it possible," Baker said, "it has happened." He picked up the phone and began to dial. "Now we're on to Gardner. This is the next domino and also the last we'll permit."

He dismissed William with a nod.

William got to work on Gardner. He leaned heavily on the language. He had typed two letters of a longer word when he felt himself decoupling from the brochure. An airplane was going by outside, and he thought of what the people in the plane were seeing as they looked back down toward the earth. More precisely, he thought of what they weren't seeing: they weren't seeing the trivial details of the day, the things that had to be moved into close range so that they would seem significant at all. People focused on what was right in front of them, perfected their ability to analyze those things, all the while growing blinder to what lay beyond it. He thought of all the people improperly used in this process, all the people whose lives depended upon being able to accumulate wisdom—or at the very least, those whose lives were hollow without it, the judge, the critic, the cleric. He was not one of those men, he knew. He had always known that. Now he knew something else, which is that he would likely never be one of them. The chirping of a bird outside recalled him to his chair, and to the screen in front of him, where he finished up the word he was typing and switched to numbers, multiplying them together to demonstrate how value could increase.

———————

As at every Gloria Fitch party, the music was too loud, careering confusingly from big band to Motown to disco. Gloria insisted Eddie was the culprit. "He has a tin ear," she said. "In the sense that it needs to be pounded flat."

The Fitch house had always struck William as comic, mainly because of the address (IIII, like it couldn't quite get started), but also because of the clash between the ornate Victorian doorbell plate on one side of the front door and the driftwood owl sculpture on the other side. The crowd was in back, small and evenly spaced, standing in groups of four or five around tiki torches staked into the grass.

The far edge of the yard was reserved for children, and they occupied it wildly, an unregimented army. Eddie Fitch emerged from among them, tousling the hair of a boy who was not his, and came toward William and Louisa. "Hi there," he said, waving from close enough that a wave was unnecessary. "You look nice," he said to Louisa. He was right: she was wearing a tight green top and black pants, both new, and she had darkened her hair close to the color of her twenties. "How about that meeting the other day?" Fitch said. "The way Baker's voice gets, I feel like he's narrating a documentary." Here on home turf, he seemed more sure of himself. He explained Southern Christmas: there was a small artificial tree, beneath which Gloria had put flamingo-colored boxes. "The boxes all had to be the same size. If you only knew how much she cares about every last little detail."

Gloria, gliding by, punched her husband in the shoulder. "Don't tell them," she said. "I like the illusion that things just come together."

"Are you talking dirty to me?" Fitch said. Suddenly his face darkened and he stepped toward the far fence. "Hey," he said. "Get down off of there now. Because I said so. I don't need another reason."

Gloria moved them across the lawn. The guests of honor were already in place, sitting in chairs in the corner by the tree. "What are we supposed to do?" William said. "They're having an audience? Is it like the Pope?"

"It's exactly like that," Gloria said. "Once again, your command of world affairs is second to none."

The Pope was surrounded by prelates. As William drew near, Graham Kenner was pointing at the tree. "Set phasers to generosity," he was saying. He was always setting phasers. Cassandra was telling Helen Hull about a fire that had gutted an abandoned hardware store a block away from her office. "Well, hello," Graham said to Louisa. He wobbled backward a bit. "Will your brother be joining us? He was the life of the party last time."

Louisa pinched her mouth into a smile. "No," she said. "I don't think this is his scene." They hadn't seen Tom much in recent weeks. He was deep into new work. "When I'm at the beginning of a project like this, I'm clean as a dream," he told William on the phone. "This is the best part of being on the wagon, the first part, before it starts to roll too fast and you have to jump off."

In the seam between Louisa and Paul Prescott, William could see the side of Emma's hip, a gray skirt and a band of leg. He experienced a pang of fear, not because he was about to come face-to-face with her, but because she was about to come face-to-face with Louisa. He wondered, suddenly, if he had even mentioned her by name. He was certain he had. Hadn't he?

The crowd cleared. William took a deep breath and a shallow step.

Louisa followed. "Hey, stranger," Stevie said. "You had to come all the way across the neighborhood to see us?"

"Well, this was where the party was," William said. He was offended when Stevie laughed. The man had that effect.

Gloria came to touch Stevie's elbow. "These are the Wheelers."

Emma extended her hand. "You're William, right?"

"I am," he said. "It's easy to remember because it's such an uncommon name."

"We met before," Emma explained to Gloria. "He came over to the house one of our first weekends in town. We were just getting out of boxes. He saw us struggling up the path, I think, and I asked him to recommend a place in town to eat."

"I hope you didn't go where he told you," Louisa said. "He has terrible taste."

"And this," William said, waiting a beat, "is my wife."

"Wait," Stevie said. "Who has terrible taste?"

"William." She pointed at him. "Him."

"Oh," he said. "Sure. I assumed that. In food, though, not wives." He showed a high percentage of his teeth. And then, to Louisa, "I think you and I get home from work around the same time."

"Ah," Louisa said. "So you've seen my one-woman show, *Louisa in the Driveway After Work*. It's doing very well. It's been extended indefinitely." She was holding an unlit cigarette now and she waggled it like vaudeville.

"Are these the new ones?" Alice Deutsch said, squeezing in next to Paul Prescott. She had been in the neighborhood for four months and was eager to be out of the spotlight.

"New one," Emma said, standing and curtsying.

William felt a surge of weakness. "Can I get anyone a beer?" he said.

"I'm okay," Emma said at his back. "I make it a policy not to get drunk the first time I meet people." Alice Deutsch led a chorus of laughter, and it wasn't until William got to the cooler that it occurred to him that the remark was not meant for the group. He took his time at the cooler. Through a small window, in the kitchen, Eddie Fitch minced garlic for Bloody Marys.

When William returned, Stevie was surrounded, eulogizing Chicago. "It was a great city, but I was a drone back there," he said. "Huge hive. Then they split us off and moved us. Someone read a study that said that marketing does better if it's semi-independent."

Gloria Fitch held up a hand to stay him. "What did you do there?" she asked Emma.

"She was a caterer, and a good one," Stevie said. "She had to stop her business, but she's so great she'll get it started again in no time."

Emma stepped forward into a smile that looked like it was already hanging there.

"Right," Gloria Fitch said. "Because it's so easy to restart a business. I'm surprised it hasn't happened already."

William felt an unexpected desire to rescue the man. "Did anyone read that article about the new convention center they're proposing?" he said. "They say it'll help local businesses." No one took the topic up, not even Stevie, and so William went back to the cooler for another beer.

He was bent down, gripping a longneck, when he saw shoes he did not recognize in legs he unaccountably did. He straightened up and offered Emma his beer. She shook her head. "Bill, is it?" she said. The vagueness was gone from her voice. Her face was turbulent despite itself. Unexpressed ideas leapt up from it in a spindrift. For the first time, he felt a tremor of Chicago. "How are you, really?"

"Good," he said.

"Good," she repeated. Was she mocking him? Echoing? Words meant nothing.

"Well, it's nice to see you," he said. "Nice to have you in the neighborhood." It wasn't true, but William wasn't certain this was a truth situation. On the other side of the yard, a girl—William thought it was the youngest Kenner—pushed a Fitch boy down roughly; he came to his feet, shoved her back, and then, almost as an afterthought, began to cry.

"Look," Emma said. "I didn't ask to come here. Stevie brought me. What's my basis for objecting?"

"You don't care for the kinds of people who live in a place like this?"

This brought a broad smile that she quickly condensed almost to a point. "I think we need a ground rule or two. You and I, well, we're not going to see each other. Alone, I mean. We'll be neighbors, fine, but there's not going to be some weird moment when you and your wife and me and Stevie get together and drink dandelion wine and confess everything and end up in bed like it's Culver City in 1969." Her fingers were interlaced and at her chest, though he didn't know if she was keeping something out or in.

"Right," William said. "I hate Culver City." He tried to open the beer bottle with his bare hand; the teeth of the cap tore into his palm.

"Good," she said. "Better than good. Great." She lowered her hands, one until it flattened against the wall, the other landing on her hip. She looked like she had in Chicago—younger, unguarded, with a fragile ridge of shoulder blade. "I welcome the opportunity to become a part of this neighborhood. You have lovely public parks, I've noticed. And one of these days, you'll have to come over to the house. We have a deck." This time she aimed the joke squarely at him, and he took it on the chin. He had his beer almost finished before she was out of sight.

Back by the tree, Paul Prescott was smoking a joint and telling a story about the nest of spiders he'd found in the basement when he first rented his bakery. Graham Kenner shook his head and said he was done buying muffins there, and Cassandra Kenner shook her head in a different way, and Gloria Fitch took the joint from Paul and put her arm around Graham Kenner's neck. "Weren't you supposed to think of some carols for the party?" she said.

"Carol was my first wife," Graham Kenner said. "Now I'm with Cassandra."

"Oh, her," Gloria Fitch said.

"She's right behind you," Graham Kenner said, doing an impression of a scared man in a movie. "Don't tell her about Carol. She's very jealous."

"I'd kill Eddie if he ever cheated on me," Gloria said, and Eddie laughed like she didn't mean it, and then Cassandra Kenner was laughing, too, screaming in like a jet.

Louisa, back now, chuckled along with them, even though she hadn't heard the start of the joke. She'd been sharing a cigarette out front with Alice Deutsch. "She wanted to talk about this guy she's been seeing. He sounds completely wrong for her. I gave her a checklist and told her, 'Don't be afraid to wait for the right thing.'"

A clatter went up from the kid corner, crying and laughing twined together into a noise William could not name.

The party wound on, high spirits floating out of bodies that were slowly sinking down. Graham Kenner and Helen Hull showed each other their stomachs. Paul Prescott showed pictures of earlier in the night. Alice Deutsch left, and then Emma and Stevie, and Louisa tugged on William's arm just as he was thinking of tugging on hers. "Let's go," she said. "Treat a lady right."

"Did you have fun?" he said in the car.

"It was fine," she said. Her posture was perfect and unwelcoming.

"You seem tired."

"I wouldn't say tired," she said. "Something at the party bothered me."

He stopped at the lip of the road. "What?" he said.

"I felt a little trapped. You and I have this big news about the house, but I couldn't tell anyone."

"Why not?"

"Because I don't think it's going to happen, at least not any time soon. You seem like you're stalling." The idea had always been there, in the shadows. She had put light on it, but too much, and now it was an eyesore.

William took a long loop on the way back, passing near the lot on Harrow, though the night was so dark that they seemed to be in no place at all.

When they got home, Louisa settled in the kitchen with a glass of wine. "You coming to bed?" William said, but then he saw the white string of the headphone cord dangling down from her ear. He went to bed without her and woke so tired he wondered if he had slept at all. Louisa was beside him, headphones still half in, one earpiece at sea on the light blue sheet.

Blondie nosed the front door to show she wanted walking, but William was in no mood for it, so he let her into the yard and went out to the garage. He smelled the sick-sweet odor the second he put his hand on the doorknob: a rat. It was small enough not to fear, fetal in death; ants crawled in a thick static over its legs and its belly. He used a plastic bag as a glove, scooped it up, and turned the glove inside out. The garbage can was wedged behind a stack of boxes, recent purchases Louisa had decided to return. The coffeemaker was among them. He threw the rat away. Next to the boxes was his guitar; he was about to pick it up when he heard the fuzz of a chord from elsewhere in the morning.

He hit the garage door opener with the heel of his hand to reveal Stevie, with his own garage door open, playing his own guitar. William walked down the driveway. He looked closer and saw that Emma was in the garage, too. Stevie said something to her and brushed a fingertip across her forehead. It reminded William that there was much he didn't know. This was not a new thought, but it was one that was suddenly large within him. He gave a salute and got his arm back down before his blood froze entirely.

TWO

The rain had eased off, but the river of the audience flowed out onto the street, churning up adjectives. "It was brilliant," one woman said. She was older and wore a dress covered with flowers. Her friend, in a blazer, tried his hand: "Dark." Then: "Provocative."

William and Louisa navigated a traffic of hats and umbrellas. "I thought the movie was slow," she said. William only nodded and said nothing. "I am telling you my opinion so that you can tell me yours," Louisa said.

"It's loosely based on *Crime and Punishment*," William said.

"That's not an opinion," she said. "You know that scene where his father went to the library to research other robberies before he planned his? That's how I would do it."

A man behind them was making a point: "Tragedy becomes trivia more quickly than you would care to admit, and then trivia is rebuilt into history."

"He's on a date," Louisa said in a stage whisper. They slowed and the man went by them: he was older than his voice, with teeth that did not quite line up properly and hands that cleared space for his words.

His date seemed not to be a date at all, but a woman a generation older, perhaps his mother.

The sun was going down over town on a Saturday. A traffic cop was posting fliers soliciting information about a recent fire at a bus station that was under construction. Louisa stopped under the coppery sky and breathed in deeply like she was taking a cure. "We could just leave," she said.

"What?"

"You know, just pick up and go."

"Go home? I thought you said dinner."

"No, I mean go for real. Forever. A woman in my office did. She and her husband sold their house and bought one they'd only seen in pictures. They made enough on the sale that they have six months to find jobs." William pictured himself in a city where they had never lived: Miami, or St. Louis, or Phoenix. He might go to work for a newspaper again and come home every night wrapped in righteousness. But Louisa was just baiting the hook. "She's going to fail, you know. I give her six months tops."

"That's nice."

"She should have taken smaller steps, the kind that don't lead you right off the edge of the cliff."

"What is it they say about the difference between falling and flying?"

"I don't know," she said. "Whatever they say, I'm sure it's wrong." They were around the corner now, in front of a boutique hotel that had gone in and out of business over the years, always changing its name, never changing anything else. William and Louisa had stayed there on what passed for their honeymoon. The place was shut now, though a sign in the window said it was just for renovation. Louisa stared for a long time at the sign, or at least at the spot in the window where it was hanging. William tried to remember what floor they had stayed on, what Louisa's hair had looked like then, whether they had fallen asleep at all. Much of life turned out to be a test of how much you could forget without losing the thread entirely.

"You know what I did at work yesterday?" Louisa said. "I reviewed snack-time procedures for classroom visits. There's actually a written set of rules. Teachers are required to submit lists of any especially slow eaters so they can be served first." She reached out and touched the window. He was still not sure what she was looking at. For a moment, William imagined that she was ten years younger, or fifteen: that no choices had been made, not even the good ones.

"All this talk of snacks is making me even hungrier," he said. Now she was the one who only nodded.

The restaurant's motif was nautical; the small framed cases on the walls held artifacts from shipwrecks. The waiter was chatty; he had a family at home, he said, "if you call a boyfriend and a dog a family." He listened to old radio dramas every night. He was writing a play about Eisenstein and thought he could take the lead. "Don't pay me any mind," he said. He disappeared for a stretch and then returned to set it all down for them: the soups, the salads, the salty fish. William had considered ordering a complicated cocktail, and now that he saw the waiter's pleasure in serving, he regretted that he hadn't. "I hope you're finding everything to your satisfaction," the waiter said, spreading his hands over the meal in benediction.

"Of course we're finding it," William said. "It's right here on the table."

Louisa laughed. "Everyone's a comedian," she said.

The waiter gave her a mournful look. "But everyone is," he said.

At the end of dinner, William went down the narrow hall toward the bathroom, took out his telephone, turned it over in his hand. Louisa was waiting for him to come back, but he loitered in the hall, watching her in the stripe of mirror. She was trying to be sad so as not to be angry, but it seemed to make her angry that she couldn't be sad.

———————

"You're a nice guy, William." Karla told him so on the phone, and she said it again when she met William in front of her house on Hardy and deposited the package in the passenger seat. William wasn't sure what to do with this information, if in fact it was information. Karla shut the door to the car and then rapped on the window until William lowered it. "I just wanted to say bye," she said.

"Bye," William said.

"Bye, Mom," the package said.

After a series of calls thick with implication, Karla had gotten to it. She wanted William to take Christopher out for an afternoon. "He's been having a rough time ever since Matthew and I split up."

"You split up?"

"About a month ago. Matthew moved on. I knew he would. It should be his slogan: 'Matthew moves on.' He got close to Chris, though, which means that now I have a boy on my hands who wonders why people get close to him, then run away. Will you take him to the park for me?"

"You want me to leave him there?"

A mix of laughter and sadness filled the line. "Just take him out there. Throw some bread at the ducks. I don't care. He knows you, he feels safe with you. Be a kind of uncle." And so William had stood looking into a cage in his garage, thinking of how little of what he owned appealed to a boy. He had a baseball glove, but it was plastic, a developer's giveaway from a promotion a few years before. He had a Frisbee that was also a giveaway, and a kite he'd bought as a birthday present for Graham Kenner's son but never delivered. He dumped them all into the trunk and went inside to find Louisa. She was in the junk room, on the computer, a catalog open next to her. "I'm heading out to run some errands," William said. "I have to get some stain for the deck and a few other things. What are you up to?"

"I'm going to try my best to do nothing."

"Okay," he said. "See you around four." She hadn't mentioned the new house in days. He wondered if the idea had moved on or if it was waiting in the weeds, ready to take him when he wasn't looking.

Small, dark, with a weight in his gestures, Christopher sat still for most of the drive, staring forward. Karla had let on that Christopher was flourishing in some regards and wilting in others. He could tie knots, more kinds than William knew existed, and he loved to read the newspaper in the old-fashioned way, and he could sketch out the history of the nation from the time of early Indians. He was a devoted if not a good athlete, especially when it came to sports where speed trumped strength. But he was lonely. "He has a hard time making friends," Karla had said. "Sometimes he'll be talking about something that interests him, and it's like his entire being is lit from the inside, and then he'll suspect that I'm not listening, or giving him my full attention, and he won't get angry so much as empty. He'll just vacate the spot where he was a minute before. If that happens with his mom, who's trying her hardest, I wonder what happens with kids at school."

William asked Christopher if he preferred music or talk radio. "Talk," he said, but the first station they found was a pastor suggesting that modern man was in exile from himself, and Christopher grew bored and started to talk about a dead turtle he had found behind his house, its shell beginning to soften. To a series of questions about class, about sports, about girls, Christopher issued brief responses and then was rigid with them for a few seconds. "You love being interviewed, I see," William said, and the boy surprised him with a smile.

At the park, William popped the trunk and told Christopher to pick out what he wanted. He went right for the kite, a red hexagon with a yellow tail. "This," he said. "Definitely."

The park brimmed with children. Teenage girls thumbed cell phones. Small boys offered up die-cast cars to older brothers. William got the kite up in the air and passed Christopher the reel; he played it out or in, trying to keep the thing aloft. Every few minutes it went into irons and came crashing back to the ground. "That's the thing about kites," William said.

"I don't mind," Christopher said. "It's fun to get it going again." He ran to launch it: a successful flight, then an unsuccessful one, then a brief stay in a birch tree. Another boy a few years younger than

Christopher came toward them from the far end of the lawn, cradling a mangled delta kite; his father followed, explaining something about inevitability. Then, behind the man, William noticed a man biking around the edge of the park: Stevie. He was wearing the same blue biker shorts he had been in at the door and a bright yellow T-shirt with an Arrow logo. Stevie spotted William, hopped off his bike, and wheeled it over.

"Hey," William said, trying for neighborly. "You here for the exercise course?"

"No," Stevie said. "Tweaked a delt the other day moving some furniture. I'm just doing laps. Who's this?"

"This is Christopher," William said. "Friend of the family. I've known him since he was this high." He kneeled down and pressed his hand down flat to the ground. The three of them smiled against the light wind. It felt almost like friendship. Then Stevie started telling Christopher how to fly the kite. "Get it up above the tree line," he said. "That way there's enough wind to keep it aloft." He was right, William knew, but Christopher was having fun running back and forth.

The wind surged, then faded, and the kite drifted into a dead patch. Christopher and William followed it as it slid slowly downward. "Make sure the bridle is set correctly," Stevie said. "I think the way you have it, the thing comes down too fast." Christopher fiddled with the kite and relaunched it. This time it went up over the trees and shone like a deep red place in the bleached-out sky. "Will you look at that?" Stevie said. "I knew it would work."

A kite up over the trees was good for a minute or so. "After this can we play Frisbee?" Christopher said. William nodded, but he wasn't sure how he was going to throw the thing; his fist was clenched so tight it felt like it was cramping.

———

The man from San Diego was named Ruben Whitfield. He was short, with large features that gave him a friendly if slightly vacant aspect. He was careful everywhere he went, the kind of man who looked at a spot before he sat down in it. On his first day, he made a point of going from office to office, acquiring one germane fact about each co-worker; by noon, when he stopped by William's office, he had a clear sense of Baker's love for Hank Aaron and Harris's ambition to sketch every skyscraper in the country and Elizondo's childhood battle with Legg-Calvé-Perthes disease. Susannah Moore had been going to night school in screenwriting and had sold a script about a young woman who had an affair with a senator during Vietnam. "How about you?" Ruben said. He had a strange accent, overly precise, as if he was passing along someone else's words.

"I've never even met the senator."

"No. What's one thing about you?"

"Are you writing these down somewhere?"

"Maybe," Ruben said. He didn't laugh at all.

"Me? There's nothing interesting about me. I'm thinking of building my wife a new house."

"Impressive," Ruben said. "My great-uncle was a prominent builder in Canada for many years." William held his left hand in front of him in a burlesque of a notepad and pretended to scribble. Now Ruben laughed. "That's not really a fact about me, is it? For me, say that when

I was eleven years old, I wrote a letter to a famous actress asking her if she would marry me, and she answered and said she would."

"Did she?" William said.

"A gentleman never kisses and tells," Ruben said. He shook William's hand a second time and went back to his office, where he proceeded to work the phones the way that William imagined Fitch or Harris or Elizondo must have when they were first at Hollister, except that none of those men had exactly reached, as Ruben did, the golden mean between patience and persistence, which permitted him to make suggestions to the unheard customer on the other end of the line and then back off of them in such a fashion that the illusion of choice was created, and William, standing in the hall listening to Ruben, felt within himself a desire, almost inexplicable, to locate ten thousand dollars of ready cash and make an investment in this product, which, as Ruben was saying, was "not a guarantee, because there is no such thing as a guarantee, really, but it's close, as close as you can get without bending the truth." He was good.

Tuesday morning, feeling inspired or some approximation of it, William arrived early to put the finishing touches on the one-sheet for Gardner, only to find Ruben already burning up the phones. Harris's new assistant said that she thought he had already signed up close to thirty thousand in new commitments. William went into the break room, where he found Fitch. "What's up with the new guy?" William said.

"I can't decide if he's the spark that will save our division or some kind of demon who's gunning for all our jobs," Fitch said.

"Not my job," William said. "I write copy."

"But he's part of something bigger. Don't you think? Maybe that's why George Hollister is here again today."

"I don't know if that means anything," William said. "He's been around the last few weeks. Probably, he's just sticking close during this Domesta transition."

This came as a relief to Fitch. "Right," he said. "Right." Suddenly he saw everything as if through sunlight. "Anyway, I'm glad the new guy's doing a good job. After two months he'll probably be down in the cafeteria with us just like Antonelli was, and I'll be not quite laughing at his stupid jokes."

William's trip back down the hallway was indirect at best; he took pains to avoid Ruben's office, paused at Elizondo's door, ducked into the copy room and ran unnecessary copies of the file he was carrying. Baker and Harris were dissecting a movie both had seen on television the night before. William left the copy room and went to the break room, where he set the coffee machine to make him a cup he knew he wouldn't drink. Louisa's new coffee machine had arrived a few days before. She had unpacked it, a sleek black cylinder, something to worship. It made coffee in perfect silence and then blinked its small red eye to signal in code that it had done all it was required to do. Drinking other coffee now seemed like a form of failure.

Finally, back to his office, where he stared at the one-sheet for a while. Outside, in the hall, Cohoe's wife had baked cookies, and they sat beneath a loose roof of tinfoil on a table. William watched as Cohoe straightened them and then wandered away. George Hollister came by, humming to himself. "Cookies," he announced, and then pointed at the plate for emphasis. He removed the tinfoil, lifted one, took a bite. "Raisin," he said scornfully, and was done with it immediately. He replaced the nibbled cookie on the plate and continued on down the hall a few steps, now whistling softly.

Cohoe returned. He was going at a good clip, eyes set on his office, but the plate caught him up short. "Hey," he said. "Who took a bite of this cookie and put it back?"

"William did," Hollister said. "I saw him."

William was at his door in an instant. "I did not," he said. "You did!"

"Don't get so angry," Hollister said. "It's nothing to worry about. It's just a cookie. He doesn't care if you took a bite out of it."

"I don't," Cohoe said. "I was going to offer them to everybody anyway."

"Fine," William said. "But I didn't. He did. I saw him." He pointed at Hollister, voice above appropriate office volume now. He could feel a hot flush rising at his collar.

"William," Hollister said. "I think you're making an issue out of nothing. Just admit it."

William stepped toward Hollister. Later, he would tell himself that he was seeing all of it hovering before him in the air—Louisa's withdrawal, Emma's arrival, Stevie's guitar, the dog, the house, the kite, the slight persistent ringing in his left ear, the way he worried whenever he saw hair in the shower drain, the hundred trivial idiocies that filled the corners of each day—but the fact was that he saw only George Hollister's small isolated nose, and his own fist as it made contact with that nose, twice, the first time tentatively, like he was practicing, the second time like he had perfected the action, feet squared and spread to shoulder width, arm straight, body twisting into the blow as it landed.

William had never hit a man in this way before, and he was pleased with the quick result: blood rushed from Hollister's nose, and though he did not fall, he staggered, cracking his head on the handle of a file drawer. Also surprising was that there was no sound, no crack or thud when fist met nose and no audible reaction from Hollister. He did not moan. He did not cry out. He receded silently from the impact, like a man being taken backward by a wind.

Noise returned. William heard Cohoe's shocked voice at his back. Susannah Moore appeared from the break room with paper towels and shoved a stack of them forward. Hollister patted the asterisk of blood on the front of his shirt. Fitch, coming down the hall, stopped about twenty yards short of the action; he looked as though he might burst into laughter if he came any closer.

William stood his ground. His fist was still out in front of him, a reminder no one needed. Then he began to sink down slightly, as if he had suffered a slow leak. He opened his fist into a hand that might help Hollister up, but Hollister did not want his help; instead, his hand still out in front of him, William turned and walked down the hall, where he used it to press the button for the elevator and then press the button in the elevator.

On the way home he stopped at a small stucco building on the corner of Torrance and Frost, a few blocks north of the pig on the pole. It had been an upscale Mexican restaurant once but was a dive bar now, filled with dirty light. William ordered a drink and tried to strike up a conversation with an older man who was trying to extract a slice of lemon from his glass with a crooked finger. "I took a swing at my boss," he said.

"You have a boss?" the man said. "That must mean you have a job." He hoisted his drink. "Here's to you."

"That's funny," the bartender said, chuckling. His flesh, which hung loose around his face, shook with mirth.

"I knew you'd think so," the man said. "You have a job, too. Laugh it up." He released his drink and went to the bathroom. William made small talk with the bartender. He wanted the older man to return. He had a sense that if he could make even the smallest part of the world right again, the effect might spread. Finally he could wait no longer and he slid two twenties out of his wallet and told the bartender he'd pay for the man's drinks. "You want to cover his tab, you'll have to do better than that," the bartender said, laughing again. He seemed like the kind of man who let nearly everything make him happy.

William stood on legs that were heavier than they should have been after a single drink. At home, on the deck, he called Fitch and asked him to keep the news under his hat. "Don't even tell Gloria," he said. "I don't want to have to answer questions about it until I know exactly what's happening."

"Of course," Fitch said. He was eager to be part of a plot, so long as it did not place him in any danger.

William watched Blondie down the yard, sniffing the bases of trees and putting her paws up on the edge of the tiger tub. "Stay away from that," William said, but worse things had been in it every day.

THREE

William wondered why Congress couldn't pass the budget. He shook the newspaper once, sitting there at the kitchen table, but nothing came loose, and he went back to the first paragraph. According to a media studies professor, it was the result of "political optics," though two senators, one a Republican and the other a Democrat, stuck to a more traditional interpretation, blaming each other. The yen was doing bad things and people couldn't stop it. In Cape Cod, dolphins were beaching themselves by the dozens, possibly because of increased temperatures in shallow waters.

On the bottom of the front page, there was a piece about a fire at the Sunny Isles Marina that too closely resembled the ones at the hardware store and bus station. The authorities were wondering whether the marina was a sequel to the depot. "Over the last few weeks, there have been a number of incidents with suspiciously similar fingerprints," said the fire commissioner. "We've asked the police department to mobilize tactical units, which allows them to hold officers on shift." There had been no deaths or serious injuries, only property damage. "But property damage is something," the commissioner said. "People work hard for what they have." William straightened up into this truth. This was the man he was, a responsible professional with a clear-headed interest in the world around him, not a disgruntled midlevel employee who had just straightened his arm into a senior executive's face. He had learned, via e-mail, that his presence would not be needed at the office while human resources and legal measured out his fate. It would take a week, possibly longer. He sipped at his orange juice and imagined the moment when he would be asked to apologize.

"Morning," Louisa said behind him. Her reflection in the sliding glass door rubbed its eyes. "Why are you up so early?"

"Busy day today," he said. "Did I tell you about this investor who bailed out of TenPak?"

"You didn't," she said. "You probably sensed I wouldn't be interested."

"Well," he said, "unless I really made the whole process clear to you, and then you'd be fascinated. People say they want a return on investment, but what they really want is the grind of the process. They want to feel their money coming or going, and most people, amazingly, don't really care which. When the feedback stops, they lose their nerve."

"You're a little wound up this morning," she said. "Is that why there's no coffee? Did you make a pot and drink it all?"

"Funny," he said. "No. I just couldn't sleep and when morning came I felt ready to go." William let a hand pet the dog's head; it was the same hand he'd used to hit Hollister. "Want to carpool today?"

"Really?"

"Sure. I'm heading in soon, and I think I'll be done on the early side, so I can even pick you up." He had worked out the angles: he didn't want to risk Louisa's coming home early and seeing his car still there, in the driveway, so for the time being he would control whatever transport he could. "Less driving, more thriving. Save the world, save ourselves."

After William dropped Louisa off at the museum, he made a right like he was headed to his office; then he pulled into a small parking lot a few blocks away, where he sat in front of a drugstore and watched a manager unlock the doors and turn on the lights. Nothing in the man's gestures suggested excitement. William bought a tube of toothpaste he didn't need and went back to the car, where he called Karla.

"What's Christopher doing today after school?" he said. "I have kind of an easy day. Want me to pick him up and take him for a snack or something?"

"Really?"

"Sure. I had a good time at the park the other day."

"Well, today he has a music lesson," she said. "How about tomorrow?"

He tried not to agree too readily. "Okay," he said.

"Sounds great," Karla said. "Thanks. But no ice cream."

"Don't tell me what to eat," he said.

The next day, a steel-gray Thursday, he arrived at school early—he had tried to drive around all day, even roamed across town in search of a sandwich shop he remembered from his youth, but he had found it too quickly—and waited outside in his car, wondering how long he had before someone grew alarmed at the sight of a man lurking on the avenue that bordered the campus. When the bell sounded, he looked for Christopher. Karla had told him exactly what corner the sixth graders used for dismissal. There was a shallow stairwell that came up from a paved play area, and at a few minutes past three a troop of children came into view, some talking to each other, some with their heads down, most looking for their grown-ups. A child with a flower on her shirt was followed by a child with confusion in his eyes, and this pattern repeated down the line, down the stairs, down through the years, forever. Christopher found the car and tried the door; William had forgotten to unlock it, and they teamed up for the lowest form of comedy, his attempt with the handle exactly overlapping William's attempt with the lock. "Want some ice cream?" William said once Christopher was in and buckled.

"That's okay," Christopher said. "We had a birthday party at school and I had two cupcakes. My stomach is small."

"Not as small as your brain," William said. "I am offering free ice cream."

They ordered for Christopher; William waved it off. "Grown-ups don't need it," he said, but he got a swirl cone when Christopher insisted. They sat underneath a huge elm that had been called the Suicide Tree since William was a child, because kids were always trying to climb it and always falling to injury.

"I would never do that," Christopher said. "I'm not stupid." He waited a professional beat. "Did you?"

"Ha ha," William said. He remembered a time when Christopher, maybe a year old, had climbed into bed between him and Karla. William had already known that things with Karla were dissolving, and from a mixture of guilt and justice, he had started to leave the bed. "No," Christopher had said, and pulled himself close to William.

The boy was a line of warmth running up the center of his chest.

"I was thinking of a swirl cone, too, but I think I'm a little old for that," Christopher said. At the edge of the shade, a little girl ate cotton candy with both hands, as if she were devouring a cloud.

Later, at home, William watched the first movie he found, a drama about a revolt in a Portuguese colony. He got up to fill a bowl with ice cream. The chocolate syrup was nearly empty; he drained the last few drops and got back to the movie. Some men fought for their life against colonial oppressors. Others finished out a bottle of chocolate syrup while they watched a movie about those people.

When the movie ended, William pulled a dining room chair flush to the front window and monitored Emma's house. Looking outward, he saw his lawn, then the street, then her house, but he also saw his reflection in the inside of the window. Who was that man? He had imagined he might travel the world. He had imagined he might squander his fortune in the most interesting and daring manner. He had read a passage in a book about how a mind of the first order accepts no limitation of its freedom, and that had filled him with a kind of spaciousness that he thought, at the time, was hope. He had imagined many things. One of the things he had not imagined was that one day he would be sitting at the front window of his house, looking across the street in search of what was not even really freedom. Blondie trotted up and leaned her head against William's leg. "Don't bug me when I'm working," William said. A bee bulled the windowpane. Rain soughed on the grass. "Go ahead and tell your mom on me," he told Blondie. "See if I care." The dog turned doleful eyes on William. Was she sad because she didn't understand or because she did?

———————

"I need you."

"I've been dreaming of this call," William said. "Well, some people would say dream. Others would say nightmare."

"I need help."

"On a workday?" William said. "Can it wait until the weekend?"

"Not really," Tom said. "I need to move to a new studio. You have a car and, let's pretend, muscles."

"Okay," William said. "I think I can make it." He tried to load up his response with reluctance, silently hint at an important meeting he'd have to miss or the duties that would accumulate in his absence. It was wasted on Tom, probably, but he considered it practice.

Tom worked in the warehouse district on the east side of town, on the first floor of a squat building whose front door was done in a crazy quilt of woods. When William pulled up, Tom was out on the curb, leaning on a street sign. It looked like he was trying to push it over. "Park around the corner," Tom said. He led William through a side entrance and down a long hall. "I've had enough of this place," he said. "They used non-drying oil in the varnish on the doors, and it blistered up so now they don't lock right. Then things started going missing from people's studios: a couple of radios, some clothes, cash. Part of me wants to stay, but the rest of me thinks I should go, and I am a democrat of me."

"So where are you moving?"

"To the school. Some space mysteriously opened up. I think they always had it, but it wasn't worth mentioning until my show started attracting attention. Now that they have a hit on their hands, they're eager to do right by the talent."

Boxes were stacked inside the door of the studio, most filled with poster tubes that contained oversize versions of Tom's charts, and Tom took the first box and William took the second, and they went until both car trunks were filled.

"I have to do a final sweep of the place," Tom said. "Entertain yourself." A few of the other studio doors were open and William could see what was inside them: sculptures made from used car parts, portraits of trees turning into women or vice versa. A back door was open; William wandered out into the narrow street behind the warehouse. The alley was a graveyard of what William assumed were once considered inspirations. There were left shoes, maybe eight of them, in every color of the rainbow; various chrome bathroom fixtures glued together; sports magazines with the faces cut out. There was an oversize wooden crate with a metal cleat at its base that five years before William might have lugged home and turned into a doghouse for Blondie. He tested the thing's soundness with the palm of his hand.

"That's a nice one," a man's voice said. William turned to see a pile of coats, and then a face inside them. He was old, his features shrunk almost to nothing, his cheeks burned red from drinking, and he had an unlit cigarette clenched between his teeth. "You going to take it?"

"I was thinking about it," William said.

"Well, for me, I like to call it home," the man said.

"I'm sorry," William said. "I didn't know."

"It's not true," the man said. "I can usually get into one of these buildings at night and find myself a corner. When these warehouses were abandoned, it was worse. They'd lock them up with big chains and I'd have to sleep outside. But when all the artists started coming, that meant people needed to get in and out, and people means me, too." He scratched his face everywhere and then covered his mouth to belch. It was shocking, the order in which people let things go. "Do you have a little spare change?"

William dug in his pockets. "Here," he said, stepping toward the man.

"Oh," the man said. He basketed his hands.

"You don't have a cup?" William grabbed an empty paint can, turned it upside down so that the loose top clattered to the ground, and deposited the change. "Here," he said. "Now you have a paint cup."

Tom was calling William from inside the building and then his head poked through the door. "You out here, Billy Boy?" Tom said. He noticed the man on the step. "Hello," he said.

"Hello," the man said with exaggerated politeness. And then, to William, "You ready? It seems like your friend wants to get going." He made a point of checking the spot on his arm where a watch would have been.

"Good luck," William said idiotically as the door closed.

Tom drove across town toward campus, and William followed. When they pulled into the corner of a small quadrangle, Tom hopped out and pressed a key into William's palm. "It's right in there," he said, pointing at the closest building. "I'm second floor, by the stairs. Get started. I'll be up in a second."

William carried boxes until there were no more. Then Tom joined him, and the two of them stood at the center of the room, admiring the clean lines of the studio and the surrounding buildings visible through the window. Quality clouds hung over the spires. Tom moved into the doorway. "You see me here at the brink of a new life," he said. "It all changes, starting now. I can already feel the ideas coming on. I am channeling." He stretched out his arms so that he filled the doorway.

"At least you're not grandiose," William said.

"At least there's that," Tom said. "Thank you kindly, sir. I'll be seeing you soon enough. I plan to call you on that favor I mentioned. Now I'm heading to the snack bar, where coeds and foodstuffs abound. I can already feel the burger coming on."

———————

On the way home, William thought he saw Louisa's car parked outside a cell phone store. The weeks since the Hollister incident had been an uncertain time for him: what he could bring into the light, what needed to stay under wraps. The day before, the parcel post man had come again. Through the window he could see the brown truck grazing in the street. He was halfway to the front door when he stopped: if he signed for the package, Louisa would know he was home during the day.

William got an e-mail from Fitch, who said he'd witnessed a whispered conversation between George Hollister and Baker. "I'm not sure what they were talking about," he wrote. "I guess it was you. I'm not sure." Even Fitch's e-mails fidgeted. Later, Baker called, and though

William didn't pick up, he listened to the message, which contained a highly vague consideration of the company's likely recourse. "I feel I'd be remiss not to be comprehensive about the possible outcomes. There is a suspension policy outlined in the employee handbook."

"You'd better get used to having me around," William said to Blondie. "Did you hear that? Suspension policy outlined." The dog tried to turn away, but he gripped the underside of her jaw. He needed maximum engagement. "Let me tell you what happened today at work," he said. Harris had worn the same shoes and tie as George Hollister and taken some ribbing for it. Cohoe had tricked Susannah Moore into believing he had slept in the office to finish up the Powell account. Or maybe he had left the office early to go to the doctor, just for a checkup. More practice: William would tell these stories to Louisa, and she would nod, not really listening, and he would be secretly disappointed that she was no closer to finding him out.

FOUR

Thursday followed suit, and Friday followed Thursday, and by the end of the week, having exhausted the rest of the house, William started spending most of his time in the junk room. He put his feet up on the couch. "Yes, doctor," he said to the dog. "I understand this is a confusing series of events." He reviewed his circumstances. He was "out of office," taking the time as sick days, because he had struck a nephew of the founder of the company. Who but a sick man would do such a thing? The phone rang. It was Baker, and William let it go through to voice mail. It rang again few minutes later and he answered without looking.

"Hollister, Antonelli, and Day," he said.

"Where can a girl go for a cup of coffee in this town?" It was Emma. "Ideally there would be no one else there."

"Oh," he said. "Hi."

"Coffee," she said. "Just tell me. I need a cup and I'm tired of waiting in lines behind people who are trading tips about how to avoid the bad science teachers in middle school. And that's not even the worst of it. Today there was a little girl, maybe seven, ordering coffee for herself. Can't parents go to jail for that?"

"Where are you?" he said.

"I'm at the mall on Gerrold Street. Do you know it?"

"Do I know it?" William said. "I know it like the back of my own hand, if my hand had lots of clearance sales. There's a great out-of-the-way place about six blocks from there."

"You have no interest in joining me," she said, hanging the sentence by a tiny question mark.

"Sure," he said. "I have a meeting but I can cancel it." He went outside. A kid was playing basketball in the Zorrillas' driveway. He vaguely remembered that cousins were visiting from Ecuador. He walked by Louisa's car, which seemed huge to him. Why had they even bought a four-door?

When he arrived at the mall, Emma was sitting on a bench outside the frozen yogurt store. "I've had it with driving," she said. "Will you do it? You can give me a tour." And then she was in his car, in his passenger seat, pulling the belt across her midsection. Her hair was dark gold where it was matted to her head by the heat. He drove north on Ashmore, past an elementary school where kids ran wild in the concrete yard. "If you were a teacher, you'd work there," he said. A block later, there was a hospital. "If you were a doctor, you'd work there," he said.

She pointed at a post office. "If I worked there, look out," she said. "Postal, postal, postal."

"What?" he said. "You're not settling in the way you had hoped?" He tried to keep the thrill from his voice.

"Stevie's out of town."

"Oh," he said. "Business trip?"

"Sort of. He writes songs, and he's always had this thing about getting them out there so that they can be heard by the people they way they were intended." She put up quotes, though he wasn't sure where they were supposed to go.

"I saw him playing guitar one morning in the garage."

"Right. Since we've been here, he's gotten obsessed with having Arrow buy one of his songs as its identity music."

"You mean to replace the regular Arrow theme?" William hummed the melody, which like most Americans he'd known since childhood: it had a run of high notes and a run of low notes, with a beat of silence splitting the two.

"Yep. That's all he's been able to talk about. And because marketing is now separate from everyone else, it means he has to go back to Chicago once a month or so for meetings with the media buyers and the outside ad people. Whenever he's there he wakes up, goes to the gym, and calls me to pump up his confidence. I'm never awake and never happy to hear from him. If Arrow buys the song, he says it could validate him as a songwriter, but I think he's mainly thinking of the payday. And money isn't music."

"Very small amounts of it jingle," William said.

Emma laughed, but not like she had in Chicago. That had been like light on the surface of water. This was like being pulled down into it. "There's a problem here," she said. "It's a place where I know nothing and I have nothing. I'm cut off from my life, my job, my friends. And all Stevie can do is talk about new starts. For him, maybe."

Emma took off her coat. She was wearing an old-fashioned pink dress, the kind of thing William would have expected to see in an advertisement from the 1950s. Beneath it there was a telltale swell of belly. He could do nothing at first. Then he could speak but had nothing to say. Then he had something to say, and he said it. "Well, that looks like a new start."

"It is," she said softly. "I'm due in September."

"Congratulations."

"I wanted to tell you at the party, but we're not telling anyone yet. I had a miscarriage a few years ago, so we're waiting as long as possible."

"Right," he said. "Good plan. Better safe than sorry. It suits you, though. That was my one criticism of you in Chicago: not pregnant enough." This time her laugh was better. "You don't know boy or girl yet, right?"

"No. I hope it's a boy. I know how much trouble girls can be. Stevie says he doesn't care. Maybe he doesn't. But the money worries him. He keeps saying that a baby is a capital expenditure, that it's a way of spending money now but earning more back later."

"I know what a capital expenditure is," William said. "I work in financial writing. That's forward thinking. Promote that man." His hands felt loose on the ends of his arms. He was still trying to see his way around the small hill.

"For me, I'm more focused on other things. I feel horrible half the time, and then the other half is like I've been plugged into some universal outlet. My hair has gotten healthier. When I drive by restaurants, I can smell what's cooking in the kitchen. My libido has gone completely haywire."

"It has?" William missed a turn.

"It has. It used to be a predictable thing, a steady line. Now there are days where sex is the farthest thing from my mind, and days where I'm at its mercy." She inspected her fingers. "Where I'm absolutely devoured. It's like being fifteen again, but this time I know what all the fuss is about."

They were on Norris now. "We're near the coffee shop," William said.

"Isn't this the turnoff for our street? Your street?"

"Sort of. It's the back way."

"Actually," she said, "can we stop here for a minute? I could use some help moving something. Do you have time?"

William pretended to check his watch. "Sure," he said. "Let me just call and shift a meeting." He banked off Norris onto Terhune, merged into Emerick, picked up Irving. He dropped Emma off on her driveway and then backed across the street to his own. He called Karla. "I might not be able to pick up Christopher," he said.

"That's okay," she said. "I don't expect you to do it every day. Just now and again."

"Can't do it now," he said. "But I can do it again."

He sat in the car and waited. He wasn't sure what he was waiting for, but he needed a short delay. He thought back through Southern Christmas, back to Chicago. He thought about how Emma had looked in the bed that second morning, about how he had gone out to the hallway to call Louisa, about how he had left a message saying Chicago was boring, about how he had walked into the bathroom while Emma was showering and she had invited him in and he had declined and she had asked him what, does this kind of thing happen to you all the time, and he had affected a tough tone and said yeah, all the time, there are lots of girls like you, and she had opened the shower door so that steam came out. "There are lots of girls like me, but I'm not one of them," she had said.

William walked across the street. Emma was still outside, shoving something from the pathway to the lawn with her foot. "Look," she said. "Some of these roof tiles fell off. That guy who sold it to us said he'd just gotten the roof redone."

"I don't think that's true," William said.

"Obviously," she said. "But Stevie didn't bother checking. He's such an operator at work, but get him out of the office and there's no one more gullible." Inside, there was a masonry of boxes against the dining room wall; the place looked like a set under construction. "Task at hand," she said. "It's a husband's job, you'd think, but he's too busy working on his song. Did I tell you the title? 'I Stand (For America).' With parentheses and everything."

She brought him water and he stood at the kitchen counter and drank it. Emma's house was like his own—the floor plan was the same, bedrooms off to the right along a narrow hallway—and so he didn't need to ask where the bathroom was or search for the niche with the garbage can in the kitchen. The differences came down to the accents: the fixtures in the guest bathroom (hers were better) or the sliding glass door that led outside (he won here).

"William," Emma said from the bedroom. "Will you bring the big box in here?"

He went into the back of the house, turned left. "In here?" he said. He slid the box against the wall. The book she had been reading when she came to the door was on a table near the bed, title covered this time by a pair of sunglasses. He turned to find Emma blocking the door. She took his hand, put it on the center of her chest, and slid it down across her belly. A fact broke through the afternoon. "Go to the bed," Emma said. He did, and watched as she swiftly popped the snaps on her shirt and unclasped her bra. The cups sat loose on the swell of her belly; her breasts were not much larger than he remembered, but they were darker at the nipples, harder to dispute. "Is there a reason you're still dressed?" It was the same voice as in Chicago, but thinner; it was as if it had been stretched from there.

"I don't have anything," he said. "You know." He made a circle with his thumb and middle finger.

"Haven't you been paying attention? You can't get pregnant on top of pregnant." She covered the distance between them, eyes beginning to go liquid as she reached the bed. William had trusted her in Chicago, without any reason but her beauty. He had distrusted her at Gloria Fitch's party for the same reason. That afternoon, in her house, he tried to make his peace with what he saw, buttons all undone, but it was too much for him; he was unable to do more than peel the fabric back to the hips and trace what was beneath. It worked for her but not for him, which worked for him.

Breaths weren't words. They were more. He turned toward her when he heard them stop. "Shit," she said, and he felt a surge of terror. "It's two. We need to get my car."

She dressed again, quickly, forgoing her bra, and he even sped a little on the way to the lot. They couldn't find her car at first ("That's because it's beyond anonymous," she said. "I don't even know the plate number yet") but she identified it by the rear passenger window, where there was a doll of a bear cub with suction cups on all four limbs. "It's waving good-bye to you," she said. "Go."

William made it home in time for a quick shower, after which he put his work clothes back on and went to get Louisa. While he waited for her outside her office, he thought back, with some effort, to the first time they had met. The guys at the paper had talked about the new writer who'd been hired from a Dallas magazine, a woman who specialized in restaurants but had also done good work on municipal corruption. They had her name as Louise, and that made William imagine someone older, to the point where he didn't even think to connect it to the tall brunette who was standing out in front of the building, squinting at the name plates, as he went out. He assumed she was there for the temp agency that shared the building and was surprised and a little embarrassed to return from lunch and find her in the small front lobby of the newspaper, filling out new-employee forms. What stayed with him most specifically was how she had folded her frame into one of the small uncomfortable lobby chairs and failed to meet his eye. Later, she claimed nerves, though nerves couldn't explain the smile she directed down into her paperwork: sly, knowing, waiting him out.

"Funny that you were thinking of that," Louisa said after she got into the car and asked him why he looked like he was a million miles away. "Guess who called me today?"

"Me, but from the past?"

"Now that's a long-distance call," she said. She folded and unfolded her hands brightly. "No. It was Jim. He's going to be in town in a few weeks. The usual drill: business, one night off, wanted to know if we could meet him and his wife for dinner or drinks."

"Sure," he said. "I don't see why not. Just tell me when."

They passed a fire truck going the other way, and when he turned onto their street he jerked his head up to signal that he had just recovered a recent memory. "Oh," he said. "I talked to our new neighbor today. She was getting into her car. She looked like she was expecting. Or maybe fat."

"That's nice," Louisa said.

"Is it?" he said. "That's all we need: another kid in the neighborhood." She turned away in hurt. Her injury was his protection.

FIVE

William was loading dry cleaning into the back seat of his car when he noticed Tom's Charger parked alongside a sagging Cadillac. A chunk of Tom's grille hung like a loose tooth. William peeked into windows. He didn't see Tom in the barbershop or the grocery. He was about to give up when he heard a tapping noise that summoned him to the Chinese restaurant in the corner of the mall. He pressed a hand to the window for shade. Tom tapped the window again with his chopsticks and motioned William inside.

A chair was already pulled out. "Sit," Tom said. He was unshaven, or at least unevenly shaven. On the table in front of him there was a bowl of white rice, a pair of empty beer bottles, and a plate with the remnants of something glutinous. "Chicken, I think," Tom said when he saw William looking. "Pork? Whatever it was, it wasn't very good." He shoveled rice into his mouth like he was stoking a coal car.

William hung his jacket on the back of a chair. "They asked for you at the Fitches'."

"Like I said, busy." Tom tugged on his own ear. Giving the sign to steal, William and Louisa used to joke when they saw someone gesturing like that.

"I keep waiting for you to call in that favor."

"Keep waiting." He slashed a finger across his throat. William wasn't sure what he was killing. "Something else is hatching. A woman, the mother of one of my students, called me. She went with her daughter to the show and she wanted to meet me."

"She's a groupie?"

"No," he said. "A publisher. She wants to do a book of the graphs." He scowled on the nouns.

"Sounds terrible," William said. "Someone likes what you do. I feel for you."

"That's not it at all," Tom said. Grains of rice plummeted from his chopsticks. "I don't know if I want my work in a book. It's like a sealed cube with mirrors on the inside."

"People open books up. They read them."

"Maybe I'm wrong to be fixating on the book. Maybe it's more about this woman. You should have heard the tone of her voice, like she'd just found the thing of value that was going to move her forward in her career."

"Maybe she did," William said. "Why is that a problem if you're the thing of value?"

"You understand even if you say you don't," Tom said. "She's just doing what all ants do, which is to go on up the anthill. You can't stop them. You shouldn't even try. What you can do is prevent yourself from wondering what a man should never wonder, which is whether you've already gone up the anthill and come back down. " Outside the window, a car alarm began to chirp. "Damn it," Tom said, pounding

the table hard enough to rattle the beer bottles. "That thing's been going off every ten minutes for the last two hours."

"How long have you been sitting here?" William said.

Tom wasn't listening. "What about these fires, Billy Boy? People are
whispering that they're being set on purpose. We were right there. We
could have seen the perpetrator stealing away."

"I heard a report on the radio yesterday where they said they don't
think Birch Mutual was linked to the rest."

"Think about fire, though. There's this absurd idea that it needs
people to set it. It's so much older than we are, so much more basic to
the planet. We have our human creativity, but it pales in comparison
to what fire does. It destroys other things and creates more of itself.
We just move along in our boring lives, boring office jobs."

"Yeah," William said. "That's where you're wrong."

Tom jerked his head up. "How do you mean?"

"I don't have a job like that. Not anymore. I punched my boss." He
had Tom's attention now. "The other day, one thing led to another.
Isn't that always how it goes?"

"Until it gets back to the Prime Mover," Tom said. "That's the
thing that causes movement but is itself unmoved. But none of us is
that. We receive one stimulus and produce another, and eventually it all
adds up to life, or what people like to call life." He seemed to feel the
vanity of what he was saying and caught himself. "Does Louisa know?"

"Not yet. Officially I'm on leave. I'm waiting to hear my fate."

"Well, she won't hear it from me. But you know what they say. *Amor
tussisque non celantur.*"

William took a stab at it. "Love and fighting can't be hidden?"

"Love and a cough," Tom said. "It's Ovid. I think what he means is that wives have a way of finding out. Though it sounds like she's a little inward these days, with all those thoughts of new houses dancing in her head. How long's it been, a month?"

"Less."

"In the course of a life, a month is nothing." Tom produced a pen and started scribbling on a place mat: arcs, lines, loops. "Figure you live until seventy. That's more than eight hundred months. If you graphed your life, you wouldn't even see this. No one would. So don't worry that it's so consequential. Contextualization is the leading cause of endurance."

"Makes sense," William said. It didn't, exactly. He didn't know whether Tom was advising him to tell Louisa or not.

Tom folded the place mat and pushed it toward William. "Do you know how I got into graphing in the first place?"

William sensed something large about to surface. "I have to go," he said.

Tom reached out for William's shoulder. His hand held William in place. "I need something," Tom said. "From you. A favor."

"Is this the one from the barbecue?"

Tom blinked and then brightened. "Right," Tom said. "That act of kindness has become a likelihood again. And this time I can tell you more. I need for you to be my wheelman."

"For what?" William said. "Are we pulling off a heist?"

Tom didn't answer. He was bent over his place mat again, scribbling madly. "There are three main shapes in a life," he said. "The bell, the L, the whale's tail." William left him there, still scribbling.

When he got home Louisa was watching TV, and he watched with her, a decorating show where they scraped sticky wallpaper off a baby's room and repainted it a pale green that even William had to admit was a huge improvement. "They said there are only seventeen kinds of patterns that can repeat," Louisa said, and William, feeling a weight in his chest, didn't answer. She got up to make them dinner, and he noticed that there was a red-brown hair on the sleeve of his shirt. He trapped it with a fingertip. It was human, but it wasn't Tom's or Louisa's or Emma's or anyone else's he knew. It was proof of a world beyond him, of questions he would never be asked, and the thought of that allowed him, suddenly, to breathe.

SIX

There had been a few brief periods of unemployment in William's life, but only one that had resulted directly from his actions. He had been a copywriter in a small advertising agency where he had a boss only a few years older than him, a slick former athlete named Frank who was married with kids and also running around with a redheaded secretary. (William couldn't remember her name; Jessica?) Frank talked about "isolating what is wanted" and "finding the center of a product," but mostly he just dumped his own work on William's desk along with unreasonable deadlines. William accepted the situation with good enough humor at first, but one night he saw his boss and the secretary fighting in the parking lot. She was crying. Jenny. He reported the incident to the head of the company, and a week later Frank fired William. "I don't know what you were thinking, guy," he said. William felt he had struck a blow for truth or morality or fairness or something like that, and it took about six weeks before it all drained out of him and he saw that he'd been a damned fool. This time it was even quicker. The sense of righteousness he had felt as he squared his feet and shifted his weight had gone out of him the second he landed the blow on Hollister.

Instead, he was fidgety, angry at himself and at everyone else, too. He couldn't tell Louisa yet, or at least didn't want to, and her manner was discouraging him even further. After the party she said she was coming down with a cold, and she was, but even after recovering she remained in a state of steady insensibility. She was a thick gray brush overpainting all other colors. After a week in the gray he needed something brighter, and that need bloomed into flesh and blood in the form of Karla.

She was at lunch first, as always. This time she was unusually casual, in a T-shirt and a brown wraparound skirt.

"Sorry I was late," he said.

"It happens," she said. "It's more or less the only thing that happens." She didn't seem angry. "Look," she said, flashing her fingers in front of him. "I got my nails done. Aren't you proud of me? It's because I have a date."

"That's nice," he said.

"I suppose it is. It never hurts to know that things are about to start happening again."

"Who's the guy?"

"A historian. He has a specialty." A newly done finger went to her mouth to help her retrieve it. "He studies why there's an uneven pace of scientific discovery across the history of civilization. I don't think much will come of it, honestly, but I can probably get in a good six weeks before I realize that. And how about you?"

"How about me what?"

"Well, the house, for starters. Are you building?"

"Not yet. Louisa thinks I'm stalling. And I think she might be right."

"That can't go on forever."

"I don't need forever. I need forty years, probably. Then it's moot."

"What are you waiting for?"

William drew a breath and then lobbed his confession into the conversation. "I lost my job," he said, "or I've set the wheels in motion, anyway. And I'm sleeping with the woman across the street."

Karla's eyes widened at the first and narrowed at the second. "Superstar," she said, nodding on the first syllable. "Tell me more." He pulled down the screen and started the projector. Certain scenes were edited; he didn't mention, for example, that Emma was pregnant. Others were reframed for close-up. Hollister's nose, he said, almost shouted with blood; he opened his fingers wide on both hands to re-create the effect. "I don't want to say I regret anything, exactly," William said. "The guy at work is impossible. She's beautiful. This is the natural conclusion for both. But I'll probably be back at work next week. And Emma and I are ending things. Things are winding down."

A little smile rippled across her lips. "Right."

"Do you remember once, when we were going out, you said something about how wrong choices were like water that's so deep you can't find the bottom?"

"Come on," Karla said. A hard shadow crossed her forehead. "I said that? Was I high?"

"Maybe."

"Well, I didn't know what I was talking about. Don't worry about stage-managing things. If they end, they end."

William looked at the damp patches on his napkin, which were making shapes he didn't understand. There was a woman across the table from him, giving him advice on intimate matters, though the two of them had long since discovered that their philosophies on such matters overlapped only slightly, and only temporarily. And yet he was hanging on her every word. How had it come to this? There was so much that was unknown to him. "That's it?" William said. "If they end, they end?"

"I guess my point is that they do end. The other morning I was in bed and I heard cabinets opening and closing and a spoon clinking against a plate. It was Christopher, getting up and getting himself breakfast. It was such a wonderful feeling, but it also made me a little wistful. Time goes." Sadness crossed her face. "But don't tell Louisa. Please. People always think honesty is the best policy, but in a case like this, it can be a kind of attack. Full truthfulness isn't always called for."

"Like I said," he said. "It's winding down."

William wasn't ready for home. He owed Emma a phone call, but he wasn't ready for that either. He drove to the coffee shop, failed to buy coffee, stood in front of the news rack, where magazines hung like dead game. He had nowhere to settle his eye: garish letters obscured beautiful faces. There was a women's magazine about hot new colors. He learned that one was white.

———

In his car, with his hand. In her car, with her mouth. In her house, a second time, with added urgency, as if Stevie might come home any minute, though he was out of town. Things were not winding down.

After the second time in her house they were too afraid to stay still, for fear that one or both would fall asleep, and so she asked him a battery of questions. Had he been inside the house when the Johnsons had lived there? Yes. Had he ever been in the bedroom? No. Had he ever had a fling with anyone else in the neighborhood? None of your business, but no. Did he have any recurring dreams? "What?" he said. "I tell you, and you look inside my head and know what I really want?"

"No," she said. "I want to tell you about mine." She was younger, maybe just a girl, and she was standing in front of a tree with a large hive in the fork of a low branch. Honey massed thick at the base, a drop in delay. As she stood there, bees emerged, flew around the base of the hive, just a few at first and then dozens, a small cloud, and then the cloud was a tornado. There were soon so many bees, she said, that they were a kind of smoke; she covered herself, preparing for the worst, but they just passed across her. "Then I wake up," she said. "Usually with my hands on my face."

"Do that now," he said. "Cover your eyes and don't uncover them until I say so. That's the game." He made a buzzing noise as he approached the hive.

———————

A few days later, he was out on his front lawn pruning bushes. He liked the feel of the clippers when they first encountered a branch, the resistance a brief moment of conscience. Emma came out to her driveway and squinted up at the roof. "Hey," he said.

"Hey," she said. "Taking the day off?"

"Working from home," he said.

"Listen," she said. "I have a question for you." She came slowly across the street. "How does recycling work here?" They were on the side of the house, hidden from view, and William began to explain the principles of separation: paper, plastic, glass. "Come on," she said. "Are you serious? I wasn't." They went into the garage and she put her arms around him and they leaned up against a stack of boxes. "You are more and less careful than other men, and one of those things, I like," she said. They sat on the workout bench he used for guitar and he ran his hands back and forth along the outsides of her thighs. "I'm so sorry I ended up here," she said.

"Stevie's job," William said. "You don't control that."

"It's only partly that," she said. "Last summer I had a thing with another guy. When that ended, I was inconsolable. Stevie felt like we needed a fresh start."

"He knew about the guy?"

"No. But he knew that the longer we were there, the more I was slipping away. It was impossible for him not to know. I was like a picture getting fainter."

"You didn't tell me any of this in Chicago."

"You say that like you deserve to know," she said. But she moved closer and kissed him, not quite on the mouth, and he put his hand at the small of her back. "I have to go," she said. "But maybe you can come by one of these days."

"Tomorrow?"

"No. And not the day after."

The day after that, he carried a spare recycling bin across the street, one neighbor helping another, and Emma met him at the door. An hour later, she propped herself up on an elbow, scissored a pillow between her legs, and started to talk. At six, she said, she had loved everything: pets, the weather, music, hats, her sister Helen, the color red, the way light flattened itself against the inside of a lampshade, poems about how children loved everything. By eight, though, she was keeping a notebook of the exceptions to this rule ("Amanda's shoes make her look like a monster"), and by ten, the notebook was filled. Twelve was the year she learned the secret: not to love everything (because it stretched your heart out of shape), not to keep a record of the things you hated (because it shrank it), but to write about the things you wanted to move past love and hate, into a place of understanding. So she composed a paragraph about the way her mother looked when she laughed. She tried to capture the way her sister's straight lines were turning like a melody into curves. "One night," she told William, "I was playing with some neighborhood kids and tore open the tip of my index finger on a stray end of barbed wire." She watched as blood blossomed from the cut. It was red, one of the things she loved. She had just started getting her period two months before, and this whole business of bleeding seemed like a paradox. How could it be that when things came out of her, she felt larger? "I wrote that down and showed it to my sister and she didn't laugh at me, which was shocking," Emma said. She put her book next to her bed before she turned the lights out, and she was happy it was there when she slept. Twenty years later there was no book anymore; it was a faint memory fading fast.

"Why are you telling me this?" William said.

"Because you'll listen," she said.

He showered at her place, opened her medicine cabinet afterward: there were vials for sleep and anxiety, along with some others whose labels he couldn't decipher. "Come on out," she said, and he did, and she rewarded him for his obedience. It wasn't until he was home that he saw he'd missed a handful of calls: Fitch, Louisa, Baker. Baker's message was uncharacteristically short and impossible to misunderstand: "You're wanted at the lawyer's office in the city. Monday at eleven." His voice was flat and William lay on the couch in imitation of it. He unbuttoned his pants. He buttoned them back up. He turned on the TV but couldn't find anything that held his attention. He washed his hands twice, once in the bathroom and again in the kitchen sink before dinner. He felt a new hostility to clues.

———

Louisa brought dinner home from a new chicken place near her office, and then they went out to the deck and William listened in vain for his favorite bird and Louisa scratched Blondie's ear. When Louisa looked at him, he looked away. When she looked elsewhere he felt a sense of loss. The difference was spreading.

SEVEN

The southbound platform was mostly in shadows and the digital sign announcing train times was covered, from William's vantage, by a tall man in lean tweeds and a hat. William stood beside a three-person bench, the rightmost seat occupied by an older woman with headphones, the middle seat by her backpack. Closest to William was a young woman reading a magazine, a redhead with tiny perfect features wearing one of the worst outfits he had ever seen: an orange leather jacket that looked like it belonged to a crossing guard, a short gray skirt, gray tights with a floral pattern, and thick platform shoes. It was like five kinds of music were being played at once, none well, but truly beautiful girls weren't undone by bad fashion. They triumphed over it. "Do you want me to have her move her bag?" she said, gesturing at the older woman.

"No," William said. "I'm conducting an experiment to see how entitled and oblivious people are." The young woman laughed. The older woman pinched the bulge on the cord of her headphones, to either change the volume or take a call.

"Off to the office," said a man passing by, to no one, but William was not going to the office. He was headed into the city, to Hollister's lawyers, to meet his maker. He moved off to a quiet spot to call Louisa. "Hi," he said. "Busy day so far. Everyone wants to meet."

"Don't be too late tonight," she said. "Tonight's the night we're supposed to meet Jim and his wife for a drink."

"Right," he said, though he had no recollection of making the plan.

"I said around eight," she said. "So let's leave here at quarter of. Though if you're running late, tell me, and we can just meet there."

"Right," he said again.

When the train came, he packed on with the crowd and took a seat next to the young woman, careful to hide his Hollister employee handbook in his shoulder bag. He got her name, which was Georgina, and this little show: first, her driver's license photograph, which she dismissed as terrible but which was far from it; then an expedition into the deeper reaches of her purse for the business card of the modeling agency she was visiting. William thought he saw a condom in there, next to a tube of lipstick. "This must be thrilling for you," she said.

"It is," he said, affecting a bored tone to cover his excitement. They talked about his work, and mostly he lied. "I'm going to see a guy from the office whose wife had a stroke," he said. "Their son just went off to college. Good kid. Interned with us last year. He's offered to skip a semester but none of us want that, so we're pitching in. I figure that by helping out Al, I'm helping out the team."

"That's a nice idea," she said.

"He's been out of the office for two weeks," he said. "I spoke to him on the phone and he's going a little stir-crazy. His wife was that kind of person, even before the stroke: won't let them have a television, doesn't go out to eat very much. They had a dinner party once, and the conversation was all about whether we deserve the things we have in life, any of us. She said no."

"Austere," Georgina said. It wasn't a word he expected. She told him about her boyfriend, who she wanted to marry her, but who she suspected would never ask. "He has to be scared into it," she said. "That's what my mother says, that he needs a wake-up call." As the train pulled in, she jotted down her phone number on the back of the agency card. She had seen his wedding ring but had not remarked upon it. Did she figure him for a wake-up call?

———————

The lawyer's office, three blocks from the station, had a poorly lit waiting room with a quartet of round brown club chairs. William had been there once before, to secure advice on a threatened suit by a freelance editor; then, like now, he'd spent most of his time leafing through fitness magazines and counting the starbursts around the edge of the rug on the floor. Across a plastic partition, a woman with big hair and small glasses tapped violently on a keyboard.

A man came into the room. He was taller than any man William knew; though he was old and stooped, he was still nearly six and a half feet. "Mr. Day," he said.

William stood. "Mr. Reeser," he said.

"Call me Marshall," the man said, as he had every time, never meaning it. Walking with practiced significance, Reeser ushered him into a room. "We have associates with bigger offices, but I started in an office this size and I will die in an office this size. Though hopefully not today." It was the same line he had used during their last meeting, but William laughed charitably. Reeser squeezed in between the desk and the chair.

"Now, listen," he said. He put his hands palms up in what seemed like supplication. "We've known each other for a long time, William."

"We have." Reeser was Hollister's head counsel and had been the kingliest presence in the company for years.

"And in all that time, have you ever known me to be anything but a straight shooter?"

"I have not."

"Well, then, let's get down to cases. We have a problem here. You struck a man. Scratch that. You struck an upper-level executive, the nephew of the founders."

William raised a palm to slow Reeser, or identify himself. "I don't know if I can explain, really. It seems trivial. But he wasn't telling the truth. It was unimportant, I realize. But doesn't it matter that he was lying?"

"I can understand," Reeser said. "I've met George. But you know: breaking a wheel for a spoke." He placed both hands on the desk. On a credenza against the wall there was a picture of Reeser, younger, with Hollister's uncle Leon, a tired old small-faced man of extreme competence. "The fact remains that the two of you can no longer work together, and another fact remains as well: he is in charge of your department." He made a flourish with the pen: more sprezzatura. "So look. Listen. Specifics here don't matter. The general picture, as painted, is bleak. He's a made man at this company, and that means that you're out."

"Out of Domesta?"

Reeser's eyes crinkled and it looked as though he might leap out from behind his desk and clap William on the back. "Can you believe it?" he said. "*Domesta*. Thirty years as Leon's lawyer and I've never heard anything so stupid. Yes, out of Domesta. But not just that. Out of the whole thing, I'm afraid. Gone from Hollister. Cashiered." Reeser pressed a button on his telephone and a young woman in a white skirt appeared with a slim sheaf of papers clipped together at the corner. "Read to yourself as I read aloud," Reeser said. " 'This letter will confirm our discussions to resign your present position with Hollister, effective June I. In light of your many years of service to the company, Hollister is prepared to offer you a severance payment equivalent to one year's salary, and to carry your full benefits for that same term. Confidential information, as defined below, shall not be disclosed for the term of two years, upon penalty of forfeit both of severance and benefits. In entering into this Agreement, the parties have intended that this be a full and final settlement of all matters, and that all related disputes be hereby dissolved. This letter will confirm our offer. Please take some time to review and consult with counsel or advisers of your choice.' " Reeser looked up. "Do you have counsel or advisers?"

"Let me understand," William said. "You're paying me because I hit George Hollister?"

"It's not just that," Reeser said. "There are matters that you might be privy to that we want to keep under wraps."

"Like what?"

"Like anything. Business strategies. Things you've heard. Anything. Everything." He lowered his eyes to the paper again and continued to read. "'If this proposal is acceptable, please indicate your acceptance by signing and returning the duplicate copy of this letter and the accompanying legal release.'"

William reached for the pen. Reeser got there first, held it out like a baton in a relay. "Counsel?" he said. "Advisers?"

"I think I've heard plenty," William said. He signed his name with as much ink as possible.

———

William had not thought of Emma most of the morning, but he thought of little else once he was out of Reeser's office, sitting in the park, watching the squirrels watch him. A girl in a blue dress fed ducks as her mother looked on with a mix of adoration and disapproval. The mother had a piece of paper folded on her lap. She was slim, pale. The girl was darker. She had the mother's large eyes and a scar on one cheek, along with something else: a focus. She looked at the ducks as if she were learning them. She tossed a few more crumbs onto the ground. The ducks rushed toward the scatter and the girl followed after them. The mother took out a cigarette, thought better of it, returned it to the pack.

William remembered back to the first afternoon in Emma's house. She had a cigarette then, in bed, and pretended to light it. "Isn't this what people do in stories?" she said.

He corrected her. "I think you mean it's what people do in movies," he said. "In stories there's usually just a break after the sex."

She propped herself up on her left forearm. He ran a finger from one shoulder blade to another. "Do it in the shape of a wave," she said.

"When you do a wave, how high and how low should you go?" he said. "I should ask Tom."

"Tom?"

"My brother-in-law. That's what he does for a living."

"Oh," she said. "Don't. I'm one of those girls who thinks three's a crowd."

"You mean four," he said, patting her stomach.

That froze her, and when she thawed, she moved without ease. He flipped her onto her back and began to trace another plot with his finger. She was cheered when the graph dipped too low.

Now, in the city, William watched the daughter, the mother, two teenagers playing cards, a gardener placidly dropping grass seed in a brown patch of the park. He came out from the canopy of trees and went to the station. Normalcy had been restored, in the sense that William was once again immersed in the mix of obligation and randomness that dominated his days and the days of nearly everyone he knew. He opened his phone to find the envelope icon blinking, read a text from Louisa reminding him of their plans, consulted the train schedule on a terminal, watched a few minutes of television in the bar, double-checked the schedule on the big board: rectangles of increasing size. The volume on the television was off, but the images were loud enough without any sound, a vulgar clutter of ugliness and beauty. There was no way to put it together faster than it was all coming apart.

"Hello," Louisa said when he came through the door. She was at the kitchen table with a mug that said FULL OR ELSE. "How was your day?"

"Got a raise, sort of," he said.

"Great," she said.

"Good enough," he said. "I got your message about Jim. We're still on?"

"No," she said. "He called to cancel. He said his wife didn't feel well."

"That's too bad."

"I asked him what the matter was and he said he wasn't sure, a stomachache or something. We had a plan and everything. Who cancels a plan two hours before it's supposed to happen?"

"Lots of people," William said. "People with sick wives. We'll catch them the next time."

"Okay," she said. "You're right. I'm making too much of it."

In bed, he couldn't sleep, and he watched her. Her eyes were closed and her fingers worked the air, untying something he could not see. He put his hands near hers and was surprised, as always, to find that they were not very much larger. He stretched a finger until it tickled the crease of her wrist and watched her eyes, which did not open. Maybe she was genuinely asleep. He didn't need any rest anymore, only a clear path out of the fog, and he was determined to stay up all night looking if that was what it took.

EIGHT

William wanted the octopus to emerge. They had teased the scene before going to commercial: a small orange fish was swimming by, largely unaware, and the octopus was camouflaged behind a pair of rocks. "I know how to cook them, you know," Emma said. "I'm a professional caterer." She was standing in front of her bedroom mirror naked, considering the swell of her belly. William was in bed, over the sheets, not naked anymore. "Not that it makes any difference. I go to the supermarket and see fliers for other businesses: the Full Plate, Ambassador Meals. There are so many and I can't imagine how I'll ever get back among them again. The other day I walked by some event hall and there was a line of catering trucks out in the street. I had to lean against a tree."

"Event halls," William said. "I remember those." He got up off the bed. The sheets did not feel right against his skin.

"I am doing my best to think impure thoughts," Emma said, "and send them across the room to you."

The transmissions didn't reach William but he got the message anyway. Sometimes he came right back at her, his face displaying the heat of attraction. Sometimes he lay out and waited for her to make a move. Usually what happened was blurry with speed, but he could keep it in focus if he squinted. "If it's any consolation," he said, "you're good at catering to me."

She scowled. "You always say the sweetest things," she said. And then, "You're an idiot, you know that?"

Emma told him that sex helped to open things up, and that they had cut a key and were in the process of using it. She had unsuccessfully tried to convince him to expand to other locations; the most he would agree to was a call while he was in his car. He stayed on the phone while she touched herself. "That was a lark," she said, but a lark was a bird, and she didn't know a damn thing about birds. William said he didn't think they could do that again. "Why are you afraid?" she said. "Don't be a little girl."

They were three weeks into it, maybe four. There was no consensus on the matter. He marked the start from the moment he had offered to take her home rather than for coffee. "Just like a man," she said. "So literal." She measured from the cooler at Gloria Fitch's house, when he'd bent down for a beer and seen her legs. "Admit that you wanted me then," she said. He pointed out that he'd wanted her—had known her—since Chicago. Why not date things from then?

"Because you're stupid," she said, showing she was teasing with a quick sharp smile. "Isn't that how you want it?" she said.

"I want it under control," he said.

"What are you worried about? Other people? Again, stupid."

She was right. William had imagined whispers in the street and women in restaurants cutting their eyes at him, but the neighborhood had surprisingly few suspicions. He'd been careful about where to meet and where to part; even when people gossiped about Emma, William never appeared in the story. Gloria Fitch had come over to drink martinis with Louisa on the deck and say several terrible things, most of them true, about the way Stevie moved his attractive young wife from one town to the next, never caring about her happiness. "He acts like he's the most important man in the world," Gloria said. "I keep thinking I'm going to see that woman dragging a suitcase to a bus and hotfooting it back to Chicago." William told this to Emma. "I would get someone to drive me to the bus station," she said. "She's a fool." She was mad at Gloria Fitch, she said, because she felt she couldn't be mad at Louisa, at least not in front of William. She was mad at Louisa because Louisa had said several nice things about Stevie. She was mad at Stevie because, as Gloria said, he had brought her out of Chicago into the wilderness. Above all, she was mad at herself for being the kind of woman who would put herself in a position where two women in the neighborhood could meet on a deck and pity her. "Like their lives are anything to envy."

"Gloria Fitch's is," William said. "She seems to be drinking all the time."

Emma stayed in front of the mirror. "Hey," she said. "You know what they showed in one of those ocean documentaries? A montage of marine animals ejaculating."

"Wow," William said. "When you talk dirty, you don't play around."

"Seriously," she said. "It's interesting how fluids go through liquids." This led directly to a suggestion regarding the bathtub. He took her up on it, to a point; she went into the tub and he sat on the edge, watching. "When I came," she said later, "I wondered about the baby. Does it feel any part of what I'm feeling?" He tried to imagine it for himself but could not even get a picture in his head. What could he think that would not be a bright light blinding him? "I know you don't know," Emma said. "I'm just saying. Don't be a fool." She used the word liberally, which took away its sting, and then she put her arms around her swollen belly and told William that she was going to do her best to make the child inside her anything but a fool.

———————

"Hey," William said. "What if I hadn't been home when you had called me that first day? Or what if I hadn't taken your call?"

"I would have moved on down the neighborhood watch list," she said. "Graham Kenner has a big bald head."

She shifted her weight; there was a creaking in the innards of the bed. They were in Tom's studio, on the narrow couch. It was Friday, one of the days that Tom taught all afternoon. William had nixed the idea of going to her house, countering with a drink at a new Cajun place and then a motel. She had scowled. "When you're from real Louisiana," she said, "you don't do that kind of fake. I'm unhappy even thinking about what they do to crawdads." The studio had a desk, a lamp, a small TV, walls covered with tacked-up charts, a minifridge filled with spring water, and nothing much else.

"I should write a children's book about marine animals," she said into William's stomach.

"A book?"

"I'm going to have a child, I read books, I know about animals. It's a no-brainer." She shifted in a way that pleased him. "After I write it, I'll take the manuscript down to the publisher's office. He'll be small, bald, with glasses. I'll probably wear something low-cut. Helps close the deal, you know." They would get down to titles. "They'll want something clever and foolish, like *A, B, Sea*. I'll hold out for *Fear Is an Octopus*, even though it sounds like a thriller. The book will come out before the baby's first birthday. It will sell like hotcakes. I'll start getting fees for media appearances and soon I'll have enough money to get my own apartment, away from Stevie, away from here. I'll get Danish modern chairs and a massive flat-screen and you can come visit me and we can try the thing with the tub again."

William repeated the only thing that fully made sense to him: "Hotcakes." He went across the studio to the window shades, which were drawn. The small tabletop television was on, showing another marine documentary.

"I like thinking the screen is a mirror rather than a window," Emma said. "We came from the water. We are mostly water." She sat in the chair, her legs apart, and William swam to her across the blue room. "You know who's afraid of the water?" she said while he touched her. "Stevie is. Always has been, since he was a kid. When he wants to overcome his fear, he fills up the sink and puts his face in it. It was something he read in a self-help book: own your phobias so they can't own you. Most of what he does began as something he read in a self-help book."

"Sometimes you don't seem to like him very much," William said.

"Thin line between love and hate," she said, huffing toward orgasm.

———

Three days later, back in Tom's studio, she put on a podcast about sharks. "When I was a kid," William said, "I loved sharks."

"Yeah?" she said. She was taking off her bra.

"Nature's ultimate killing machine," he said in an announcer's voice.

"I think maybe you've misunderstood," Emma said. Her pants were off now, and she was standing in front of him. "Sharks kill a handful of people. You know how many sharks people kill? A hundred million a year. That's a whole Mexico of sharks." She got up on the bed, on her knees, and guided his hand between them. "Let's get back to me. Do this, okay?"

"Should I keep moving or else you'll die?"

She set her expression in a prim frown, almost marmish. "That's another myth. They need water flowing over their gills, but they can move it with their mouths. Quiet. Let me concentrate. And go a little slower, and with a lighter touch." Her marmishness receded. She gripped him hard by the shoulder, drew in a breath that she couldn't keep, relaxed her grip.

The shark show had given way to a survey of microscopic organisms, narrated by a woman with an overripe British accent. She needed switching off. On the far side of the desk, there was a folder marked, in Tom's hand, "NEW." William opened it. It contained a set of charts, all burned, some along the edges, some in the middle. One had a charred arc that stretched fully from lower left corner to lower right, riding high in the middle. That one was labeled *How Much Fire Liked This Piece of Paper.* "Look," William said, holding it up. "It's like he collaborated with nature."

Emma didn't care, and said so. "I think I've reached my limit."

"With what?"

"All of it," she said. She had been coming across the street one afternoon, not to go to William's house even but to retrieve a garbage can lid that had blown up onto the Eatons' lawn, and an older woman on the Zorillas' driveway, the mother-in-law maybe, had seen her. "I didn't feel guilty about it. She doesn't know enough about the neighborhood to know where I should rightly be, not to mention that I wasn't doing anything wrong. But I felt hemmed in, and kind of exposed, like I wanted to run back inside. It was a combination of claustrophobia and its exact opposite."

"Agoraphobia," William said, happy to help.

"The load I carry," Emma said. She stood and showed it. "What will you do without me?" she said.

———

They were together in public only once, a few days later. Louisa was home sick with a cold and Stevie was out of town, so William and Emma let their lust and optimism ferry them across town to a park, where they sat with the sun at their back and watched the purple shadows of their heads upon the black paved path.

Then they went to an Indian restaurant, where she asked the waitress to bring her the hottest entrée and then, after one bite, fanned a hand in front of her open mouth like she was waving to someone in there. He was beginning to like her again as he had before.

But then after the meal, when they were standing outside the restaurant, she gripped his hand hard and brought her face so close to his that she could be heard even if she whispered, though she spoke loudly. "I need you to listen," she said. Her eyes were down to slits as if anything wider might harm him. "I'm turning this off."

"Right," he said. He spoke casually, to hide the fact that he was heartsick.

She smacked him across the cheek, trying to look playful as she did it. "Do you hear what I'm saying? This is it, William. What's the matter with you?"

"Everything about me is matter," he said.

She showed her teeth but did not laugh.

He was joking, but also dead serious. People were matter and not the good kind: they bore the burden of their consciousness. Unconscious matter had the right idea. It just *was*, and continued to be. "Take me home," she said. The sidewalk was unconscious, and he stood on it and did his best to be like it. The car was unconscious and he leaned on it and did his best to be like it. "Now," she said. The radio was unconscious and he fiddled with the knob. "Take me home now," she said, and he covered the distance quickly and looked away from her as he pulled up just around the corner, in the spot they'd agreed was safest, and as she left the car he closed his eyes and listened to the click of her heels as she went from unconscious car to unconscious street. When she passed out of earshot he was suddenly conscious again and found he was gripping the wheel hard on both sides, as if he were trying to keep himself from washing away.

NINE

Louisa had a family friend who had died of cancer in her early thirties, and Louisa made a point of visiting the grave every year, a little more frequently when she became older than the woman ever did. The cemetery was twenty minutes beyond the new house, and one afternoon, after they stopped by the building site, she told William she wanted to visit Sylvia. They stopped to buy flowers. "She liked marigolds," Louisa said. There was no rain yet, but the sky was the same color as most of the tombstones.

Louisa stopped in front of a small stone that had mostly melted into the earth. "There she is. Or isn't," she said. "She wasn't the strongest woman I ever knew, but she had a certain quality. She always seemed like she was telling you the truth, even when she wasn't."

"I wish I could have met her."

"You did," Louisa said. "When we were dating the first time. She liked you. She said you had a way of putting her at ease."

Louisa stood by Sylvia's grave, talking to herself. William couldn't hear much of what she said, but he thought she was apologizing. He remembered something from a college lecture: burial had started with the Neanderthals, who may have had at least a vague belief in an afterlife.

He wandered off down paths that were like alleys and avenues in this planned city of the dead. He found a child who died before he was ten, a baby who died before he was one. He found a woman who had ascended nearly to a century. He imagined his way down into the graves, holes that held back all light. "Ready?" Louisa said, and he didn't answer, because he wasn't sure what the question meant.

What it meant, it turned out, was that she was ready. That night in bed she reached over and took his hand, and happiness went through him like a current, racing across pathways that had become accustomed to confusion. She woke before him the next morning and made breakfast, and she was whistling when he came out of the bedroom. In the invisible choreography between them, she had taken a step he hadn't expected; she seemed happy to be with him. And the happiness wasn't desperate or frenetic or insistent; rather than trouble every room with this new energy, she let it ripen into what could only be described as a state of happy relaxation, wineglasses left out on tables, kitchen happily disarranged. "I don't know," she said when he asked her. "Perspective check, I guess. When you see what death really is, how still it is, it makes you want to move through life instead of resisting it."

If there was to be any alienation, it would have to come from him, and so it did. One night, he found a T-shirt of hers heaped in the corner of the couch and snatched it up in sudden rage. "Just because you don't want to be in this house doesn't mean you have to treat it like a garbage dump," he said, and she smiled until it was clear that he was serious, at which point she took the shirt and left the room. Another night he got on her about an open jar of peanut butter and how ants would find their way to it. He wasn't sure what explained his sudden volatility, except that it was a form of distraction, both from Louisa's new contentment and from his own growing sense of unease, shading faster than he wished into a kind of terror. He had located the source. It was no mystery. He had lost his job and he had agreed to build a new house and he was remembering Emma's face and the yearning softness he had seen in it, once or twice, when she wasn't determined to show him how strong she was. While he had been with her, he'd been able to put her out of his mind, but now that she was gone he could not. The farther the flame, the worse it burned him. Emma did not ignore him. That would have been rewarding. Rather, she saw him across the street or once in the supermarket and said hello, with a quick smile and wave. She was free to be friendly when friendly was no longer a borderland to something more dangerous. He resented the wave and the smile but would have been ravaged by their absence, and that was the real problem: not that he couldn't stay with his true feelings, but that he didn't know what they were anymore.

———

One cloudy evening, William looked out through the attenuated light and saw Emma getting into her car. She was holding a parcel and dressed casually; he figured it for a quick trip. "I'm going for a walk," he said to Louisa.

"Looks like it might rain."

"I can see that," he said. "I'm not concerned, and you shouldn't be either." He tried to slam the door between the hall and the garage but it just eased shut on spring hinges. He shuttled up and down the block in what was turning into an impotent drizzle. A bicycle belonging to one of the Kenner kids was abandoned at the edge of the Morgans' yard. William wheeled it back and left it under a tree. In the middle of the street he saw a broken bottle and threw it away in the Eatons' garbage can. The wind was picking up, and William was about to head for home when Emma's car came around the corner. He saw a head in the passenger seat: Stevie. She parked in front of her house, got out, gave William another eviscerating wave. "Holy God," he heard her saying to Stevie. "I felt like I was in half." On the rear window of her car, the bear doll was hanging from a single arm. William knew just how it felt: melodramatic.

He marched back inside, passed through the house, found Louisa in the kitchen making sandwiches. "So," he said. She tilted her head at him, squinted happily. Behind her in the window a leaf bounced on an updraft. "I need to tell you something." And then he did. There were two stories that needed telling, Hollister and Emma, and he told only the first. It was a tactical operation, not a kamikaze mission.

She bit her lower lip, shook off a thought. "So," she said, possibly not mocking him.

"So," he said. "That's the situation as it stands. I am not working there anymore." He braced himself against the counter. "We're okay with money for a little while," he said. "At some point, later in the summer, I'll have to start looking for something."

She set the sandwiches on the table and straightened the plates before she spoke. "I'm less bothered by this than maybe I should be. I didn't think you were happy there."

"Who could be?" he said. But he had been, so long as he'd been left alone.

"And now we can make more serious plans about the house." He must have looked stricken; she seemed very surprised for a moment and her forehead bunched in worry. But then her face relaxed into a smile and she didn't look like she wanted to leave the room. "It's something constructive to think about." She hadn't meant the joke but she took credit for it, a quick bow. "You'll see." Then she blushed and ducked her head and said, "I wish you could see what a good idea this really is."

TEN

"It was disgusting."

William was spending most Tuesday afternoons with Christopher, and sometimes Thursdays as well. They went to the bowling alley. They went to the movies. They went to the arcade in the mall, where William dominated on a deer-hunting video game. The days shaded into one another as if in a montage. Even Christopher sensed that. "We should have theme music," Christopher said. He hummed a wobbly melody.

"You should have seen it there," Christopher said. "Just dangling on the end of her finger."

William had taken Christopher to a birthday party. It was uneventful, at least from the adult perspective. In the kitchen with the other parents, William repeated his boilerplate: not my kid, belongs to a friend of mine, no, not my girlfriend, known her forever. Sometimes he rode this last phrase longer than was necessary to acknowledge what was being danced around, the sex. Then he stood in the kitchen, with the one other dad and the three other moms, and talked about school and athletics and all the other things he didn't care about. When one of the moms raised the question of how stability might come about in the Middle East, he was relieved, until he realized he didn't care about that either. He drank more beers than the other dad but fewer than one of the other moms, who started to flirt on her third and was now at five. William slid down to the open end of the kitchen to give her a wider berth. He called Louisa, couldn't reach her; called Tom, whose line went straight to voice mail; called Karla to tell her that the party was rolling along. A little girl with blond hair and a Band-Aid on her shoulder skipped up to William. She was eleven or twelve. "Have you seen my dad?" she said.

"Is that him?" He swung the bottom of his beer bottle toward the dad at the far end of the kitchen, whose name he thought was Randy. The girl shook her head. "Well, if that's not him, he's probably not here. The grown-ups who dropped kids off haven't all come back yet."

"Okay," she said. "He said I could get a bracelet on the way home," she said. She pointed at his phone: "What's that?"

"It's a telephone."

"I know," she said. "I mean on your hand."

He looked back down. There was a tiny bug on the knuckle of his thumb. "Oh," he said. "Not sure. A fly?"

"It's an immature wasp. We studied them in fourth grade. In England, they brought them in to kill whiteflies."

William shook his hand until the assassin dropped off. "What'd you study in fifth grade? Mature wasps?" She didn't laugh. She stared up at him instead, and he wondered what she saw. "I wish my dad would get here already," she said. "He's always late. So disappointing." She was hard-hearted; there was no one she loved. Even her father was only a way of getting to the store.

This was the girl Christopher was describing as the ringleader.

They were sitting with the windows down, on the edge of the duck lake, where William had stopped on the way home from the party. Christopher sipped a milkshake. Directly in front of them, an older man was on a park bench, throwing pieces of bread to the ducks. He seemed to be aiming for them. "We were tossing this ball back and forth, and this one kid just ran in and kicked it," Christopher said. "It went over the fence. He was laughing, and that girl, Alana, walked right up to him and slapped him in the face. And not a play slap either. Hard. He started crying and snot came out of his nose, and instead of wiping it on his sleeve he pinched it and it hung there."

"A gobbet."

"What?"

"That's the word. A lump of it."

"Doesn't it mean a cup?"

"Not a goblet. A gobbet."

Christopher pinched his fingers together and held his hand away from his body as if it wasn't his. "It was disgusting, but the kid didn't know what to do with it. Eventually he brought his hand back and wiped it on his pants, and Alana started pointing and laughing at that." He frowned. "Last summer at camp, she picked on a girl so bad. She's going to end up in jail or worse."

Out in the park, the old man on the bench stood up. He was hulking, Reeser's height at least, and he moved unevenly, as if one leg was damaged. As he went through the park, parents near him began to collect their children. "He's big," William said.

"Yeah," Christopher said. He sounded unconcerned. "Then we had to sit and watch a stupid movie. It was animated, with a dog, and it was for kids at least three years younger."

"I wish somebody told me about it," William said. "I was trapped in the kitchen with adults I didn't know."

"You wouldn't have liked it. Like I said, it was stupid." He wasn't ready to move on from Alana. "People like her for no reason, even though she acts like an idiot. Her parents got a divorce last year and kids said that was the reason. But what's the reason now?"

"You didn't act worse when your mom and Matthew split up."

"Matthew wasn't my dad," Christopher said. "I didn't like him."

"Why not?"

"When my mom wasn't around he made lots of jokes about how rich she was, even compared to him. And then he always said something about how it didn't matter. Why would someone keep talking about something if it didn't matter?"

"Maybe he was trying to teach you a lesson."

"I doubt it." He swirled what remained of the milkshake around the bottom of the cup. "Did you know my dad?"

William drew a breath. He weighed the value of honesty and could not, in the end, find any. "Yes," he said. "He was a great guy. You're very much like him."

"I am?"

"You look like him, for starters."

"You know what I read in a book? In ancient Rome, more than one-third of children lost their fathers before the age of ten."

William didn't know what to do with that information. "And there's a kind of quiet he had that you have also. He didn't always want to talk, or want other people to. You seem like you feel that way sometimes."

"My mom thinks I'm sad when I don't talk, but actually I'm happy. Mostly I like watching people, and talking gets in the way of that."

"It gets in the way of watching?"

"Of noticing and then thinking about what you notice." The conversation had become, unaccountably, meaningful. "Like Matthew. On the last day I saw him, he was dressed up fancy to impress my mother, but he had food in his beard. A gobbet."

"Ew," William said. "I'm so happy I taught you that." The man in the park was pointing up into a tree, gesturing more broadly now. He had one long finger extended in front of him. William started the car but did not put it in gear. He did not want to be the kind of man who left a place simply because someone he didn't know was doing something he didn't understand. But when the man turned and came toward them, William backed out. He had a child to protect.

————

Louisa was in the kitchen, reading a catalog. He moved until he was right above her and bent to kiss the crown of her head. "I'm ready."

"For?"

"For the house," he said. "I'll do it. We'll do it."

She angled her head back until she could see him. "Really?" Her eyes were bright.

"I just figured that if the wife wants, the wife wants. Who am I to stand in the way?" The edges of her eyes began to cloud with gratitude, or possibly suspicion, and he advanced the frame. "I'll call a contractor tomorrow."

William went to sit on the deck. The evening was clear and cool. His favorite bird sang in the tree above, piercing notes going up, and then, like a heavenly visitation, it appeared at low branches, still singing, and landed on the corner rail of the deck. It was tiny, with brown-streaked feathers and a red cap; its head moved in quick flicks. William wasn't sure he had ever seen it before, and if he had, he hadn't known he was seeing the bird he loved so much to hear. He froze, afraid to move, and he and the bird stayed like that, looking at each other. That was when he heard shuffling in the kitchen and the glass door dragging open. At the sound of Louisa's foot against the deck, the bird flew out into the yard in a perfect sight line. It was going away, but it looked like it was only getting smaller.

Part V

———————

THE LOW WALL

Once, when they were young, William and Louisa had gone down-state with another couple, a woman from the advertising side of the newspaper and the woman's boyfriend. It was the culmination of a few months of light complaint on Louisa's part that they never vacationed. "You're content to stay here in town," she said. "And I am, too, for the most part. It's just that sometimes I like to get away. It gives me perspective. You know: see how the other half of my mind lives." William had started collecting brochures for scuba getaways and hiking trips, but then one afternoon Louisa had called him to announce that she had, on both their behalf, accepted an invitation to drive into the foothills for a long weekend.

The house belonged to the other couple, or rather it was the man's family's vacation home, so William and Louisa were guests. They played their roles willingly, taking off their shoes at the front door, agreeing to predetermined meal times, happily packing into the car whenever a destination was suggested. The other woman, Marilyn, was dour and had eyes ringed by worry, but she came alive in the country; the man, Mike, who was timid in most of the rest of his life, did not mind lecturing them about the region, about which he seemed to possess an endless storehouse of information. And so the two women drank wine and cooked a little, and the four of them drove to antique shops and farmers' markets and then to a red cliff nearby that Mike insisted offered the best view of the river that wound through the countryside. It was a midelevation alluvial river, he said, and as a result very rare. "This is a backseat kind of vacation," William said the first night, when they were in bed in the guest room, which had been Mike's room in childhood.

"If we're going to have a chauffeur, we should at least have that glass that goes up between us," Louisa had said, but by the next morning's breakfast, she too had settled into easy obedience. All that was left of her disapproval was her nickname for the couple: Eight Eyes, because they both wore glasses, and both made a big show of misplacing them and then saying they'd be lost without them. The second night, the four of them played a board game that no one understood very well. Marilyn insisted that each player had to roll the dice, move around the board, and then draw two cards and act them both out simultaneously. Mike said that was impossible. "What if you drew left and right?" he said. "Or up and down? How would you act those out at the same time?" His voice was rising to a pitch that suggested he was going to lord it over her.

William said he thought he knew and then stood still in the middle of the room. "See," he said, "both up and down, both left and right. Easy."

Marilyn laughed warmly and this softened Mike, who refilled everyone's wineglass and then told a series of long, sentimental stories about his family, which included two sisters and an older brother who had died in a car accident in college. "We have an agreement that if we have a boy, he'll be named after Jerry," he said, his voice catching, and Marilyn, sitting on the floor next to his chair, reached up and squeezed his hand.

———————

The third day, the last day, Louisa woke William up early. She was wearing what looked like a tennis outfit, a short white skirt and a tight yellow top. He squinted against its brightness. "Come with me," she said. "The rest are sleeping."

She led him out behind the house, where a path ran the length of a long low wall. At the end of the wall, almost like a mark of punctuation, there was a giant oak tree with a tire swing tied to a thick low branch. She climbed into the tire and he pushed her around for a while. The cold morning sharpened them. "Can't you just imagine living in a place like this?" she said. "Me and you and the twelve kids."

"Twelve?" William said. He made a sputtering noise.

Louisa laughed, and even when she stopped the laughter stayed on her face. "Okay, six," she said. "It's settled. I'll be the hausfrau. You can go to work at the newspaper and come home early, or late but with tales of heroism. It'll probably be three boys and three girls, and they'll line up on either side of you and listen with saucer eyes."

She hopped down from the swing and put her arms around the trunk of the tree like she was embracing it. Then she reached behind her and lifted her skirt. "Hey," she said. "Why don't you come over here and fuck me before Eight Eyes wakes up?"

William had rarely heard her use the word except in anger. It excited him, and he did his best to bring it off despite the cold. Louisa kept herself steadied against the tree the whole time, grunting lightly into the bark. Then she turned and kissed him. "I forgot to brush my teeth," she said. "I hope that's okay."

The sun was beginning to burn off the morning mist and she asked William to push her in the swing for a few minutes more. He sent her off with a little thrill, knowing she'd be right back. When they returned to the house, she balanced on the low wall, arms out like she was flying.

———————

Monday night, they drove home. Mike apologized for getting them back so late. "It's going to be hard to spring out of bed for work," he said. "But this way, no rush hour." He pulled up in front of William's house and popped the trunk so that William could get his suitcase.

"You've got a good one there," Mike said.

His tone was too fatherly by half and William clowned him off. "The suitcase?" he said.

"No," Mike said. "Louisa. Marilyn thinks very highly of her and I can see why. She's pretty and sane."

"Pretty insane?" William said, because that's what he had heard. But then he looked at Mike and saw genuine affront in his expression and he was sorry that he was taking it all lightly, their generosity and Marilyn's cooking and the way the drive home was latticed with good feeling. "You're right," William said warmly. "She's a keeper. I won't screw it up. I promise."

He reached out and shook Mike's hand and they went their separate ways, Mike and Marilyn to suburban Pittsburgh, where they married, raised a family of three boys, separated over money trouble, got back together when Marilyn was diagnosed with cancer, and celebrated their twentieth anniversary the week before their oldest son's high school graduation. Louisa never mentioned that house again, said she didn't remember it very well when William brought it up, and William learned, slowly, a lesson, which was not to take seriously any desire that did not recur. People were filled with whims, with wants that fit perfectly into a moment, but only that moment, and that had no broader application. And so they never had gone out to the country for that low wall or any other, instead staying in town, more or less rooted to the spot, moving always both up and down, both left and right.

Part VI

———————

SOMEONE ELSE'S MIRACLE

ONE

In the wake of their visit to the cemetery, Louisa had become suddenly ardent, and William had receded. Then, after he agreed to move forward with the house, he settled back and waited for another wave of good feeling, only to find that for her, his decision was the conclusion of a struggle, one where she had emerged triumphant, and to the victor went the spoils, which in this case included the right to be quiet again, careful and inward, refusing to reveal too much by word or gesture. When he tried to reach her she did not pull back, exactly, but stayed right where she was, giving up nothing, not even interest.

He tried to rouse her with planning. He spread an oversize sheet of graph paper on the kitchen table. "Come," he said, and she did, silently, and he took a pencil and drew Harrow, running east to west, and a large rectangle for the lot. "Circular driveway?" he said, and Louisa made no objection, and there it was, a rainbow rising off the horizon of the street. He made a line to indicate the front wall and a notch for the doorway. The rest of the page was only empty space and he felt claustrophobic and agoraphobic all at once. "That's just the beginning," he said. Louisa's eyes shone unhelpfully.

He drew again the next night, and then a few nights later, neither time with any great success, though Louisa did start to pitch in with minor suggestions. She wanted a flower bed out in front, and an asymmetrical fence. The fourth time they drew, there was a ring at the door: Tom, coming to return Louisa's extra pair of car keys. "This is the old homestead I've heard so much about?" he said. He smelled beery.

"It's the new homestead," Louisa said. "And you've heard nothing about it." She went into the kitchen to watch the high-tech cylinder make coffee. William wondered if she'd noticed the beer, too, or if she was taking the edge off her own wine.

"It looks kind of traditional. Is that a white picket fence, or off-white?"

"It doesn't need to be untraditional. It's not one of your charts," William said.

"Charts are for water," Tom said. "Maps are for land."

"You know what I mean. It's not an artwork. It's where we're going to live."

"I just think you could do something more interesting," Tom said. "How about radical verticality?"

"What do you mean?"

"Stories and stories. A tower."

"The neighbors would love that," William said.

"Who cares what they say? There's no kids, so stairs aren't your enemy. Go up, young man."

"Zoning doesn't permit," William said.

"Get an easement."

"That's not what an easement is," Louisa said. She had come out when Tom said stairs weren't their enemy. She had no coffee and now she wasn't going to get it. "It's late and only getting later. Isn't there someone at home wondering where you are?"

"If you're trying to hurt my feelings, I'm just going to stay right here and take it," Tom said, but he left a few minutes later.

Louisa lifted the floor plan by its corners and told William to open up the junk room. She had prevailed on him to carry out the filing cabinets and break down the exercise machines and throw away any electronic device not in perfect working order. "I now declare this the pin-up room," she said, and William was gratified by the phrase.

He taped the floor plan to the wall. "Come to bed," William said, and instead Louisa pulled her knees up onto the couch and began to take liberties with what remained of the red wine. The whole thing seemed chancy at best.

———

"Running out," Louisa said. "Back around noon." William lay on his stomach in bed and sorted through the burr of a lawn mower, a mating cat yowling, the ting-a-ling of a bicycle bell. He was reluctant to get up, not because he was still tired, but because he knew the risks out there.

He went to the deck, coffee in one hand, phone in the other. He had gotten the name of a contractor from Graham Kenner, one he recognized from signs around the neighborhood. "He's the father of a woman I work with," Graham said. "Great guy. Loves to talk politics." That had been enough reason not to call. Paul Prescott had another recommendation, a "true genius" whose addition to Paul's lake house upstate was "equivalent to the finest work of modern sculpture." He charged accordingly.

Instead, William dialed a man who came recommended, conditionally, by Eddie Fitch. "My sister used him a while back," he said. "She liked his work but said he could be a little closed off." He giggled. "On the other hand, you could say the same thing about my sister." The man picked up after two rings.

"I'm looking for someone to build me a house," William said.

"How big?" The voice was Southern, rickety, scarred by cigarettes, at least.

"You mean bedrooms? Square feet?"

The man sighed. "Let's meet," he said. "Do you drink?"

"Sure," William said.

"I don't, anymore," the man said. "But I can't stand those coffee places. I'll meet you at the Sit Inn on O'Farrell and Randall."

William didn't know the place, and as it turned out, almost no one else did either. There was only one other patron at the bar, a white-haired gentleman with a high brow and a squashed nose.

"Mr. Day?" he said.

"Call me William."

"Wallace," he said. His rheumy eyes suggested an almost comic surplus of self-doubt. But when William described what he had in mind, Wallace nodded crisply. "Sounds very similar to the first house I ever built," he said. "More than thirty years ago now. That's one of the things you learn: no matter how much you think things are changing, you always end up right back where you started."

"Maybe I can get the prices from thirty years ago," William said.

"I don't joke about money," Wallace said. "My estimate, when it comes to you, will be ironclad." Something like anger rose into his eyes and washed out against the water. "There's something I have to tell you," he said. "I tell this to every client before I start working with them."

"I hope it's something encouraging," William said.

"People will tell you that building a house is an emotional experience," Wallace said. "That you're providing shelter and future, that it's the closest male equivalent to childbirth." William nodded. His heart quickened. The man was articulating his feelings exactly. "Well, that's bullshit," Wallace said. "It's a matter of squaring risk and reward, costs and benefits. That's all. Don't get sucked in by the mumbo-jumbo, or the first house you build will be your last."

The next morning, the two of them drove out to the lot. Wallace was semiretired, living in a small clapboard house not far from William. "I didn't build it," he said. "I built the one I raised my kids in, but that went to the wife when we split up."

"Sorry to hear that."

"You shouldn't be. It was the best thing that ever happened to me." He threw back his head and gave a sharp staccato laugh. They were in his truck, going Kerrick to Francis to Harrow, driving too slow the whole way, radio tuned to classic country, which he played at maximum volume. It had rained lightly the previous night, and a layer of gauzy fog hung low over the land. At the lot, the two of them got out. Wallace said he would start by building an office in what would eventually be the corner of the house. "It'll be a wooden shack and then we'll tear it down and it'll be the gap between the house and the garage," he said.

"Like a command center?" William said.

"Exactly," he said. "I'm too old to be outside in a folding chair or leaning on a truck." He tromped to the edge of the property and pointed. "Right there," he said. "It'll go there." Then he did what he said he would not do and leaned on his truck and went through the list of steps with William: grading the site, preparing it, foundation footings, framing of floors and walls, installing windows and doors, attaching the roof and siding, roughing in the electrical and plumbing, adding insulation, putting up drywall, underlayment, painting, counters and cabinets, sod. "At that point you can put a cherry on top of it," Wallace said.

"Is there any chance we can get the deck up early?" William asked.

Wallace smiled like he was dealing with a sharp customer. Yes, of course, it could go up fairly early in the process, he said; like the command center, they could use it for things like storage and so forth. Wind was picking up. "I'm cold," Wallace said. "Should have worn a jacket. Or pants, for that matter." He threw back his head again. Wallace hadn't said that he loved the land or that he thought anything built on the spot would be a palace, which suited William fine. Wallace opened the door of his truck and the music he liked poured out.

———

William's week was a series of holes he could not fill, and he had to be careful not to fall into them. He devoted the morning to minor repairs around the house, and he drove through the afternoon, skittering from station to station. The news that week was about another fire, this one in a used-car lot, where a large cardboard display in the parking lot had gone up in flames at the same time a small blaze broke out in a corner of the roof. The phrase "intentionally set" had now been replaced by the word "arson." "We use the term because it has legal ramifications," a fire department official said. "It has to do with whether or not we can prove the intent of the fire setter." The language was moving them all toward a new awareness.

That night the doorbell rang. Tom stood there with a bag of chips and a six-pack. "There was another fire."

"I know," William said. "So we're celebrating?"

"Yes," Tom said, "I *would* like to come in. We don't have much time." At eight, he explained, the local news was running a special report. They were reviewing the full set of fires, repurposing old footage, even clips of the anchors reporting the story on the nightly news. "Pull up a chair," he said. "Would popcorn be inappropriate?"

The fire commissioner came on first to introduce the hour. He had eyes like pinpricks and a habit of turning to the side to point at his whiteboard, which exposed the collop at the back of his neck. "We are looking at a distribution that radiates out from the northeast side of town," he said. Yellow diamonds appeared on the map.

At first, it was just William and Tom watching the show, which meant it was mostly Tom holding forth. "It's strange to see the news report of the arsons long after the fact," he said. "Fire's supposed to be something primal, but this puts it on a delay, which is also a remove. It's like Mark Twain said: 'Words are only painted fire; a look is the fire itself.' In a way, you wish the cameras would just get there and shoot the fire as it burns. Or that someone would put a camera in the fire even before it starts." He had raced through a pair of beers. "There should be a whole channel devoted just to that. I'd watch it all the time." William thought of mentioning the fire graphs he'd found in Tom's studio, but he caught himself before he did.

When the special broke for a commercial, Louisa joined them. She perched on the edge of the armchair and watched silently as happy children clambered into the new family car. "Hey," she said. "Does anyone want pizza? I'll order."

"Sausage," Tom said, and she went to call in the order. After she left, Tom said, "She doesn't seem to hate you as much these days."

Tom was wrong: she didn't seem to hate him at all. The floor plan in the pin-up room had restored him to her good graces. "You know what else?" Tom said. "I was reading around in Latin and I found the original for 'Out of the frying pan, into the fire.' *De calcaria in carbonarium.* It's Tertullian. He was also the first one to explicitly formulate the idea of the Trinity. Oh, and he praised the unmarried state as the highest state of man. I don't like his reasoning, celibacy and all, but you can't argue with the conclusion."

"News is back," Louisa said, resurfacing to rescue William. The female anchor, cool in considered blue, reviewed the timeline, gave tips for reporting leads, warned against taking suspicious figures lightly. The camera panned to the commissioner, parked massively behind a tiny desk. "Pay attention, as well, to the crowd," he said. "People gather to watch a fire, and sometimes the arsonist himself is among them. I use the masculine pronoun because that is, more often than not, the case." A short feature on Karim followed: though most of the investigators did not think Birch Mutual was the work of the same man, Karim's was still the only death, and so, however imprecisely, he was the face of the problem. Tom stood up and showed the way he'd run, legs almost straight like stilts, and Louisa put a hand over her mouth and asked him to stop.

Tom's clowning, Louisa's horror: between them, William took the role of analyst. There was one car that caught his eye, a black Pontiac with a decal on the back; he'd spotted it in the reports about two different fire sites, the marina and the nursing home. "Maybe that's something," he said. "You heard the fire commissioner. People gather to watch a fire, sometimes the arsonist among them."

"That seems unlikely," Louisa said. "A guy sets a fire and then comes back to rubberneck?"

"That would be like me going to my own art opening," Tom said.

"You do go to your own art opening," William said. "I should call this in."

Louisa lifted a slice of pizza emphatically. "It probably belongs to one of the reporters or a tech."

"Oh," William said. "Yeah. I didn't think of that."

"That's why I'm here," she said. "To be the smart one."

Two nights later, the commissioner was a guest on another local station, on a panel show hosted by a severely handsome black man who seemed like he was already auditioning for the national networks. Tom dropped by for that show, too, and Louisa protested lightly that the rubbernecking made her uneasy. "Come on, Mom, can we watch, please?" Tom said, and she relented and brought a Chinese takeout menu in from the kitchen. They switched on all the lamps and overhead lights in the den and sat in the center of the warm glow. "I hate to say it," Louisa said, "but Tom was right. This is fun."

"Tom is always right," Tom said. "This is the life: food, friends, and things burning down to the ground."

"Friends?" Louisa said. "How about family?"

"It's not a word I like," Tom said. "But have it your way."

They weren't the only ones who were captivated. The fires, nine in all now, were bringing everyone together. Fitch called to say he'd been at a local service station when the police had questioned and then released a young man buying a can of gasoline. Stevie, outside one morning watering the lawn, joked that he was going to wet the house down to protect it. Even Karla was hooked; she and Christopher were watching the coverage together, and she was using it to teach him about the difference between crimes against persons and crimes against property. "Did you hear the commissioner's press conference today?" she asked William on the phone. "He said they've pretty much decided they're not looking for a juvenile, based on the sites of the blazes. We've had a marina fire and a hardware store fire and a train station fire, and juvenile fire setters tend to target institutions—schools, churches, that kind of thing."

"Why?" William said.

"They seek control," she said.

"Who does?" Christopher said from the background.

"Nothing," Karla said.

"Tell me," Christopher said. "Please."

"See?" Karla said.

TWO

Among the many things William didn't understand was himself. When Emma had moved to town, he had pushed a chair against the dining room wall and stared out the front window for hours, and when he saw her, it only intensified his desire to see her again. Now he never saw her and hoped he never would; only by remaining absent could she be as important to him as when she was present. One morning in the coffee shop, he thought he spotted her standing along the back wall, looking at a painting of a girl on the beach. He shut his book, stood, and left without picking up his drink from the counter, though he had already paid for it.

He achieved his aim, in part, by staying away from his house, and that meant, increasingly, visiting the site of the new house and asking Wallace questions whose answers he didn't understand. What were his options for supporting floor joists? Did new wireless technologies mean that the electrical phase would go more quickly? "It's almost like you have a job again," Louisa said.

"Except that instead of getting paid, I'm the one doing the paying."

"Six of one, half dozen of another," she said. "But see? I was right. It's the thing that's keeping you sane."

"I'm glad you think so," he said.

Nine was too early, and even nine thirty slightly obsessive, so William showed at ten. Wallace was there, along with Hank, his architect, and two other men William could not exactly tell apart. Hank was a rockhead, six feet tall, two hundred pounds, with very few ideas but perfect certainty about how to express them. He had a hand with at least two mangled fingers, which he held up whenever he counted things, which was often. "We've just done sill plate anchors," Hank said, "and now we're putting in the soil cover." William nodded, and Wallace told Hank to show him what he meant, and Hank smiled sharply like someone's unkind father and spread a blueprint out on a bench. He touched one spot and then another and William nodded again, quicker this time, like he was absorbing everything, when in fact he was watching the two workmen saw boards for the deck. The sky was clear of clouds and the sun was bright and the men joked over the sounds of their work. "I can see your house from here," one of the men said to the other. "And your wife, too. I think I see the two of you screwing in front of the window." The other man laughed and said something William couldn't hear.

Wallace and Hank conferred in the space above the blueprint. "It's the vapor retarder," Hank said. Wallace shook his head. "I'm telling you," Wallace said. "Joints have to be lapped. I don't even know why there's any discussion." Hank nodded and Wallace turned to William. "And we might backfill the retaining wall," he said. "And Hank has some ideas about the landscaping."

"It's too early for that," Hank said, shocking William by flashing a quick smile that looked a little shy.

"Or is it too late?" Wallace said. He hummed a B-movie suspense cue.

———

William wondered why Louisa wasn't visiting the lot more often. "Frankly, I'm a little insulted," he said. "Boy meets girl, girl asks for house, boy agrees to house after being unjustly accused of dragging his feet, girl doesn't seem to care." He shook his head slowly enough for comedy.

"Work's been crazy," Louisa said. "Pick a day."

There was a calendar hanging alongside the phone, and he stabbed a finger blindly into it. "How about . . . today?" he said. Wallace had finished the deck at the new house, and William couldn't wait to see it.

"As long as you drop me off at work and then pick me up. No point in taking two cars all the way out there."

"Deal."

Louisa was waiting outside her office, sun starting to set behind her, when William arrived. He rolled down the passenger window. "Would you like some candy?" he said.

"Only if you're a total stranger," she said. "It doesn't taste as good when it comes from someone you know." William's laugh iced over; the joke had run away from him.

The traffic on Oswald was awful, so he cut over to Pemberton—no better—and then to Rockwood, which moved at a slightly faster creep. Cars coming the other way flowed easily through the afternoon. "There's probably an accident," Louisa said, pointing vaguely ahead of them, and William noticed a plume of smoke snaking over the roof of a house up on the right. "Look," he said, and Louisa did. But it wasn't the house: the smoke, dense and black, was coming from the discount-retail mart with the statue of a pig on a pole.

William pulled the wheel and cut across a parking lot. A fire engine was already there, and one of the firemen was fitting a hose to a hydrant. They found a spot close enough that they could hear the firefighters talking to each other and he and Louisa sat and watched the place burn. The Bond Street façade was already charred; heat had melted half the struts under the sign that overlooked Lucas Avenue. The firemen were carrying cash registers and other equipment out under the sign with the huge plastic pig. William rolled down the car window to get a better sense of things, and rolled it back up immediately when he smelled the smoke: it was chemical, acrid, unvirtuous. Then one of the retail mart's windows blew out, and the flames went like a vine up the side of the building, and the sign, its last struts melted, gave way and crashed to the pavement. The pig, thrown free, skidded out into the center of Lucas Avenue. William inched the car forward. Heat reached them through the doors. Cold air inside the car bulged to keep it away. The pig, defenseless on the pavement now, had lost a leg and one side of its face had melted flat. Louisa took his hand and touched her knee with it, and then moved it higher up on the inside of the thigh. "There's something about a fire," she said, burlesquing but also really feeling it.

"Prove it," he said. But she let his hand fall free, and by the time they made it out to the lot she was stood chastely before the house like a parishioner who had come to church at off-hours just to feel the holiness of the place. That night there was another fire. They were coming closer together now. A corner of a warehouse on the east side of town had burned, damaging the contents but harming no one. "Isn't that right near my brother's studio?" Louisa said, and William nodded, though he had no idea. The fire had started in a trash can. A coffee cup had been stuffed with toilet paper that was dipped in gasoline. It was significantly cruder than the others, but that didn't mean it wasn't connected. "Sometimes, a perpetrator will try to break his own pattern to throw us off," the fire commissioner said. It didn't make the six o'clock news but it led at eleven.

————

William expected to meet Tom at Stevie's event, but Louisa, twisting in small silver earrings, asked if they could pick him up. "There's something wrong with his car again," she said, fluffing her hair and frowning.

He was standing outside already, wearing a red sport coat that came off as clownish. "Hey ho," he said, sliding across the back seat. Something sloshed in his hand.

"Is that a beer?" William said. "In my car?"

"Life just gets better."

"That hasn't been my experience," William said.

"Oh, because you have it so bad," Louisa said.

"Mom and Dad are fighting," Tom said, and crushed the can.

The event was in a temporarily converted garage a few blocks from Louisa's office. A sign hanging in front said SPECIAL EVENT in red letters. William parked in the side alley and they went in through the back door. Eddie Fitch was the first to greet them, in a narrow hallway by the bathrooms. He kissed Louisa hello and shook Tom's hand and then hung back as they went on up the hall, bugging his eyes out at William like a bad spy in a movie. "Something's up with TenPak," he said.

"What do you mean?"

"I'm not sure." His eyes darted from side to side. "Baker's been having lots of closed-door meetings, some with Hollister, some with the new guy, and no one looks happy when they come out." He spotted Gloria coming down the hall. "Can't say any more," he said. "She'll never stop asking questions. I'll call you."

Gloria leaned in, kissed the air near William and Louisa. "Are you guys going to see the talent?" she said. "He's backstage. There's a door over there by the stairs. I'll take you."

Backstage was a tiny room not much larger than a closet. The walls were a pale yellow; the floor was old tile, no longer clean; the black leather couch was the only piece of furniture, unless you counted the folding tables with a tray of carrots and celery and an ice bucket filled with beer. Emma was standing in the corner; Stevie was next to her, talking with a young female reporter who was holding a digital recorder under his mouth. "I moved here because my company said so," Stevie said. "It was a marriage of art and commerce." He was wearing an olive sweater, tight at the cuffs, and loose black pants. William wondered if he had his blue bike shorts on underneath.

"Art and commerce got married?" Gloria Fitch said in a loud whisper. "I know a perfect present for them: it's a painting of a coin."

"I just wanted to do justice to music that I loved as a child," Stevie said. "I hope I make people remember it better rather than forget it."

The reporter moved the recorder back under her own mouth. "Well, it seems like it's all worked out," she said. She pressed a button. The device beeped.

Louisa stepped in to hug Stevie. Emma was showing now, well beyond the concealing power of any outfit, and that meant that she received a different kind of hug, hands on shoulders, faces briefly brushing. William didn't even try; he just wished them both good luck, and Stevie gave back a salute and Emma curtsied cutely, as she had at Southern Christmas.

It was time to go, but Louisa had struck up a conversation with Stevie. She was telling him how she liked what he was saying about the tree and the branches. "No one ever thinks the tree can fall," Stevie said, and Louisa nodded, and Emma, standing behind them, met William's gaze and slowly rolled her eyes. It was a comic gesture but also somehow seductive and Emma, sensing that, retreated behind Louisa. William watched them standing there next to each other. It gave him a sense of power, but also a sense of doubt. They were opposed: the power and the doubt, but also the two women, the taller brown-haired one he'd seen year in, year out, from nearly every angle, and the shorter, paler blonde who slipped out of focus even when he stared directly at her. Neither of them was really saying what she meant. Who was withholding the most? William was.

A young man came in to call five minutes. Stevie put his face down into the ice bucket and came up breathing hard. "See you out there," he said.

The neighborhood lined the apron of the stage. A woman in a pantsuit came to the microphone first. She explained how Arrow Automotive had used the same theme music since 1947. "It served us well," she said. "But last year we all agreed it was time for a change. That's when we first heard this marvelous song. It only made things sweeter to learn that it was written by one of our regional marketing managers. Please give him a warm welcome." Ominous electronic music swelled and dry-ice vapor floated across the stage from right to left. Then, on the screen at the rear of the stage, the image of a firework bursting open, along with a sampled thunderclap. "*Flamma fumo est proxima*," Tom said. Stevie sprang up the shallow steps. He had changed into a black Arrow T-shirt. He looked like he'd been lifting weights. His guitar strap was patterned Navajo. "Rock star," Graham Kenner yelled.

"Hardly," Gloria Fitch yelled, just as loud.

Stevie basked in the glow of his specialized popularity. He picked out a note or two, then stilled the strings with the flat of his hand. "How are you all doing tonight?" he said. "I didn't write this song with cars in mind, but maybe the cars had me in mind." He strummed a chord. "This song is the new theme of Arrow Automotive, a leader in quality American automobiles since 1931. I hope you like it."

The first thirty seconds were purely instrumental, and William almost found himself humming along. Then Stevie lifted his head and started to sing:

When times are dark, it fuels our pride
A light that's shining nationwide
It keeps us walking on the straight and narrow
We don't need a second chance
To make the most of circumstance
The truth comes straight ahead just like an arrow

When Stevie reached the end of the verse, he paused. A floodlight doused the room in blue, revealing a drummer behind him, previously unseen, and Stevie grabbed the microphone with his right hand for the chorus: "Every time I stand, it's for America," he sang. "It stands for every single thing I love." A man with a gray goatee held a plastic cup aloft, his index finger extended. A woman, her face lit by her cell phone, took video. There was a second verse that had an even higher incidence of patriotism than the first, and then a second chorus. Afterward, Stevie played an instrumental version of the original Arrow theme.

"I read that it was composed to mimic the sound of a car coming across a bridge," a woman next to them said. "It was Pittsburgh and they have hundreds of bridges." She had freckles on both cheeks and plenty more to say but William didn't catch any of it; it was as if someone was cutting a lawn of words and those were the clippings that were flying out of the top. Tom leaned in and said something, and the freckled girl wandered off.

"What did you say?"

"I told her to go by the bar and I'll meet her there," he said. "Now I'm going to get a drink."

"And I'm going to get rid of one," William said. He passed Graham Kenner, who was too close to Helen Hull in the corner of a booth. William couldn't hear what he was saying, but it was putting a dreamy smile on her face. He went farther down the hall, turned at the end, and there stood Emma, in the dogleg by the bathrooms. She was as round as a raindrop. William stiffened from shoulder to shoulder. He considered running. But when she turned, he was still there, and he waved with a hand that felt suddenly tiny. "Hi," he said.

"Did you enjoy the show?" she said. Her face had grown fuller with her body.

"Did you?" he said.

She considered him for a minute, pursing plump lips, and disappeared into the nearest door. William glanced around the hall: its red paint was peeling to show other colors underneath. A corkboard advertised upcoming shows, as well as items being sold by musicians. Would he pay three hundred dollars for a "used amp almost new"? The wall was giving him a headache.

Emma emerged, too soon for almost anything. She had a piece of paper in her hand, and she thrust it toward William. "What is this?" William said.

"A note," she said. But it was a paper towel with a childlike drawing on it that he slowly came to recognize as an octopus. "I want you to read it." A button popped high on her sweater and one heavy breast swung toward him. She seemed drunk but that was impossible. "Listen," she said. "I have a story for you."

"Okay," William said.

"It's going to take a minute."

"A minute's not going to kill me," he said, hoping he was right.

She took a deep breath. "A few weeks ago, I was driving by that park where we spent the afternoon," she said. "I was thinking about you, wondering about why I spent time with you. I couldn't think of any reason at all, not at first. But then in the park I realized: it was because you gave me freedom. I loved the idea that I could change my life, and I liked you for helping me get closer to that idea." He started to agree, but she waved him silent. "And now the baby's close, and the bigger I get the smaller I get, and I don't see how I'll ever be able to change anything again." William held the octopus paper out to Emma. She stepped back, just one small step, but it was enough to prevent her from taking the paper from him. The relief in her eyes was enormous, like someone thrown free of a wreck. She went back into the party without tears or anything else.

The Fitches were dancing in a corner of the club, moving to different music than the music that was playing over the loudspeakers. They were bathed in a lunar blue. Gloria swung her head from left to right and back again. "Look at them," Louisa said. "Want to dance?"

"I think the party's over," William said.

A look came over Louisa's face like it was the saddest thing she had ever heard. "Okay," she said. "Have it your way. Let's go get Tom." Louisa said. Tom was firmly installed at the bar with the freckled girl, and he patted the stool next to him to show William and Louisa where to sit down.

After that, William remembered little: two beers, then another, then a glass of whiskey pressed into his hand, warm and mean, then Tom's knees snugged around the freckled girl's calf. Eventually, they left Tom there, entangled, and Louisa complained bitterly the whole way home that he needed to grow up, that he would never grow up, that he was worse than a child, that it was her job as a sister to point it out and she didn't know why the freckled girl couldn't see it.

———

The whiskey tugged on William's sleeve to remind him of the beers. He was out on the deck, and Louisa was in the house, still sleeping.

When he called to wake her up, she hung up on him, and he listened to the Buddhist drone of the dial tone.

Earlier in the morning, he had seen what he thought was his favorite bird, the high-whistler, perched on the edge of the lion tub, and when it reappeared in the grass by the eagle he decided to go down into the yard for a better look. When he came back up, Louisa was in his chair. "I'm feeling a little woozier than I'd like," she said. "How about you?"

"Same," he said. "A little worse before, a little better now. Sunlight is the best disinfectant."

"Alcohol is a pretty good disinfectant," Louisa said. "I was all snugged in last night when we got home. That's the best thing about drinking. It changes the outside by changing the inside."

"Sounds like something your brother would say."

"I think it's something he has said," Louisa said. "Listen: I had a dream. Well, an idea."

"Shoot," he said.

"Let's have a party," Louisa said. "Over at the new house."

"Well, sure. But it won't be done for a while."

"That's my stroke of genius. I thought of it last night at Stevie's thing. You know how you and Wallace are putting up the deck first?"

"I do know, yes."

"Well, that's perfect for a party. We can bring over some of the furniture, and those scenic lanterns, and the grill. And Tom's birthday is right around that time."

"Maybe I'll bring over a tub to help him celebrate."

"Sure," Louisa said. "We can put bottles of beer in there with him and he can hand it out to people." Her face was taking on daylight now. "Imagine. Our first party at the new house."

William tried. The only party he could imagine was the one he'd just been to: Gloria and Eddie dancing in a blue wash, Graham Kenner flirting with Helen Hull, Tom ordering drink after drink for an unknown freckled girl. There were blank spots where other people had been. "Sure," he said. "Let's do it."

"Great."

"Right," he said. "Great. And if we get right up to the day of the party and I decide I'm too fragile, I can just hide out in the command center the whole time."

She started to reply but held her fire. They let the sunlight beat down on them, a silent cleansing.

THREE

On the radio, a candidate for local office promoted a spiritual brand of environmentalism. "We all must share the earth," he said, tone honeying. No one would have wanted the bit of it William was passing across: a small river of filthy metallic water and a bridge stretched over it. And yet there was something comforting about the scene, the way it communicated its decay honestly. The small lot beside Tom's studio was constellated with broken glass, so William parked on the street. He smelled acrid air the second he opened the car door; this was where the warehouse fire had been, in the building that backed onto Tom's studio. William got out and wandered down into the alley, past a Dumpster loaded with burned boards and bolts of cloth.

A man's voice hailed William from the side of the alley. "Look," he said. "It's Paint Cup." By William's reckoning the other man was Paint Cup, but he wasn't about to quibble. "How's tricks?" the man said.

"Can't complain," William said.

"Me neither." He coughed a laugh. He looked a little worse for wear, clothes grimier, hair knottier. A scratch on the back of his hand glowed hot-tempered red.

"I think I might take this after all," William said. "Build a dog-house."

"Suit yourself." He gestured toward it the way a king might. "I have no need for it here."

"Thanks." William tipped it onto its side. "Hey," he said. "I saw there was a fire here."

"There was," the man said. "Pretty exciting. I almost got myself an autograph from a firefighter. A hook-and-ladder was parked right over there." He pointed. "You ask your friend about it?"

"Who?"

"Your friend. The one who was with you last time. I saw him go in there about a half hour before the place went up."

"No," William said. "I doubt it. He doesn't have a place here any-more. Must have been someone who looked like him."

"Must have been," the man said, mouth curling into some kind of smile. He rooted in the pile next to him and withdrew a blanket. "I think I'm going to take a nap," he said. "All this fascinating conversa-tion has tired me out." He disappeared beneath a stretch of blue.

"Okay," William said. He got his fingers beneath the edge of the crate and lifted.

At the house, all he had wanted to see, he saw the moment he set down the crate behind Wallace's command center. The doghouse mimicked the shed, which was itself a miniature of the larger house, which was now a frame standing between William and Harrow Street. The upmost third of the skeleton, done in cedar, was a graph that rose from left to right. Things, at last, were looking up.

———

Out in town, buying things he didn't need, William pushed open a drugstore door into bright afternoon and ran smack into Fitch. "Oh, hi there," Fitch said. He checked the face of his phone. "I'm late." He angled his phone up again, squinted against the glare. "I'm late."

"For a very important date?" William said.

"I meant to call you," he said. A woman rolled her stroller up to him. Fitch smiled shyly, and the woman frowned, and then Fitch frowned, too, unsure why his smile hadn't been matched.

"I need to get by," she said. Fitch nodded but stayed put. William, in a show of leadership, moved off into a shadowed patch nearby. "I was going to call you," Fitch said again.

"So you say," William said. "About what?"

The afternoon sun had bleached out most colors. The car parked just beyond the overhang was slightly yellow, Fitch's face slightly red. He shook his head, a displeased little tic, and tried to fit his hands together. "Things are bad at work," he said. "Worse even than before. There's a serious problem with TenPak. When O'Shea pulled out, and then Loomis, there was a run by smaller investors, and it turns out that Hollister doesn't have the money to cover the customers. And all the while, the new guy's been selling harder and harder, which means the process will only repeat. There are at least two lawsuits being threatened, and every day Baker makes it clearer that he's not going to take the fall for this."

"So who is?"

"I don't know," Fitch said. "All of us, I guess. When there's a storm, it rains down."

"Maybe I'll turn out to be the luckiest one of all." Fitch didn't even smile; he just stared at his own hands, which were fidgeting faster now.

A horn honked. "That'll be Gloria," Fitch said, and rushed across the panhandle of the lot and vanished into a slightly green sedan, looking around as if spies were everywhere.

FOUR

William's phone buzzed with a text from Karla. "Turn on news," it said. "Ch 9 now." The fire commissioner stood at a podium, a bouquet of microphones in front of him and a whiteboard behind him. "We are now prepared to release a comprehensive profile of the man we think is responsible for the fires."

A woman in the front raised her hand. The gesture displeased the commissioner, but he pointed at her anyway. "You're sure it's a man?"

"Reasonably so."

A man in the back blurted out. "Can you tell us anything else?"

"I can," the commissioner said. "I was about to." He turned toward the whiteboard, scribbled in a blank space, and then turned back. "Based on the way the crimes have unfolded, we have determined that our suspect is a white male, almost certainly in his early to mid-forties, likely well educated. There's a high probability that he is either unmarried or childless."

A man in the front row leaned forward, taking his time with his question. "And what's the motive?"

The fire commissioner sighed. "That's where I was going next. He appears to be motivated by economic resentment rather than a personal grudge. These are only educated guesses, though, or interpretations."

The woman in the front raised her hand again. "But definitely a man?" she said.

"They usually are," the fire commissioner said.

"And what are we counting as the arson set?" said a man in the back.

"Clearly, it's not every fire in town," the commissioner said. Laughter surged briefly. "It's the ones we've been talking about all along: the depot, the marina, the hardware store, the dollar store. There are erroneous reports about this last one, the warehouse." That was the building adjacent to Tom's old studio; William leaned closer to the screen. "That fire seems to have been set by a copycat," he said. "This isn't uncommon: a case starts to get publicity, and someone wants in on it. The warehouse fire was significantly smaller and significantly more amateurish, a kind of experiment."

An experiment? The word went icily through William.

After two days of rain, the sun and heat had returned. The afternoon cooked the inside of the car. William found Tom's Charger parked right outside his studio, fender now double dented. He went inside and knocked on the door, once, then a break, then again, as if it was a secret code. He heard shifting and scraping and then Tom came to the door and opened it. "Who is it?" he said, though he saw William's face. Tom's hair was in an uproar.

"Hey there," William said. "I was just driving by. Thought I'd stop in to say hello."

"Busy," Tom said.

"Yes, I *would* like to come in," William said. Tom opened the door a little more, maybe a foot wide, and William pushed his way in. Chaos possessed the studio: pencils snapped in half and disarranged on the desk, books open upside down next to beer bottles. The only work visible was a large-scale oil painting of one of Tom's charts—a gradually descending line titled "How Well You Understand This Graph Over Time."

"Wow," William said, sitting down on the narrow sofa. "The place looks good."

"Yeah," Tom said. "I've been busy. But nice to see you. It's been a while."

"Not really," William said. "Stevie's thing was just last week."

"It was?" Tom said.

"How did that go?" William said. "Last I saw, you were doing pretty okay with that girl by the bar."

Tom bunched his brow and searched for the memory. "Katy? Karen? I don't know. It was a twenty-four-hour flu. She was a nice girl, if you like that kind of thing, but I had to get back to work."

"Right," William said. "I see. What are you working on?"

"'New pieces' is what I've been telling people. But that's not exactly true. I've been going through old work and reconnecting with it. Sometimes I've been pulling it into a different medium." Tom pointed across the room. "Like that canvas over there. When I have to repaint the graphs, I remember them completely, in ways I thought weren't possible anymore."

William hunched forward and leaned his forearms on his knees, a

technique he'd seen TV cops use to put suspects at ease. It was time
to get what he'd come for. "Can I ask you something, Tom? You know
that graph? The one about how much fire liked paper?"

Tom had started off toward the canvas. "Of course I know it. I
made it. To me, it's part of a larger comedy about the human arro-
gance that makes us think we control things—or rather, our refusal to
believe what we're shown repeatedly and conclusively, which is that we
control nothing. I don't believe in God, but I believe in the universe.
And I believe that when the universe looks down upon us, it doesn't see
a species with an acceptance of its fate. It sees a species raging against
that fate, and maybe it admires that stubbornness just a little."

"Right," William said. The sense that he was not quite listening
was strong enough in his tone that Tom turned around. "I was out by
the warehouse where you had your old studio," William said.

"Oh?" There was a light in Tom's eyes that seemed to make it difficult for him to see what was around him. "Why?"

"I wanted something from the alleyway. When I was out there, I
talked to someone who saw you."

"Who saw me?" Tom repeated.

"Who saw you going into the building the day of the fire."

Tom was, all at once, as still as a Buddha, head down. He spoke
finally, in a hushed voice that William couldn't hear at first. William
moved closer. "Cranston."

"What?"

Tom's head snapped up. "That was the name of my psychology
professor in college. He used to talk about how people project their
own negative ideas onto others. He wrote a whole book about it. He

said that suspicion was like a black butterfly, and that what darkened it was the shadow of the person looking."

"Okay," William said. "The next time I'm in a library or a bookstore, I'll check it out."

"You could use a copy right now," Tom said. Now he was staring at William intently. "Unless I'm wrong, you're accusing me of something."

It sounded stupid when Tom said it. "No," William said. "Not accusing. Just being overly curious."

"I'll say. Can I ask how you know about the fire graph?"

"You must have mentioned it to me."

"And yet, I didn't," Tom said.

William's scalp tightened. "Never mind. We don't have to talk about this."

"We don't have to do anything," Tom said, his voice louder. "We all have choices. So what I'd like to know is why you chose to end up in my studio on a day I'm teaching, and why you somehow found your way into a folder that I'm not showing anyone." Now he was almost thundering. "How does a man come to be in a place like this, looking at things he shouldn't?" He paused, as if at the top of a hill, and then started down it. "And not looking at them alone, either."

Silence sealed the room. William sat down. "Oh," he said. "That. It's not happening anymore." He paused.

"I'm not going to say anything to Lou or anyone else," Tom said. "It doesn't matter to me who you spend your time with. What does matter to me is what you're saying right now."

William struggled for a foothold. "But you were there that morning, right? In the studio?"

"I was looking for something," Tom said. "I found it and I was gone from there by noon. When was the fire? Early evening?"

"I don't know."

"That might be useful information when you're building a case," Tom said. He picked up a brush, pointed the handle at William. "I don't want to talk about this anymore. The next time we meet, let it be under better circumstances." He turned his back on William, lifted the brush to his canvas, left it there to make a growing point. When William's hand was on the doorknob, he spoke again. "And count yourself lucky that there will be a next time," he said. "I don't know if I should feel proud or ashamed that I'm letting you get away with acting reckless like this."

"Like I said, it's not happening anymore."

"Not that," Tom said. "I mean the way you treated me." He turned back to the canvas and painted a horizontal line that ran to the end of the canvas, where it went straight down along the edge. William went out to sit in his car and wonder what he had done—or rather, why he had done it. He had misread the available evidence and then perpetuated the delusion just because it shone brighter than everything around it. It was a distraction from the blunt, dull expanse of the rest of his life. Without Emma, he had entered a kind of poverty. The currency was energy, and he was not able to hoard it or spend it. He turned on the radio and left it tuned between stations, trying to make out the words that bobbed to the surface of the static.

Four days later, out in Jerroldtown, police surrounded the home of a sixty-two-year-old retired professor named Thomas Lareaux, who promptly came to the front door with a gun. Lareaux fired at an of-

ficer, who fired back. Wounded, he fell to the ground. He was arrested
and placed in an ambulance. One wall of his small house, according
to a department spokesperson, was papered over with photographs of
the buildings that had been set on fire over the past months, including
the bus station, the hardware store, Sunny Isles Marina, and the East
Side warehouse. The car dealership and Birch Mutual were not among
them. Lareaux drove a blue pickup truck, said an undercover policewoman, who may well have driven a black Pontiac.

———

Lareaux was scheduled to be arraigned Thursday afternoon. William
cut short his meeting with Wallace out at the lot and picked up Christopher at school. "Special unplanned stop," he said.

"Okay," Christopher said.

"We are going to see a master criminal of our time," William said.

"Okay," Christopher said.

They joined a knot of people at the base of the courthouse steps,
at first only about a dozen, but then twice that, and then they were
at the center of a lake whose shore was receding. The first police car
that pulled up discharged a young black man, who passed the crowd
without incident. The second contained Lareaux.

The gunshot had winged him in the left arm, and he wore a sling,
which made him easy to spot. He was escorted by a policewoman toward the crowd, and voices went up as he approached: jeering voices,
scornful voices, but also curious ones. "Why did you do it?" one
woman said. Her tone had an unimaginable innocence.

Lareaux wore glasses in life, but they had been taken from him, and he stared obtusely into the crowd with sad, far-wandering eyes. "I have a political agenda," he said. "Those who think they are in power must be taught otherwise. We are too beholden to self-appointed masters. We must tear them down." The papers had uncovered their own rationale: Lareaux had a grown son who had been in and out of mental facilities his whole life; he had worked at four of the sites and been fired from three of them. The names of his son's former supervisors were neatly lettered beneath the photographs on his wall.

A man from the rear of the crowd ran out and tried to shove Lareaux. "I had a friend you almost killed," he said. "If he'd been on time to work, who knows what would have happened?" Someone else flung a paper cup filled with ice at Lareaux's head. Then, suddenly, a section of the crowd surged forward. William was jostled. He caught sight of Christopher taking an elbow from a big man bumped by an even bigger one; the boy went down into the middle of the lake of people. A young woman, also teetering, stepped on Christopher's hand, and William heard him cry out in pain. When a space opened up, Christopher was gone.

The woman who had stepped on him was following Lareaux up the courthouse stairs, yelling now. William went up the steps too. He tried to get an elevated vantage. He looked at his side of the street, at the other side. He checked both corners. Christopher was nowhere to be found. William called his name and waved, first one hand and then both, already imagining the news report: the missing boy had been in the company of his mother's friend, who was unemployed as a result of a workplace assault.

Lareaux was inside now, and the people who remained on the stairs were yelling at each other. William paced from one edge of the court-house to the other until he saw Christopher, or at least a spot that was the same deep green as his shirt, sitting on a bench far down the block.

He hurried over.

"I didn't know where you went," Christopher said, his voice thin with panic.

"I didn't go anywhere," William said. "You did."

"Not my fault," Christopher said. He was pressing his right thumb into the center of his left palm. William moved it aside and found a deep bruise. The ridge of the palm was swollen. "It's fine," Christopher said, trying to hide the hand behind his back.

"We should get it X-rayed to make sure it's not broken."

"But it'll be okay?"

"What do you think?" William said, but he was asking, not tell-ing, and he could see that Christopher could see that. And so William said yes. When they pulled up in front of the house, Christopher said nothing, just took his backpack with his good hand and dragged it behind him up the front path.

Tom came over that night, unannounced, the anger of the previ-ous week evaporated, and joined William and Louisa in front of the television for what they all knew was the end of the line, in a sense. They ordered food and watched footage of the courthouse riot, and Tom said he thought he saw William, and William said he hadn't even gotten out of his car, and Louisa said he should have gotten as close as possible, that things like that didn't happen every day, and then the news was on to sports, and Louisa switched off the set and started picking up plates, and Tom left, and the two of them sat there in silence and William watched his wife, wondering what would happen next.

———

Karla called for lunch. "Tomorrow," she said crisply, not quite asking. When William arrived at the restaurant, she was sitting, menu already closed.

He started in with something he had just heard. "My old company is about to take a fall." Fitch had called him early that morning from the stairwell at work, breathless in his act of espionage, and brought him up to date. "The new salesman was sent back to San Diego without an explanation," William told Karla. "Independent consultants have been to the offices at least twice, guys in dark suits who look like Secret Service and don't talk much to anyone. Apparently, the company made false and misleading statements regarding their investment properties and didn't vet investors properly. And that's not even the worst of it. The worst of it is, there's a paper trail."

"Business, even immoral business, is distinguished from casual deception by the presence of records. My father used to say that all the time."

"That's a big thing to say all the time."

She didn't smile, not even a little. She fingered the collar of her blouse. "What were you thinking, William?" she said finally.

"About what?"

"About yesterday. A child in a mob scene like that?" She leaned forward, hands up underneath the tabletop as if she was weighing it.

"I'm sorry," he said.

"I'm sure you are." She kept her eyes on him. "I'm just not sure it matters."

"How's his hand?"

"It's okay. Soft cast. He can't really eat or write, which is going to make it a rough week." She put her head down. When she looked up, her eyes were wet. "I don't think you should spend any more time with Chris."

He slid his hand across the table, but Karla stiffened. "Stop," she said. "I think partly I was using you to spend time with him so that I wouldn't have to. As he gets older, I get more worried that I can't do this alone. I can't worry about that anymore."

"That doesn't mean I can't help out now and then."

"It does," she said. "You're not his father."

"But this isn't fair to him."

"It's not fair for him if you stick around this way," she said. "This is something I mismanaged. Let's change the subject."

"There's nothing to change it to."

"Well, then we're done here."

William paid, desperately, as Karla stayed at the table. Her tears were already over. He walked her out to her car, and she got into the driver's seat and put on her sunglasses. "You know you'll have to forgive me," he said.

"It's not about me," she said. "Also, you know that thing you did where you told Chris you knew his father?"

"Yes?"

She shook her head and said nothing, with an expression that made it look like there was nothing more to say.

At home, William went into the junk room and looked through pictures of Lareaux's arraignment. One of them had been taken as Lareaux stepped out of his car in front of the courthouse. All the drama was in the right half of the frame, while the left was clotted with a disorganized mass of courthouse visitors, some fixed on the source of the tumult, others occupied with other business. At the leftmost edge of the photo, William spotted himself, with his arm around Christopher, coming through the fringe of the crowd. He printed a copy of the picture, folded it up, and put it at the bottom of the drawer of his bedside table.

FIVE

Tom was already jabbering as he got into the car: about how skillfully he had deceived Louisa, calling her Wednesday night to complain about a meeting with a cross-state curator that had been called for too early Friday morning ("I even made up a nickname for him to make it seem more real," he said); about his calculated but entirely believable weariness as he explained that his car was in the shop again; about the silently counted pause before he proposed that William take the trip with him. "I copped to being a terrible driver," he said, "although I admitted that I don't mind your company. She gave her blessing. Go ahead, husband, go off with my crazy brother for a road trip where God-knows-what will happen. Who knows, maybe another boss will get punched." He was looser than usual, almost happy.

The expressway was mostly clear, and the directions Tom gave were surprisingly direct: head north for an hour and west for a quarter of that, at which point there would be a lake and, just beyond it, a town. They passed through gridded suburbs, a large town studded with church spires, a designer village that seemed to be composed solely of historically preserved mansions and bespoke wine shops. They traced the curve of a river and split a grove of trees. The afternoon sun was still strong. "Don't you want to know where we're going?" Tom said.

"To see a cross-state curator," William said. "At least that's my understanding."

"Ha ha," Tom said. "The trip is art-related, actually. We're going to see one of the greatest painters I know." They were approaching their destination, and Tom seemed to be feeling the nearness of it. He rocked his weight against the armrest. He rubbed the tips of his sneakers together. He thumped a thumb into the pleat beside him.

"Hey," Tom said. "I need a place where I can get a little present. Maybe when we stop for gas." The gas station was next to a modest garden center; Tom settled on a dwarf bottlebrush, which he balanced in his lap like a child. The towns got smaller and the space between them larger. Houses crowded the winding roads. William focused past the windshield, tried to learn from the land, from the people who filled it, but everything seemed behind glass rather than beyond it.

Finally, they pulled up beside a modest, immaculate inn: two stories, a screened porch, a hard-carved sign overhanging the front door that showed two ducks in a pond. As they entered the lobby, heads rose to consider them, then settled back into the business at hand: conversation, magazines, chess. Tom walked to the back of the room, disappeared into a paneled office door, and returned with a tall, thick man, dark skinned and severe of feature. He wore a black poplin shirt with a black suit coat; a stickpin went diagonally through his green tie. "This is Kenneth," he said. "He works here."

"That's a poor introduction," Kenneth said. "I am the proprietor of this establishment." His voice rose and fell in a gentle lilt.

"I got you something," Tom said. He motioned to William to hand it over.

Kenneth took one of the blood-red blooms between his fingers appreciatively. "I like plants."

"More than people, from what I recall."

"Can you blame me?" Kenneth said. "Have you met people?"

"This is William," Tom said.

Kenneth laughed. "Present company excepted, of course," he said.

They sat at a long table in the lobby. A lamp watched over a stack of tourist brochures. A bottle held a browning mum. "I reread your message this morning," Kenneth said. "I want you to know that I support this course of action." His voice was low and level; he seemed like he spoke that way no matter who was in the room.

"I haven't been able to reach Jesse for a day or two," Tom said. "I assume things are still on." His mouth got small when he spoke, as if he was nervous. Was Jesse the man Tom had mentioned on the drive?

"There's a party tonight," Kenneth said. "We're expected to be there." He turned to William. "You too," he said.

Kenneth showed them to a room on the first floor, where William flattened himself on the bed. Pen-and-ink birds flew diagonally across the wallpaper, and William imagined them peeling away and circling the room. He must have fallen asleep, because he came awake with a start at the sound of the door opening. The birds went flat again. "Let's go," Tom said.

They all packed into Kenneth's truck, Kenneth and Tom in the front, William in the back. "Sorry for the tight squeeze," Kenneth said to William. "It's only a mile." But a mile meant something different in the country, something bumpier and more vertiginous, and by the time they came to a small house at the round end of a horseshoe driveway, William had to stagger out to steady himself against the truck.

"Come on, city boy," Tom said. "You have to meet Jesse."

William heard a voice before the door opened. It was a woman arguing playfully with someone—someone on the telephone, it turned out. She pulled the door open with her free hand and waved them in.

When she saw Tom her eyes widened, in either joy or misgiving. "Gotta go," she said, and hung up the phone. She was darker than Kenneth, with a tiny frame and nearly perfect features. She could have been a teenager except for the weariness in her eyes.

"This is Jesse," Tom said. "She was a student of mine. One of the first, in fact."

"That dates me," Jesse said.

"That's what Tom does," Kenneth said. "He dates you. Or at least he did. All those nights I had to stand on the porch with a shotgun." Kenneth, William was coming to understand, was Jesse's father.

"By 'shotgun,' I think you mean 'paintbrush,'" Tom said. "Before Kenneth got into the inn business, he dabbled as an artist."

"Dabbled?" Kenneth said. "I taught you everything you know."

"Which is, about painting, exactly zero," Tom said. "Nice work."

"While the banter is flying, let me give you a tour of the place," Jesse said to William. She and Tom still hadn't really looked at each other.

———

The tour led through the whole of the house, which was hardly anything, only a living room, a bedroom, and a small yard, but there were careful details everywhere that attested to the vibrancy of the place. The wooden chairs had been carved with a story that went up one arm and came down the other, continuing on the chair beside it. Each of the lampshades had been dyed a subtly different shade. "Sit here," Jesse said, directing William to a brown leather couch. It was draped in green fabric, like a young woman trying to conceal her beauty or an old woman trying to conceal its absence. A few other guests milled about in the room: two women who appeared to be a couple, two women who did not.

On either side of the front door were two vast canvases, almost floor-to-ceiling, depicting roughly the same scene, an Old West desert with scrub brush in the foreground and distant cliffs. In one, an Indian sat proudly astride a horse, and everything about him was done in vivid color, from the red tips on the feathers of his headdress to the blue squares on his buckskin pants. The other canvas was nearly identical—same desert, same scrub, same horse—but in the Indian's place was a white man in modern business dress. William wondered if these were the paintings Tom had wanted him to see.

Jesse passed three jelly jars filled with gin to William, who passed the first along to another guest but kept the other two. He felt certain that the real party was on its way, that at some point the front door would fly open and dozens of artists would pour into the house. There would be young men in high spirits and young women pretending at first to resist those high spirits. But the doors never flew open, and William grew more and more drunk, there on the brown couch with the green fabric draped over it. He spoke to a young woman with a shock of orange hair who didn't complain when he put his hand on her leg. "A cousin," she said, though he didn't know whether she was saying that she was Jesse's cousin, asking if he was Tom's, or introducing another detail altogether.

The stereo was singing about dancing and good times. Tom passed through the room, whispering, with Jesse at his side. William pulled himself to his feet and followed them, at a distance, into the backyard. They had different music out there, wordless, slower. Kenneth was sitting in a chair talking to a girl who was wearing a beaded vest. She was laughing. Tom and Jesse were in the near corner of the yard, talking closely, and then Tom leaned on the fence and drew his hand back sharply. William saw a line on his palm, a red rivulet. Kenneth stood and produced a handkerchief, which he held out to Tom in a courtly manner.

William went back inside to sit with the cousin on the couch. She was talking about God now. More gin was brought his way.

The last thing he remembered was standing with the cousin in the yard. She was still on God, and he was marveling at the way the black lace of brassiere overlaid the brown skin of breast. Tom and Jesse were at the corner of the fence again. Now they were standing at a distance from each other, and she was talking excitedly, pointing at the ground. William thought he saw tears on her cheeks, and Tom's hands were in the shape of a cage, as if he were protecting a seed.

————————

"And so," Tom said, swinging his arm over Kenneth's shoulder the next morning, "I make my good escape. I thank you for your hospitality. Sometimes I don't know what you see in me." They had been offered breakfast, declined, accepted coffee in its stead.

"Whatever it is, I don't want to see it around here much longer." Kenneth laughed and embraced Tom. "I am sorry that you didn't get what you came for," he said more softly.

Kenneth had already loaded their bags in the trunk. Tom told William to drive off, but about a minute later, he told him to pull over. "Pop the trunk," he said. On top of their bags were two large flat rectangles wrapped in cloth.

William peeled back a corner and saw that they were paintings. "Take them out," Tom said, and then he shut the trunk and unwrapped them so William could see. The first was a landscape of a placid little town, where two children played in the street and a short, dark woman with long hair stared into a store window at a blue dress pinned to a white backing. The second showed a red boat in a harbor and a man tying a rope around a brown piling. In both, the framing was off center and the colors were subtle but forceful. Tom moved his hand over the face of the woman in the second painting. "What do you think she's thinking?"

"That she wants the dress?" Like the man in the other painting, the woman wore an expression of casual concentration.

"Exactly," Tom said. "But the title is *Mexican Village, One Minute Before Earthquake*. The other one is *Florida Town, One Week Before Hurricane*. That's what's makes these painting so great. They are acts of colossal misdirection." William looked at the woman's face again, tried to retrieve her thoughts about the dress, if that's even what she was looking at. Would she buy it? Would she ever get to wear it? The questions were a close circle around him.

"These are Jesse's?"

"She only paints Indians," Tom said. "These are Kenneth's. And now they're mine. I bought them with the money from my book advance." He shut the trunk. "Supporting him is the least I can do. You know what they say about talent: if you don't have it, help it."

"You don't have it?"

"Not like Kenneth. I have a way of seeing that's unshared by most people, and then a way of seeing my seeing. I look at things the wrong way and then stubbornly insist it's the right way, all along holding out hope that I'll make a few converts. When I do, it'll help the idea that the things I've made are art. But talent?" He shook his head. "I don't think so. When I see paintings like this, when I really start to feel what they're doing, I get weak. And not the kind of weak when you look in the mirror after a bad haircut. Serious weak, soul weak, like there's something in the universe that can make you better but that you don't possess, and won't ever." He tapped the car with two fingers, as if he were telling a driver to take off.

———

There were two YOU ARE HERE signs before the highway, one in front of a craft outlet, another by a scenic overlook, each temporarily true, and then a diner with a banner that said EAT HERE NOW. "It makes a good argument," Tom said. The restaurant was in a shack connected to a small convenience store. On the far wall, there was a lunch counter; next to it there was a bar, a garish pair of abstract oils, and a lottery ticket machine that flashed out a series of numbers. The whole scene was like something of Tom's, a graph of increasing despair.

They sat beneath a mirrored clock in the shape of a guitar. The obese bartender was talking to a balding man about his youth as a skier. "Two-day blizzard," the bartender said. "Couldn't even get out on the slopes."

"You made me think," the balding man said. He tapped his head to show the site of the injury. "The snow that year was up to the window in my garage."

Tom brought two sandwiches and two beers to the table. "Just water for me," William said. "It's a little early."

"Right," Tom said. He moved both bottles in front of him. "I don't think there's a menu, even. You stand there and after a little while they push food at you." He bit into his sandwich and made a face. "I hope you're not expecting some kind of best-kept secret."

Behind Tom, the balding man pressed a series of buttons on the lottery machine. "So how long has it been since you've seen Kenneth and Jesse?"

"That's a story," he said.

"I have time," William said.

Tom set down his sandwich. "Well," he said, "I first moved up here right after college, to study with Kenneth. She was just a girl, the daughter of my painting teacher. She was seventeen, maybe. But she had this unearthly glow. I would go to Kenneth's house to drop something off or have a drink and I would spend the whole time looking at her. Have you ever read Rousseau?" William hadn't. "Well, there's a passage about when he was young and in love with a young woman. She starts to eat some food and he calls out to stop her. There's a hair on it, he says. She puts it back on her plate in disgust and he grabs it and gobbles it down. It's the closest he can get to her. That's how I felt about Jesse. Then I got a job teaching, and I left town."

"Was there a romantic farewell?"

"No, not at all. Kenneth drove me to the airport. She was in the back seat. I think when I was out on the curb she waved and told me to have a good time. I loved her, though, and the idea of her stayed with me wherever I went. You know: St. Louis, Belize, New Zealand, Timbuktu. My world tour. I had girlfriends, but they were substitutes, except that they didn't do what substitutes are supposed to do, which is distract you from the original. They just reminded me of her. Now and again I came back to visit Kenneth, and I saw her then."

"So then you got involved?"

"That would make sense, but it didn't happen then either. I didn't want to disrupt her life, or his either. But I kept coming to see her, and at some point I started to see that she felt the same way about me that I felt about her. It wasn't a flash of lightning or anything that dramatic. It just became clear to me. At that point, I felt strong enough to stay."

William was confused. "To stay with Kenneth?"

"To stay in town. I quit teaching. I took a job at a store, started sculpting a little. Within a month, everything was in place. Jesse and I did the whole thing, moving in together, forsaking all others. We were going to get married." He fell silent. The story was over, except that it wasn't.

"So what happened?" William said. "It ended?"

"It did."

"And now you're reconsidering? She is?"

Tom ate a little more of his sandwich, seemed to taste it less. He scratched along his chin. "We had a son," he said.

William started to speak, but Tom, having started up again, wasn't stopping. "It was about a year after we got together. We were ecstatic. He was the last piece of the puzzle. Big baby, laughed all the time, a real bruiser. He started walking the day after his first birthday, and we used to joke that you could feel the ground shake when he put his foot down. Then he started fainting. We took him to the doctor, who said it was convulsions from high fever. One morning Jesse went in to wake him up. His lips were blue. We got him to the hospital right away, but right away wasn't soon enough." William understood now; Jesse hadn't been pointing at the ground, but rather beneath it. He was one and a half, Tom said, and that's the age he stayed. "He had an underlying cardiac problem, something called long QT syndrome. It's named after the part of the cardiogram that widens." His fingers, deft from practice, drew a graph on the table. "When people say 'dead and gone,' what do they mean? Where do they think people go, exactly?"

William didn't know what to say. "Louisa never mentioned anything."

Tom let William wait for a while. He was looking past William, into the middle distance, and for once he didn't seem as if he wanted to be seen. "That's because she doesn't know," he said. "We weren't talking for a few years there before I moved upstate: sister with happy, settled life doesn't seem to care about brother with unhappy, unsettled one, to the point where, even when brother moves a few hours away and his life starts to come together, he doesn't feel comfortable calling her. And then, when Jesse and I split up, I did anything I could not to think about it, which included not mentioning it to anyone. I got rid of most of the photographs, kept only one where he was sleeping in the crook of Jesse's arm and one of him sitting up in bed. I didn't want the rest of them because I didn't understand what they were documenting. That's when I started making charts, in fact. It was my way of struggling with facts and what happens to them when they're no longer true in any measurable way." Tom made a funny birds-fly-away gesture that didn't belong to him at all, or to any man William knew. Maybe it was something Jesse had done. "When Louisa told me about the job at the college, I wasn't sure I wanted to be only a few hours away from Jesse, wasn't sure I could. But I took the job and didn't think about her, except to think that maybe one day I would go see her. I got my courage up, lost it, got it back again. Once or twice I called but hung up when she answered. It was a mess. I was a mess. Then, a few weeks ago, I was here working. I was trying to think of what the baby looked like and I couldn't," he said.

"What was his name?"

"Michael." The word crossed the space between them. "That was the day I went to the old studio. It wasn't there. I broke down and called Jesse and managed to say hello when she answered. We started talking, carefully at first, about why we ended things, about how our lives had gone, about what we remembered and what we needed to remember. She agreed to let me come and see her. You were my ride. I had all the hope in the world. Then, last night, she said she didn't think she could make a go of it." He finished off the second beer, closed his eyes, and sat back in his chair. He looked completely bereft and, despite the fact that his eyes were closed, more like Louisa than ever. "So that's that," he said. "I guess it's what the experts call closure."

"I'm sorry," William said, hearing the words emerge without any sense or meaning, and gradually the rest of the room returned: the men at the bar wrapping up the conversation about their ski trip, the intolerable sandwiches, the lottery machine strobing green.

Tom threw a twenty and two fives on the table. "Let's get the hell out of here," he said with great spirit.

The convenience store connected to the restaurant was stocked densely with chips, candy bars, sticks of meat, and a rainbow of sugared waters. The woman at the counter was speaking in rat-a-tat Chinese but understood enough to hand William down the pack of gum he wanted and to give Tom a small envelope of aspirin. Out in front, on a bench, there was a man about William's age and a boy, no more than ten, stroking his father's arm and looking impassively into the parking lot. One of them might have been blind. In the car, a few miles later, William mentioned them to Tom, but Tom was no longer with him. He had been musing on the passage of time, wondering whether people moved through it or vice versa, and he quoted Shakespeare on the matter, "I wasted time, and now time doth waste me," and that last word had launched him into sleep.

SIX

And so William was back home, which meant planning the party Louisa had suggested, and checking on progress at the new house, and sitting on the deck of what would soon be the old house and watching the trees whose names he did not know sway in the breeze. He was trying to do some reading, too. Tom had encouraged him to pick up Cranston's self-help book; the first time he had dismissed the suggestion, because it was the afternoon when he'd accused Tom of arson, and that day was best discarded wholesale. But on the drive home Tom mentioned it again, and William was in no real position to resist. He found a used copy, a compact paperback with a burnt-orange cover, and dipped into it whenever he had the time.

It was mostly unreadable, or rather readable only in bursts so short that the process could not fairly be called reading. The text was densely uninteresting, filled with bromides about life's triumphs and trials illustrated with anecdotes drawn from Cranston's own unremarkable experience. Still, something in the third chapter had caught his eye. "Life," Cranston wrote, "is a series of substitutions designed to distract you from the fact of your deprivation." The idea stayed with William. He had tried to forget about the loss of his job by spending time with Emma, and tried to forget about Emma by spending time with Christopher. Now, without Christopher, he was substituting again, with Cranston. But that would go soon, too, and something else would take its place. None of the options was satisfactory, but none was any less satisfactory than the rest, and even the first link in the chain, his job, was only helping him to cope with some other absence or emptiness. Recognizing this all as an endless cycle made him feel marginally less deprived, and he wondered whether he actually was laying down the foundation for a better understanding of himself. It was a cheering proposition, and it propelled him through the wasteland of chapters four and five.

In chapter six, another insight came forward. "An unhealthy impulse," Cranston wrote, "should never be discharged in action, but can never be completely defeated by inaction; rather it should be concealed from the view not only of others, but of the possessor of that impulse." A feeling of recognition circulated hotly through William, who underlined the passage and put a star in the margin.

For weeks during the summer, William had been keeping two secrets, one professional, the other personal, and he thought that when he came clean about his job, it would be easier to withhold the facts about Emma. Instead, when he disclosed his professional secret, he felt the personal one growing inside him with increasing pressure, trying harder with each day to break free. After the trip upstate with Tom, though, the count was back to two again, and he was calmer. "Maybe the second acts as a kind of buffer," William said. "This way, if I have a sudden attack of honesty, I'll just spill the thing about Tom and Jesse. Don't you think?" Blondie didn't answer.

William was going through the neighborhood with her, late at night, on a walk no one needed but him. It was cold and cheerless and he walked quickly, toward the open mouth of the cul-de-sac. He passed the Kenners', saw the blue glow of a computer screen. He passed the Morgans', smelled something baking. He passed the Zorillas', heard the faint sound of a woman either crying or moaning, but flattened, like it was coming from a television. At the end of the street, he took Blondie left and came back up the parallel street. He stopped in front of Annie Martin's house, which backed Emma and Stevie's. It was dead quiet, which meant that Annie Martin was awake; when she slept, she ran the radio loud so that people would think there was life in the house. He passed through her yard to the border of Emma and Stevie's lawn, where he looped Blondie's leash around the low half branch of an oak. He whispered the dog's name. He went farther into Emma's yard until he could see her bedroom window.

Emma came into the frame in her underwear, brushing her hair. She wore a white T-shirt but then she took it off. Her breasts hung heavy, and her belly was emphatic beneath them. She traced down the middle of her stomach with her index finger and he remembered doing the same. She turned away from him, toward the mirror, and he felt the nearness of her body through the window, through the wall. Then a noise spooked him, a rustling in the bushes, and he crab-walked toward the right side of the house, where he encountered another noise. It was Stevie's guitar playing, coming from the rearmost window of the garage. He was playing a series of notes, slowly, tidally. Each note had a shape, most round, some jagged, and yet they all seemed to fit together. It was beautiful until Stevie began to sing, and then it was something else. William shifted his weight forward, and just at that moment a cat scampered across his path, flashing eye-shine up at him. Blondie chuffed and rolled a bark in the bottom of her throat, and William untied her and hurried along the strip of lawn to the street.

The next day, he saw her again. He had stocked up for the party—rum and vodka, plastic cups and paper napkins, chips, dip, peanuts both plain and flavored, olives as big as eggs—and the young cashier had remarked upon the purchase, and he had said that it was all for him, and the girl had laughed, a bell in the afternoon.

At home, he unloaded the bags into the garage and leashed up Blondie for a walk. "You look awfully familiar," he said. "Do I know you from somewhere?"

A shadow overtook him at the head of the street, just outside the Roth house, which had a paper scarecrow hanging in the great window that overlooked the front lawn. It was Emma. "You weren't going to invite me?" She tried to sound indifferent, but she was out of breath from coming up the block. It was warm and humid, and half circles of sweat darkened her green blouse under the arms. Her hair was matted to the sides of her head. It occurred to him, for one crazy moment, to tell her that he'd liked it better through the window the night before.

"To what?"

"This party at your new house. I didn't get an invitation." They went under a shade tree that was either dead or close to it; Blondie circled the trunk as far as her leash allowed. "Look," Emma said before he could talk. "Maybe I shouldn't say anything. But Stevie asked me and I don't have a good answer."

"What about the truth?"

"Hilarious. He's under the impression that all of us are friends. He talks to Louisa some evenings, driveway to driveway, just the kind of neighborhood chitchat that normal people do."

"How do you know you'd even be able to come?" He indicated her belly. "You won't want to bring a baby to a boring party."

"Why not?" she said. "Just make it right."

"And if I invite you, that will be right?"

"Sure," she said. "Neighbors at parties of neighbors. Normal."

"Okay," he said. "Especially since the occasion is that we won't be neighbors for long. I lived here for ten years and you chased me out in four months."

Her expression cracked a bit, and what came through was sadness mixed in with a little bit of triumph. "Don't be mean," she said.

"Not mean," he said. "Just saying."

"We might not be long for this place either," she said. "Corporate creative has really taken a shine to Stevie."

"Corporate creative? A shine?"

"The less said, the better," Emma said.

"I'm not saying anything," William said. "So that should be best."

"Hey," Emma said. "Look." Higher up on the tree's trunk, William could see the edge of a honeycomb protruding from a hollow. "They usually use bigger spaces than that," Emma said. "They smooth the bark near the entrance. Can you see?" She angled her head up. The wind freshened and gusted behind them. A spot appeared at the corner of the hive and bombed down at Emma. "Ouch!" she said. She hit at her own hip. "Damn it." What looked like a bee's corpse tumbled to the ground.

"It's exactly like your dream," William said.

"Yeah," she said. She frowned. "That's what I think about my life every day. Just like a dream."

William wasn't up for more conversation. He tugged on Blondie's leash and headed for home, counting twenty steps before he turned and looked back. He wasn't sure what he expected to see, not exactly, but what he saw was a woman he had known for a few weeks, at most, staring up at a tree as sunlight dappled the grass beside her flatly.

SEVEN

He was deep into the invitation stage now. Fitch had said yes. Wallace had said yes. Tom had said no and laughed and asked if William minded if he set the phone down while he thought things through and then, without setting the phone down, said he couldn't be sure because Jesse had reconsidered his offer, and then laughed again, with a hope that was also a fear that the hope was misplaced, and said that he couldn't control the pace of that reconsideration and didn't want to, because he wanted to fully deserve whatever came to him. "I'll put you down as a maybe," William said.

The phone rang back right after he hung up with Tom. "Hello?"

"Is this William?"

"It is," he said, suddenly unsure.

"This is Bonnie Travis." He couldn't place the name at first, and then he remembered: the short, moon-faced woman who was married to Jim, Louisa's ex-boyfriend. They lived in Seattle with a boy and a girl. She did something in sales. Bonnie.

"Hi," he said. "How's Jim?"

"That's why I'm calling," she said. "He's dead." Her voice, high and fluted, misshaped the word.

William caught his own reflection on the inside of the glass door that led out to the deck. It looked like a mirage. "What?" he said. It didn't seem like enough. "How did . . . ," he said, and then stopped. Now it seemed like too much.

When Bonnie spoke again, her voice was frayed. "He's been having a hard time. It started as money trouble and it spread. We haven't been getting on."

"We heard from him about a month ago, when you two were in town visiting. We were going to have a drink."

"No," she said. William let the line fill with silence. "He never even made that trip. He just wasn't able."

"But he said he was here. He said that you weren't feeling well and that's why he couldn't come out to meet us."

"He said lots of things, for lots of reasons." She coughed a sob. "The funeral was small, just family." It hadn't occurred to William to think about the funeral until then. "I just thought you should know," she said.

William was overcome by fatigue at first, but then he was overcome by the opposite. He walked down the hall to the bedroom, came back to the garage, ended up in the kitchen, uncertain what he was looking for. In the bathroom William looked at himself in the mirror. He saw a man who preferred illustration to photography, winter to summer, South America to Europe, basketball to baseball, who thought often of death, preferring to divert it into metaphor, and dreaded the days when he could not, who frequently experienced a violent hatred of the ways that people asserted their own importance, who wondered if he knew anything, especially the things that he once thought he knew completely. He flicked off the light and watched his reflection in the dark.

When Louisa came home, he greeted her at the door and said he had coffee in the kitchen for her and that she needed to come and sit. "There's news," he said.

"Are you expecting?" she said.

He laughed because he thought anything else, even a grave face, would be a kind of ambush. He let her get halfway through her cup of coffee. When he told her about Jim, her hand flew up to her mouth like a bird, and she began to breathe shallowly through her nose. Then she pulled her arms tight around her, each palm matched to its opposite shoulder; the muscles stood out in her forearms but they were not very strong muscles and the effect was one of failure. "When did we see him last?" she said. "He looked good, I thought." She dragged an index finger through the wet corner of her eye. She looked like she would be wiping her eyes like that all night.

––––––––

William wasn't expecting a second call from Bonnie. "I feel like I owe you some more details," she said. Her voice was thick and thin at once. "I found him." She paused, though not long enough for William to say anything, which was a relief, and then she tipped forward into the rest of her explanation. "He was sleeping on the couch in the guest room. He was doing that more and more, at first because the kids snuck into our bed at night and woke him up, but then for no reason at all. On the night I'm talking about, they weren't even there: they were at my parents' house. But he never came to the bedroom, and I figured he was on the couch, like always. He was sensitive to noise and to light, so it was always like a cave in there, door shut tight, lights off. I came to get him in the morning and the door was open a crack and all the lights were on. There was a bottle of pills on the table next to him. I went to shake him, and the second my hand touched his arm I knew. It wasn't just that I guessed. I felt it. The absence of it. I didn't even try to revive him. I just called the police."

A question stirred dimly within William, and he brought it into the light. "Did he leave a note?"

Bonnie made a harsh noise that sounded almost like a laugh. "Not just one," she said. "Evidently this had been on his mind for a year or so. We were in debt and he wasn't telling me. He was addicted to pills. He couldn't sleep because he felt like everything was vanishing. He was worried that he had cancer. It's hard to even tell what parts of what he said were true." She drew a deep breath and this time when she spoke her voice was steely and tearless. "I have two kids," she said. "A man with children shouldn't be allowed to do that."

"Terrible," William said, meaning all of it. He kept most of the information from Louisa, except the fact that Jim had thought that he was sick, because that seemed like a plausible explanation for an impossible act.

———

The next morning, Louisa made coffee that she didn't drink and started in on how Jim had looked the last time he had visited them. "He'd lost some weight," she said. "Not too much, though. He said he'd been working out regularly, that he was cutting out red meat.

Why would someone let vanity rule them, even a little, if they're think-ing of ending it all?"

"He probably wasn't thinking about it yet," William said. "Or he was putting on appearances. Or he was fighting to stay afloat."

"He had an uncle who killed himself," she said. "Jim always said he couldn't imagine ever doing anything like that."

"That was twenty years ago," William said. "Why would what he said then matter now? The person he became might not even be con-nected to the person he was."

"If people are going to change so much," Louisa said, "then we shouldn't be able to remember them as they were. It's too awful." She got her things and went to the front door. It all seemed like labor and William suddenly felt that he, too, was moving with difficulty.

William called Wallace. He needed to arrange a time to pick up some paperwork from him out at the site. "Haven't seen you in a lit-tle while," Wallace had said on the phone, sounding a little forlorn. He told William he had to go survey a new site at some point, but that he'd leave the papers for him in the command center if he wasn't around when William got there.

It was time to walk the dog, who wasn't in the yard or in the kitchen or in the bedroom. William tried the garage, but no luck there either. Out of the narrow window facing the street he saw a shape flash by, and then another. Each darkened the window for only a fraction of a second, and the series of them signaled like a code. He opened the door and saw that it was a pack of boys on bicycles, racing and shout-ing each other's names. "Your mother," one of them said, laughing. Across the street, Emma and Stevie were getting into their car. William waved and Stevie nodded in return. His face was set, not exactly grimly, and he had a zippered duffel slung over his shoulder. He pointed at Emma and said something to her, though the words didn't carry to William. They backed their car out and drove up the street. Was it the baby already?

William went back inside. "Blondie," he said, louder this time. No claws scratched on door. No tags jingled on collar. He called Louisa but she still didn't pick up. "Do you have the dog with you?" he said. "Call me." That's when he thought to go out in front and check on the gate, which he found slightly ajar, wide enough to fit his entire forearm.

William started off down the street, whistling sharply for the dog. He knocked on neighbors' doors, but two houses in a row were empty, and at the third Cassandra Kenner answered, wearing an extra-large men's T-shirt and possibly nothing else. William asked after Blondie, received an invitation inside to call the neighbors, declined politely, and got out of there quick. He hopped into his car and looped through the neighborhood, up Albert and down Briar, up Pence and down Garth.

On Elster Street a dog idled against the flat wall of a hedge, but when he got closer he saw that it was a dark brown shepherd at least a third heavier than Blondie. Hinton: nothing. Cedar: no dogs, but a pair of cats and a little girl presiding over them in what looked like an extremely important meeting. Then, on Fallows, he saw Blondie crouched beneath a tree, nosing in a patch of high grass. He pulled to the side of the road. "Hey," he said. "Come here." She barked but stayed where she was. William got out of the car. Blondie had clawed into the under-soil; ants fled over her paws. "They might think you're their god," William said. He tugged the god by the collar, pushed her into the back seat, and sped up Fallows to Kenmore, and then Kenmore to Harrow.

When William pulled up to the house, he noticed that the deck was done. The finish had dried. It was beautiful, the color of dark beer. Wallace's truck was gone, so he walked to the small office; the lien waiver was folded up inside an envelope and centered on the desk. He turned back around just in time to see Blondie leap from the car and sprint toward the edge of the lot, where the land was soft from recent rains. "Hey," William said. "Come back here." He sprinted after the dog. It felt good to run, and particularly good to be running after something. He caught Blondie, or she let herself be caught, and he led her back along the dry high grass that led up toward the hillock. When his phone rang, he reached for it with his free hand, which meant going across his body. His next step was wrong. He did not fall, but he stumbled, and Blondie tore free and went down into the thick bluish mud up to her hocks. "Goddamn it," he said into the phone.

"What?" Louisa said.

"Wait," he said. "Hold on." He got the dog by the scruff and dragged her toward him.

"I can't really hear you."

"Where are you?" he said. "I'm out looking for you."

"For me? What about Blondie?"

"I have her."

"Oh," she said. "Well, you should come looking for me. Soon."

"Why? What's wrong?"

"William," she said. He hoped this was not her answer. Then the connection went to pieces and he could hear only a few stray words, "me" and "why" and "get."

"Where are you?" he said again.

"I'm at the coffee shop, on a bench outside. I'll wait for you here." Her voice slightly trembled.

The dog was matted with mud and William had no time to wash her and he wasn't about to let her back into his car like that. He led Blondie out to the doghouse behind the office, clipped the leash to the metal cleat, and wrapped it until it was short enough to keep her close to the crate. He found a dish in Wallace's office, filled it with water from a bottle in the fridge, and set it beside her. "Good girl," he said, hoping the dog would believe him. "Back as soon as I can."

He went around the back way to the car; from behind the deck, the frame slanted down from left to right. Blondie barked hoarsely, a glimpse of her head protruding above the edge of the desk.

Louisa wasn't at the coffee shop, though Gloria Fitch was. "No," Gloria said. "I haven't seen her. If I had, I would have asked her to stop me from beating that kid who made me the wrong drink." She sipped it happily. "Hey," she said. "Did you hear? Emma Wheeler went into labor." William nodded and said he'd seen her and Stevie driving off to the hospital. "Can you imagine?" Gloria said. "When will people learn? A kid seems fun when you're making it, but then . . ." She threw a hand up.

William called Louisa. No answer. He drove slowly home through the hardening dark. She wasn't there either. Inside he stood in front of the television, watching baseball. He made himself a sandwich and ate just half indifferently. He switched channels and caught a few muted minutes of the movie about the aging cowboy trying to connect with his daughter. He dozed off and woke and saw that two more hours had passed without any sign of Louisa, and then he really started to worry. When the home phone rang at eleven, he picked it up and said, "Where are you?" But it wasn't Louisa. "Someone from the crew just called me from the lot," Wallace said. "You'd better get over there now." His tone had no give in it.

———————

Ennis, Gerrold, Oliva, Finster, Deacon: William was crossing roads so fast they began to blur together, and then he was racing down a long straightaway, and then he was swinging onto Harrow. What he saw in the distance put a fist around his heart. The house was burning.

Men walked around the edge of the lot, keeping an almost respectful distance from the cauldron of orange and white that beat like a heart in the rib cage of the house. They were heavy in slick yellow, with enormous black stripes stretching across the middle of their uniforms. There were eight men on the perimeter, and two had hoses, and there were four more who stood back slightly from the burning frame, and there were two more even farther back pressing buttons on their walkie-talkies and speaking numbers. William looked around, at the ghost of the frame of the house, at the lumber charred and at points eaten fully through, and he was not willing to believe anything he saw until he saw Louisa sitting on the hood of a car across the lot.

She was wrapped in a blanket but still shivering, and a fireman was on one side of her and a policeman was on the other, and there was a siren just behind her that gave off red light and then blue light, echoing the two men.

The heart beating in the rib cage of the house slowed and everything else did, too. A man on William's left said that for a few weeks there he thought he'd never see another fire, not after Lareaux was arrested, and that in some strange way he welcomed this one, though he felt bad for the poor sap whose house was coming down. The poor sap made his way to his wife. When he reached her she did not cry or even blink, just repeated his name as if casting a spell. "William," she said. "William, William." He brought his face close to hers, tried to smell the skin beneath the soot and smoke, failed. There were bandages across the tops of her thighs and some kind of foil pack cinched to one calf.

The two men who'd been speaking numbers into walkie-talkies had set them down; now they were loading something into the bed of a pickup. It was a lump covered in canvas. William's scalp pricked with fear, suddenly terrified that it was Louisa under the canvas, but Louisa was right in front of him. "Who is that?" William said, but the men couldn't hear him, and so he ran for the pickup, shouting, or maybe he just thought he was shouting. "Wait," he said, but the men loading the lump would not wait. The men bumped the gate of the truck and William saw a paw poking out from underneath the canvas. He turned back toward Louisa. A tear streaked her face in negative, a channel carved in the soot. William found another truck with the gate down and fell against it. Blood rushed through his head. He could not stand but he could not do anything else either. Policemen stretched tape across the front of the property. A small man in a suit spray-painted silver spots on the ground, describing a circle in three points. A rope lay like a snake in the middle of the circle, its tail indicating the blackened doghouse.

Louisa spoke William's name again. Years before, when they had worked together at the newspaper, William had interviewed a man who had been a hero in the Second World War. He was being devoured by dementia, and all he could do was speak his late wife's name, after which he buried his face in his hands. Louisa buried her face in her hands. The fireman helped her to her feet. The policeman helped her to his car. The pickup truck with the something in it drove away. An ember floated down from the burning house like an unused wish.

———

For the first time in months, William could stand at the edge of the lot, facing away from the street, and see the entire sky, a gluttony of blue. He walked around the space where the house had almost been, just as the men in yellow with black stripes had done the night before. The left half of the deck was still intact; the right, where waterproofing had started, was gone, and a light rain pattered onto the smoldering lumber, sending up strands of steam. Wallace arrived soon after William and stood next to his truck, leaning on it, unwilling even to take a single step forward. "I used the space under the deck to store flammable materials," he said helplessly. "It never occurred to me that it was anything other than safe." He started explaining what he knew about builder's risk insurance, and how as far as he knew it covered this kind of thing, and that project disasters were not as rare as he might think, and just when William was going to say he understood, Wallace gasped and brought his hand up to his mouth. With his other hand he pointed to the charred snake of the leash in the grass. "The dog," he said.

The hospital was only ten blocks away from their old house. If they had moved already, it would not have been convenient. William spotted Stevie and Emma's car in the visitors' lot and he took a space a row away. Louisa was up on nine, eyes open. "Hi," she said. "I am so glad it's you."

There was an orderly in the room, a young man who identified himself as Jeffrey and extended a hand that William did not shake. Jeffrey talked like a car whose brakes had been cut. "As far as I know she has not slept yet, sir," Jeffrey said. "She has no serious injuries but we're going to want to keep her here under observation. And after a little while someone may want to come by and talk to her about the fire, though of course they'll have to wait until she's ready. She was very lucky, sir, to have gotten out the way she did, with only a few minor burns and some smoke inhalation. We've seen so much worse." A phone somewhere on Jeffrey buzzed. "I have to go attend to that, sir. Will you be staying or going? Visiting hours end at eleven but immediate family is welcome at any time."

"I'll be right here," William said, trying to keep his voice level but failing. He sat in the chair next to Louisa's bed and brushed a strand of hair from her forehead. Her hands lay balled in fists on the white of the sheet. "Do you need anything?" he said, and she said that she could use a change of clothes but that she didn't need it right away and would he stay and sit with her, and he said of course. He gently squeezed her hand and she closed her eyes but he felt her squeezing back.

———

Soon, there were others in the room as well: an administrator who brought William a large plastic bag that contained Louisa's wallet and shoes, along with some papers; a nurse, corpulent and capable, who lectured Louisa on the treatment of minor burns, first painkillers, then makeup when the skin grew back with uneven pigment; and then a young Chinese woman, Janet Chen, who identified herself as a city fire investigator. "I just need to talk to Mrs. Day for one moment," she said, producing a clipboard. "I'll be taking notes but the clipboard is also a recording device. Do you consent to this interview?"

Louisa nodded.

"We'll try to keep it brief," Janet Chen said. She pressed a button on the clipboard. "Can we consider this an official statement?" Louisa nodded again. "You'll have to speak out loud," Janet Chen said.

"Yes," Louisa said.

"Why don't you just tell me what happened," Janet Chen said.

Louisa lifted her right hand, tugged at the tube that extended along her forearm. She closed her eyes and then opened them. "We had gotten some bad news about a friend of ours," she said. "I went out for a drive to think about it and then I stopped to get coffee. Around four, I think, I spoke to William on the phone." She tilted her head toward him for confirmation. "The connection was bad and I guess we got our wires crossed, except that there weren't any wires, which was the problem. He thought I wanted him to come and find me at the coffee shop. I thought he wanted me to come meet him at the house. Just a stupid mix-up. I got out to the house and I wasn't very happy about it."

"About the house?" Janet Chen said.

"About the fact that William wasn't there," Louisa said. "I needed him there. I was in the car, getting more and more anxious, and my phone battery was run almost entirely down, and I didn't know where he was. So I went to the deck to sit on the railing and look at the trees. I thought it would calm me down. Which is also why I was smoking." She rubbed her fingers together to recover the memory. "I don't do it anymore, almost ever, but I had an old pack in the glove compartment and I was smoking it. I had a few cigarettes, and then I decided it was time to go. One of the cigarettes must not have been out completely. Or maybe it was just a spark. I don't know. Obviously I didn't notice. I went to the car. I was getting ready to drive away when I saw the start of it in my rearview mirror. It was an orange glow, maybe yellow at the bottom." Her tone made it sound like something beautiful.

"And what happened moving forward from that?"

The tenses seemed to throw Louisa off balance. "Next, you mean?" she said. "I got out and ran toward the house and then I ran back to the car. I drove across the street, to get farther away from it, and I called the fire department." Her voice caught. "I didn't have any idea that the dog was there." She lowered her head into her hands. "She didn't make any noise at all."

"Yes, ma'am," Janet Chen said. She pressed the button on the clipboard again. "I just have a paper or two for you to sign, and then we'll be finished."

Then it was just the two of them and Louisa turned to William, gave him the full of her eyes. "The phone battery should have lasted longer than it did. I was sitting in one of the chairs where I would have sat at the party. You think you're building toward something, but it's just an illusion. You put things on top of other things, but then everything can come apart just like that. Poor Blondie." She had the rhythm of a ranter but everything she said was thuddingly lucid.

"Wallace says we're covered," William said. At this, finally, Louisa began to weep. "We can start over. It'll be okay."

"I'm sure it won't," she said. "I don't want to be the villain but I don't see any other way to tell this story." She closed her eyes again and would not open them. By degrees, sleep drew a curtain of relief across her face.

———

William backed out quickly, careful not to hit Stevie and Emma's car, and hurried home. Louisa had said the fire was an accident, and it had to be. She had been smoking a cigarette, which had fallen. A cigarette was more earth than fire. It had dropped into the space below the deck, where chemicals were stored. Chemicals became fire if only given the opportunity. But then the black butterfly passed close enough to him that he could feel the beat of its wings on his face. Maybe Louisa knew about Emma. Maybe she had found the letter. Maybe she hadn't been out there thinking of Jim but rather cursing William. Business, even immoral business, was distinguished from casual deception by the presence of records. His legs were matchsticks that could hardly hold his weight.

He went into the house, into the bedroom. He was moving slower than he had at the lot, but his mind was moving faster. He sat on his side of the too-high bed and opened the drawer of the bedside table. The picture of him and Christopher at Lareaux's arraignment was flat on top where he'd left it, and he drilled down into the drawer, down through the old postcards, through the dirty magazines. But the letter was still there, just as he had left it, untouched and undetected. The fire was an accident. His wife had been in an accident. He put the letter back in the bottom of the drawer, closed up the table, and went to the deck. The tubs were in the yard. The lanterns were on the rails. He thought he heard the boy in the adjoining yard admonishing his parents, proving their unfitness by exhaustion. He took a seat in one of the large wooden chairs, lit one of the lanterns, the cactus, and everything that had been waiting for him, like a policeman around the corner, now appeared to make its arrest, and he touched his elbows to his knees, and he did not dare to breathe.

———

When the phone rang, it was Tom, returning a call William didn't remember making. "How could something like this have happened?" he said. "Where are you?" His voice was sharp with worry.

"I'm home," William said. "Getting her some clothes."

"Where is she? I tried to call but it went straight through to voice mail."

"She's in the hospital. For observation, mostly. She seems to be okay. Are you going to visit her?"

"First thing in the morning," Tom said. "I'm upstate. I've been here all week. This is crazy, though. I can't imagine how she must feel."

"She feels terrible," William said. "She's been pretty clear about that."

"It's a shock," Tom said. "It's nothing anyone would have thought. What a terrible accident. We're thinking of you." William heard a woman's voice in the background, Jesse's voice, and he understood that the clarity in Tom's voice was not from worry alone. It was from happiness. "And tell her I'll see her soon." Tom left the line open long enough for William to hear him tell Jesse they'd have to leave at dawn.

At the hospital, Louisa's clothes balled up in his backpack, he took the elevator up to six, where he squared up in front of the water fountain and pressed the button. He stayed with his head down and let the water run over his lips and chin for a long time. He traversed the hall, glancing left and right, until he found Emma's room, which was the first beyond a second elevator bank. He heard Stevie asking how far apart they were. "My legs or the contractions?" Emma said. "Tilt the TV so I can see it better." William took a brochure about vaccination from the wall rack and tried to look busy. "Sir?" a nurse said with polite hostility. "You can't be in the hall here, sir." He let her see him press the elevator button, but when she was gone he slipped into a side room, bought a soda he didn't want from the vending machine, and clasped it between his hands until his palms were cold from the metal. He found a niche near the elevator area where no one could see him and pretended to talk on the phone. He heard Stevie's voice again, this time saying something he couldn't make out, and then a doctor came up the hall, striding purposefully, and went into the room. Sometime before three, a baby was born, not his, never his, a capital expenditure, someone else's miracle.

Part VII

———————

THE LAUNCH PARTY

Six months later, a lifetime, William's car was in the shop, and he was driving Louisa's car home from Tom's book party, and Louisa was saying how surprised she was that Tom had gotten back together with Annika, and wasn't it strange that he didn't look happier, and William was murmuring vaguely, neither agreeing nor disagreeing, careful not to reveal what he knew about the situation, which was that Tom and Jesse had quickly settled on a wedding date, and just as quickly fallen to fighting, and that a bitter month had ended with her decision to leave him for good, and that she was now pregnant by another man upstate. Instead, William said that Annika looked as though she had aged five years in the year since she and Tom had last been together, and that was when Louisa put both her hands on the dashboard in front of her in a gesture of conspicuous steadying and told William that, during a particularly bad stretch in the spring and summer, she had been sleeping with a man who worked at her office.

They were on Loomis Street, near Harrow, only blocks from the empty lot where their new house would have been. There was a pond to their left and a small park to their right. The windows were down because the temperature was mild, and crickets called out through the perfect night.

William turned into the park's paved lot. There was one other car there, an old VW Beetle with two teenage girls in it, smoking. A third girl was in the back seat; William glimpsed a strip of bare shoulder. He pulled past the Bug and into an empty space at the far end of the lot.

"So," he said. The word was like a hole in the air.

Things had been going well since the house burned down, more smoothly than William had any reason to expect. He had celebrated a birthday, and then Louisa had, and in both cases they had taken quiet dinners at new restaurants downtown and talked frankly about how, despite all that had happened, they were lucky. William had found work at a large bank, a job that was a natural continuation of what he had done at Hollister. He described investment opportunities and nudged customers toward those that seemed to best suit their needs. His new boss saw him as a quick study, was always saying so, had already moved William into a bigger office and after only six months had already given him a substantial bonus. Louisa's boss, the museum's top administrator, had retired for health reasons, and the board had asked Louisa if she would consider taking the position on an acting basis, and she had, and though they were still negotiating whether they could come to permanent terms, Louisa felt that even if it all fell apart she'd be assured of a position at least that good at another museum. They had buried the dog in their yard, in the corner near the little girls who liked to sing, and they had stood on the deck afterward, afraid to sit for fear that might make it seem more real, and he had folded her against his chest.

The park light over them, a metal drop at the top of a metal stalk, blinked erratically. William sat for a minute with the engine going, pushed the pads on the seat down with his hands. In his rearview mirror he saw the Beetle pulling out of the lot. The radio was on the same station it had been on that afternoon, but the program had changed from talk to music, gentle jazz whose effect, paradoxically, was to make the anger rising in him even hotter and sharper. He didn't know what to say, so he said nothing.

Louisa had made her admission matter-of-factly, responding, William figured, to some internal train of thought: maybe something Gloria Fitch had said about errant spouses, meaning Graham Kenner, who had been drummed out of the house when Cassandra had discovered him with Helen Hull; or maybe she was thinking about the cover of Tom's book, *Graph Zeppelin*, and how it had a line that sloped diagonally downward and ended in a fiery crash; or perhaps she was simply observing how Tom put his arm around Annika like he was keeping his distance from her and lamenting the way that unhappiness could bloom between people like a black flower. She hadn't taken a deep breath before speaking, or told William he should brace himself, or done anything at all in prelude or preparation. She had just clicked the clasp of her purse closed and then open and put her hands flat on the dash and told him the news. As the light flickered above, she elaborated slightly: the man was a lawyer working for the museum on a lawsuit brought by a woman whose son had been injured when part of an exhibit had fallen on him. The man had come by the office, which seemed entirely necessary given the case. Louisa thought nothing of it until he invited her to coffee. They had flirted for six months or so. "This was a while ago," she said. "Last spring."

"Before I went to the trade show?"

She squinted. "I had met him, yes. It wasn't why I sent you to Chicago, though when you were gone the thought did occur to me. Nothing happened then, though. Then he went away on another job and I didn't see him for a while, and then one day he came by for lunch, and one thing led to another." William asked where; Louisa said a motel. "It happened one time after that," she said. "Two total. That was all. He didn't keep after me to continue, and I was relieved because I wasn't interested at all. At some point I felt that I had never been so uninterested in anything in my whole life."

William rolled down the window. It was colder outside now, which seemed to focus the noises of the night. William put his hand down on the fabric of the seat and started to make a fist. At first it was purely theatrical; he wanted Louisa to see his hand clenching and unclenching. But the more he did it, the more he thought maybe it was accurately reflecting what he felt inside: the anger, the confusion, the need to hold tight to something certain. He believed he should speak, and probably with a question. She had told him who, and how long. Should he ask why?

He must have, because Louisa turned toward him, her expression now opened up. Silence slowly closed it. She crossed and uncrossed her ankles and laughed, or made a noise close to it—not nervous, he didn't think, but more in the fashion of a tipsy wife. "Well," she finally said. "Are there ever real reasons?" This question didn't seem rhetorical, and so William started to answer her, but he managed only a few words before she interrupted him. "I wasn't running toward him, not for a second. I was running away from my life." Again, William started to speak, and again, she interrupted. "Maybe that's the wrong way to say it. I needed to know that I existed. Was I even casting a shadow? John was a nice man, but weak." She cocked her head to one side. "In fact, I think you met him once. In the mall." William did not remember. "An older guy, kind of gaunt." William thought suddenly of long, bony hands, which he did his best not to picture sliding up his wife's leg, or worse. "Before him, I wasn't sleeping well for a while, and then I wasn't sleeping at all. I started to drink more than I wanted. Remember the mail? I was afraid I might vanish and I started setting it aside as proof that there was something only I knew. This was just a version of that."

A light shone in the rearview mirror. It was a car coming into the lot, the kind of full-size station wagon William didn't see much anymore. It lurched heavily into a parking spot a few spaces down from William and Louisa, and three teenagers piled out noisily. The girl walked around to the hood, looking angry, and leaned against it. Two boys followed her at a delay; one seemed to be pleading with her, the other mocking her, both slightly, and as William watched he wasn't sure he didn't have it reversed, because she seemed to be receptive to the one who was mocking and dismissive of the one who was pleading. Both boys produced cigarettes and started to smoke them, or were they joints? The car radio was on too loud, playing a song William had loved when he was their age. Louisa noticed it too. "It's like we're watching a time machine," she said.

"Which one am I?" William said.

Louisa did not answer. Something in William's tone held her silent. And then William was silent again, also, and the girl put her arms around the neck of the mocking boy and then hooked a finger through one of the belt loops of the pleading boy and then took his cigarette from him and flicked it an impressive distance across the parking lot. It went like a shooting star through the darkness and sent off a shower of sparks when it landed. Then the mocking boy got back into the car and changed the radio and the girl started to kiss the pleading boy and the pleading boy clasped his hands at the lower part of her back and the two of them went at an angle against the edge of the hood.

"Is this for our benefit?" Louisa said.

"Doesn't seem so," William said.

"I'm sorry," she said. "I just needed my strength back. Do you know what that feels like? I was doing it for us, in a strange way, for you and me. I wanted to be better. For the first time in years, I felt like we were building toward something."

"We sure were."

She winced, her face childlike and mournful. "I didn't mean the house."

"I know what you didn't mean," William said, and turned the key to start the engine. But before he backed the car out of the space, he lifted his right hand, as if he were indicating the height of something or someone, and then brought the flat of his palm down as hard as he could on the top of the steering wheel. It juddered and for a second he thought he had broken something.

"Jesus," Louisa said.

"I hate this car," he said. He said it like the assault was purposeful. But the act had surprised him, and when he went to back up he bumped the lower half of the wheel and the horn honked, once, for a fraction of a second at most. The girl and the pleading boy turned toward them and turned away just as quickly and that's when William thought he recognized her: she looked like the cashier at the Red Barn, the daughter of the owner. But then she stared defiantly at William and Louisa as if she could see them, though he didn't think she could, and this time she didn't look like that girl at all, and William backed out and left the parking lot. The boy in the car shouted something at them, and William waved good-bye with his hand, which was beginning to hurt.

Louisa started to speak a few times. She asked him if she'd made a mistake by saying anything. She told him that it had been less than nothing. She reassured him that she was happy with how things were, now that all the trouble between them had evaporated. William was hardly driving anymore, just resting his left hand on the wheel as they rolled onto their street. The Brookers were hosting a small gathering in warm light and everyone was smiling. The Morgan place looked just like William's but wasn't. Stevie and Emma's house was dark, and was no longer theirs at any rate. They had moved to Arizona, baby in tow, so that Stevie could oversee corporate creative. On the day the moving truck had come to cart their things away, William had walked across the street and given Stevie a handshake and a pat on the back, feeling as though the two of them had shared something, even if he was the only one who knew it. "Hold down the fort," Stevie had said. William had saluted, just as he had at the garage door, not feeling as idiotic about it this time.

William pulled into the driveway and got out without turning off the car. An orchestra of birds tuned up in the branches overhead. He unlocked the front door and pushed into the house with his shoulder.

He heard claws scrabbling on the tile; the dog bounded out of the hall and hit William hip-height. "Good boy," he said, bending down to scratch the dog's head. This one was black, with a white streak running down the forehead to the nose, and he slept in a crate in the garage. William went into the bedroom, where he lowered himself onto the bed and looked out to the driveway. Louisa was sitting in the SUV with the door open, illuminated by the interior light, still as a statue.

He closed his eyes and time passed, not very much, maybe, but enough that he began to feel its weight upon him. When he opened his eyes Louisa was out of the car, facing him, just a few feet from the house. She was backlit by the headlights of the car, which meant that she was looking at her own reflection and he was lost behind the glare. He wondered if she could see him at all. She made a spider of her hand and pressed it to the outside of the windowpane. William stood and went to the window. He waved with his sore hand, receiving no acknowledgment in return, and then lowered the hand to hip height, made a spider of his own, paired it with hers, across the glass, and stood there squinting at her silhouette as the light ran away from her in streaks.

ACKNOWLEDGMENTS

Movies have credits, as do record albums. The contributions of others are recognized explicitly. Books, being strange, operate under the fiction that they're produced by a single individual. As that individual, it falls to me to recognize the rest of the people who helped this book into being, in ways both large and small, subtle and straightforward, abstract and concrete, willing and somewhat less than willing. I'd like to thank my wife, Gail; my kids, Daniel and Jake; my parents, Richard and Bernadine; my brothers, Aaron and Josh; my friends Lauren and Rhett and Nicole and Charlotte and Nicki and Todd and Harold and Steve; my agents, Jim Rutman and Ira Silverberg; my boss at work, David Remnick; my colleagues at work; and, finally, last and most, my editor, Cal Morgan. I'd also like to thank all married men and women for living rewarding, frustrating, comforting, and disconcerting lives that are frequently in flux and too infrequently in focus.

About the author

About the book

Read on

Insights,
Interviews
& More . . .

A Conversation with Ben Greenman

Where do you live?

In Brooklyn, right near where the spacecraft Barclays Center landed.

And yet, you chose to write about the suburbs. Why?

Well, I grew up in the suburbs, and I think I'm still there in some ways, in my mind. I got conditioned to believe certain things about human interaction, or the lack of it. In the suburbs, distance works differently. There's more silence (which can be either paralyzing or erotic) and more meaninglessness (which can be either liberating or crushing).

But that's about the book, and this is about the author. Let me ask you about the relationship between your life and your writing. How do you feel about writing autobiographically?

Generally, I've been against it. But as I've gotten older, I've wanted to look more closely at the kind of life I have, even if that doesn't exactly mean looking at my own life. As life goes on, it becomes more and more about weighing responsibilities against diminished (or narrowed) freedoms. I have accepted that in my marriage, in fatherhood, in work. But I haven't explored the same principle in my writing. For a long time, I wrote with a maximum of freedom, meaning trickery and metafictional evasion. I told myself that taking fairly straightforward aim at the lives of my characters was less exciting, though maybe I was just avoiding it because it was less comfortable.

Do you worry about hurting people close to you when you write?

Yes. I know a writer (I won't say who) who seems to take delight in calling out friends and lovers in his or her fiction. Is that bravery? Is that narcissism? I suppose I am not answering the question so much as asking more questions.

How else have you changed as a person, and how has it changed you as a writer?

When I published my first book, I was just recently married. I had no children. Now I've been married more than a decade and I have two children. Somewhere along the way, I crossed an invisible line that made those things more important than books. Or at least more important than what happens to a book once it's published. At times, I would agonize over every little detail of a book's publication and reception. Now, it seems like a somewhat arbitrary process that shouldn't really be overthought, because it's not purely predictable and not an enjoyable source of speculation.

How do you handle reviews?

At first, I read them all. Now, I try to avoid them all. I know lots of reviewers. ▶

A Conversation with Ben Greenman
(continued)

I have worked as a reviewer. I respect the profession and think it's vital to the future of literature that people continue to have conversations about books: what works, what doesn't, why certain trends intensify while others wane. But I'm not sure it's vital for the future of authors. More specifically: investing too much in reviews can be fatal for authors.

*You have written a wide variety of kinds of books, from a collection of experimental short stories (**Superbad**) to a novel about a funk-rock star (**Please Step Back**). Do you have a mental list of other kinds of books you want to write but haven't yet?*

Sure. A political novel, a crime novel, a purely comic novel, a form of scripture, a novel in verse, a single-word novel, a memoir of a word, a travel book about imaginary places. ◠

Plotting a Point

WHEN I WAS YOUNG, I went to see an author read at a bookstore. He was older, though probably not as old as I am now. He was not exactly famous, but he had done good work for years. He was proud of what he had achieved, and rightly so. I sat on an uncomfortable chair with two dozen other youngish people and admired his reading for the clarity of vision, the lack of histrionics, and the evident pleasure he took in his sentences. He was not self-satisfied. He was not foolish. He did not talk about things like advances or sales. He was a good role model for a young writer.

Afterward, the audience asked questions. Two of them have remained with me. The second, I'll talk about later. The first came from a young woman in the crowd who stood to ask it. She asked the writer why he wrote at all. The audience laughed, but it wasn't a combative question. I think she just wanted to know why an intelligent person with other options would devote his life to the art of prose, which is often a prescription for obscurity. He thought about it. He scratched his not quite beard. "Well," he said. "I guess to connect with people."

At that moment, my heart fell a little bit. I didn't measure it, but I'd guess a centimeter. It fell because his answer was incomprehensible to me, and it ▶

5

was incomprehensible to me because, up to that point, my own fiction had approached the question from the opposite direction. I wrote not to connect with others, but to prove the impossibility of connecting with others. One of the first stories I had finished was from the perspective of a dog about to get put down in an animal shelter. The dog was uncertain what his life had meant, if anything. The dog had loved the human to whom he had been attached, or thought he had, but his current state cast that entire set of memories into doubt. The dog was exiting life with only slightly more information than he possessed when he entered it, and less certainty that any of that information had value. I'm not sure the story was any good, though it contained at least one nice touch, which was that the dog could express himself, but only within his own head. He was narrating, but not communicating. He had thoughts, but no one understood him, or even heard him.

It is possible that if I had stayed after the reading and approached the author to talk about his answer, he would have reconciled his worldview and mine. He might have said that the impossibility of connecting was exactly what motivated his attempt to connect. We might have been speaking the same language. But I left. I thought I was proving my point by leaving, but maybe I had proven his point by going to the reading in the first place. Maybe I had proven his point by reading at all, his work and the work of others, or by feeling, as I encountered any book, a mix of attraction and repulsion: to the prose, to characters, to an author's ear for language, to imagery, to plots. Maybe I had proven no one's point.

The story about the dog was published in a college literary magazine a few years later. The writer from the reading got a little more famous, then a little less famous, then a little more, then a little less. It was and remains an admirable course. A while later, I got a deal with a publishing house. When the first copy of my first book came off the press, I flashed back to that reading, and to that question. Was writing about connecting with people, or about erecting a monument to the fact that connection was impossible? In that first book, and for many years afterward, I answered that question indirectly: aggressively, but indirectly. I wrote high-concept short stories, often comic, that had a certain amount of alienation or ruptured communication baked right into the dough.

Then it came time to write a more traditional novel. "The time has come," said a voice from on high. It turned out to be my editor. The first thing I did was reject the suggestion out of hand. Instead of taking up a traditional story, or a traditional mode of storytelling, I created a new character who was the enemy of tradition: a conceptual artist ▶

Plotting a Point *(continued)*

who distilled his fears about the way the world (mal)functioned into a series of graphs. His approach, I decided, would be to burlesque any attempt to make sense of the chaos and randomness of the world. Shortly after I thought of him, I started to make graphs on his behalf. One of the first was a recursive commentary on the way comprehension slips away from you even as you reach for it.

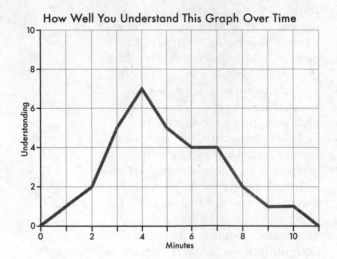

How Well You Understand This Graph Over Time

That graph made me laugh, once, and then it made me sad. It contains both sadistic and masochistic elements. It has also landed differently in my mind at different times: it has seemed like a superficial paradox but also a profound abyss. A little while later, I was looking at it upside down and thought of a companion graph.

How Much I Had To Manipulate the Data To Make It Seem Like Things Were Looking Up

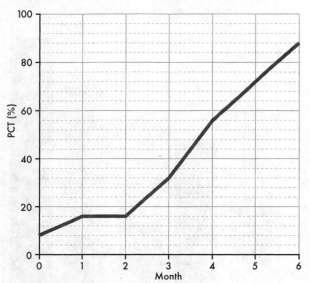

That one was also sad, maybe even sadder. Look at the line: It goes up like something optimistic: a bird on the wing, an answered prayer. But it's measuring the dishonesty needed to falsify that optimism. I tacked that one up next to the first one and looked at it until the gray line went even grayer, at which point I made another graph about dishonesty. ▶

Percent Chance That In the Original Full-Color Graph, Each of These Bars Was the Color It Claims to Be

At around that point, the idea of a novel-length work based on that character fell apart. Maybe that's an exaggeration. I found myself backing off of the graphs slightly. It wasn't because my editor and I had talked about a more traditional novel. It was because the graphs were comfortable for me in every way. They were habit. I made dozens of them. And while part of creative work is doing the things that you do well, part is deciding when to disrupt your own habits. In terms of that question from the reading decades ago, the graphs were not a way of connecting with others, or even a way of admitting that connection was impossible. They were a way of forestalling the question by communicating primarily with myself.

I printed out the graphs, set them aside, and moved forward with the novel. It became something different, less a staging ground for conceptual pieces, more a straightforward investigation of marriage, of childlessness, of emotional and sexual infidelity. These were common topics, I knew, because they engirdled the lives of many people I knew.

Then a strange thing happened. A guy I had communicated with a little bit online started posting the graphs on his website, and the graphs began to acquire some measure of popularity. People responded to them. There was, briefly, some talk of making a book of the graphs.

At that point, I knew I had to abandon them, or at least move them farther and farther away from the novel I was creating. I went back to the book. The conceptual artist became a secondary character. His sister and her husband came to the fore, along with those questions about marriage and fidelity and suburban emptiness and disappearing youth. The charts were still over my desk, addressing some of the same questions, but they were no longer presiding over the book. The charts were now a set of ideas that had ▶

been abandoned by another set of ideas.
What better way to explore loneliness?

So, what is loneliness? It's everything
except for the few things that it is
not. Last year in the *Guardian*, Teju
Cole made an excellent list of books
about loneliness. He picked works by
W. G. Sebald, Ralph Ellison, Lydia Davis,
and more. All his selections were good,
but they were also primarily books
about solitude, books about lives without
connections. The deeper I got into this
book, the more it seemed to be about the
opposite: a highly connected life that was
nevertheless lonely. (I started to write
"that was full of loneliness," but it
seems strange to say that something is
full of loneliness. It's like saying a room
is full of emptiness.) The main character,
William, is married, without children.
He works at an office with coworkers he
sees nearly every day. At some point, he
starts sleeping with a woman who is
not his wife. Does he ever make a
meaningful connection? Is it even
possible? (There is a moment in the
book where he forges a relationship with
a boy, the son of an old friend. Briefly,
that nourishes him, but it is short-lived
as well.) Some might argue that William
does what everyone does: he enjoys a
series of temporary connections that,
over the course of a life, add up. They
would not necessarily be wrong. But
I would ask them a follow-up question:
Add up to what?

So is that the real question? Is *The
Slippage* an attempt to discover life's

ultimate purpose—or, alternatively, to discover that there isn't one? That seems grandiose, though it may also be accurate. For most of my own life, I have assumed that the thing that makes life tolerable is meaning, and that the thing that makes meaning is art. Facts are necessary things, but they are just the footholds in the wall you use to climb higher so you can see (or hear) art. And even when you get within reach of art, there's often not enough of it, or at least not enough of the right kind. I don't mean to say that you can't find art you like. That's not hard to do. But liking is only the beginning. Each and every piece of art, whether a short story or a painting or a pop song, has a specific effect on a certain reader/viewer/listener at a certain time. And art, like medicine, can save or doom. Sometimes the art you like isn't the art that challenges you. Sometimes the art that challenges you isn't the art that enlarges you. Sometimes a piece of art grabs you tight but lets you go too soon: disappointment. Sometimes you depend on a piece of art to rescue you and it leaves you cold: more loneliness. If you could locate exactly the right kind of art exactly when you needed it, that would be great. But believing in that kind of efficient delivery requires an implausibly optimistic view of the world and how it operates. How things really work, I think, is that we need to clear away much of what's created so we can find ►

Plotting a Point *(continued)*

the things that are meaningful to us.
And so, in the novel, I found a role for
the chart artist by setting up a subplot in
which two forces are locked in battle: art
and fire. Both are refining forces, though
one is an agent of creation and the other
an agent of destruction. At one point,
following a rash of arsons in town, the
chart artist develops what some might
call an unhealthy obsession with fire,
and then translates his obsession into
artwork:

I liked that graph when I thought of
it. It seemed funny without also being
mean. I even considered making it the
sole graph in the body of the novel,
reproduced below a normal old
paragraph of prose. Instead, it ended
up here. Later, it occurred to me that it
(along with many of the other graphs)
actually encodes a great deal of anxiety

on my part about how artwork is received. This graph, the fire graph, is a metaphor of enthusiasm. It speaks to the odd process by which an audience (of critics, say, or students, or the reading public, whatever that means) does or does not take to a book.

What happens after a book comes out? People read it and have reactions, and some of them express those reactions, in print or online. It's a perfectly workable process. But it's also a strange process, reductive and confusing. Earlier, in telling my story about the reading I attended as a young writer, I mentioned that audience members asked two questions that have remained with me. The first, as I have said, was about connection. The second was this: "Is this your best book?" A young man asked that question. I believe he was wearing overalls, which is neither here nor there. The older (but still young) writer tilted his head as if he was thinking. He scratched his not quite beard. His answer was this: "No." The audience laughed. "What I mean," he said, "is that I think the best is yet to come." Once more my heart fell a little, not because I didn't see the wisdom of the writer's answer, but because I thought I saw something false flickering at the heart of it. The chances that your next work will *always* be better than your last are slim indeed. Over the course of a career, work both draws closer to ▶

Plotting a Point *(continued)*

inspiration and moves farther away from it. Believing in steady improvement is an operating fiction. And yet, pride tells you to be more proud of the most recent work than the work that came before it, and to pretend that it is the most completely realized portrait of your inner state. Again, much of this becomes irrelevant if an artist signs up for a lifetime subscription to his or her own artwork. Long fallow periods can be followed by a new flowering. Movements can be profitably lateral instead of aggressively, deceptively vertical.

After I left that reading, I went to a restaurant and did some doodling on a napkin. One of the things I doodled was a graph that later inspired a piece of work by the conceptual artist who did not quite become the center of this book. It seems like an appropriate place to end. ⌣

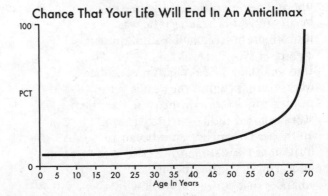

Chance That Your Life Will End In An Anticlimax

Author Recommendations

THIS BOOK IS ABOUT MARRIAGE: other things, too, but maybe mainly marriage. Here are some other works that also look closely at the idea.

Frederick Barthelme, *Second Marriage*. Frederick's brother Donald has a grand literary reputation, deservedly so. Fewer people, maybe, know about Frederick. His novels are more realistic and also more comic, which combine to make people feel that they're somehow miniatures. They're not. They see sharply and they say what they see just as sharply.

Frederick Busch, *Harry and Catherine*. Busch is one of my favorites, for his clear-eyed prose and his devotion to real people. This novel takes place solidly in the real world, with politics and history underlying an adult love story. It's beautifully written and expansive when it comes to ordinary human emotions.

Lorrie Moore, "Real Estate." For years, Moore has been putting up good work on this particular plot of land. This story is about illness and compromise and violence and the importance of humor in dissolving all those things, at least temporarily. It also contains a great working definition of marriage: "a fine arrangement generally, except one never got it generally. One got it very, very specifically." ▶

17

Alison Lurie, *The War Between the Tates*. This, in a way, is the counterweight or countermovement to the Moore story. The people may be specific, but the world they inhabit is very general, satirical in the broad sense. I thought about the Lurie book often as I wrote my own, though they have very little in common. Oh, also, Mick Jagger is in the TV-movie version of the Lurie book.

The Bible. My book is a book about infidelity, at least somewhat, and it raises the question of whether it can be part of a healthy marriage. Statistics say yes. The Bible says no. But what else does the Bible say? Let's look at Deuteronomy 22: "If any man take a wife, and go in unto her, and hate her, and give occasions of speech against her, and bring up an evil name upon her, and say, I took this woman, and when I came to her, I found her not a maid: Then shall the father of the damsel, and her mother, take and bring forth the tokens of the damsel's virginity unto the elders of the city in the gate: And the damsel's father shall say unto the elders, I gave my daughter unto this man to wife, and he hateth her; And, lo, he hath given occasions of speech against her, saying, I found not thy daughter a maid; and yet these are the tokens of my daughter's virginity. And they shall spread the cloth before the elders of the city. And the elders of that city shall take that man and chastise him; And they shall amerce him in an hundred shekels of silver, and give them unto the father of the damsel, because he hath brought up an evil name upon a virgin of Israel: and she shall be his wife; he may not put her away all his days. But if this thing be true, and the tokens of virginity be not found for the damsel: Then they shall bring out the damsel to the door of her father's house, and the men of her city shall stone her with stones that she die: because she hath wrought folly in Israel, to play the whore in her father's house: so shalt thou put evil away from among you." Family values, I guess.

Donald Westlake, *Drowned Hopes*. Westlake's the best, and this is one of his best, a heist book with a nearly perfect hopelessness. Why is it also a book about marriage? Because there's one little subplot involving Bob, a guard at a reservoir, who is thrust into a hastily arranged marriage with his girlfriend, Tiffany. The marriage and its accompanying pressures proceed directly to Bob's brain and attack it via nervous breakdown. Bob's story only takes up a few short chapters—they're central to the plot, but marginal to the main characters—and it functions like the cartoons around the edges of *Mad* magazine. Still, it's one of my favorite portraits of American marriage. ∿

Don't miss the next book by your favorite author. Sign up now for AuthorTracker by visiting www.AuthorTracker.com.